Circles in the Sand

~ A Dog's Tale ~

Kathryn Crofton

ORIGINAL WRITING

© 2011 KATHRYN CROFTON

Cover photograph of 'Ragsy' by the author

All rights reserved. No part of this publication may be reproduced in any form or by any means—graphic, electronic or mechanical, including photocopying, recording, taping or information storage and retrieval systems—without the prior written permission of the author.

978-1-908024-26-8

A CIP catalogue for this book is available from the National Library.

Published by ORIGINAL WRITING LTD., Dublin, 2011.

Printed by CAHILL PRINTERS LIMITED, Dublin.

Dedication

This novel is dedicated to all dogs, cats and horses, be they lads or lassies, be they princes or paupers, who make every day of our lives a little special for having known them.

For Sheila, Poochie, Pirate, Sweetpea and Maxim who enriched our family in every way imaginable and for Steel, Millie, Jasper, Laurel, Hardy, Charlie Chaplin and Balthazar who continue to do so, but, most of all for Ragsy, who was a prince amongst paupers, my greatest hero and best friend.

Dearest Marie,

I hope you enjoy the book. You are a very great lady and a wonderful friend. Please spread the word about the book.

This is the beginning of the fight against animal abuse in Ireland. Please God, we will win the war with your help & prayers.

All my love

Acknowledgments

Thanking you, my dear friends and family, for your emotional support and encouragement is a monumental task. I hope you enjoy this novel, inspired by a true story and told through characterization. My purpose is to shed light on the ramification of acts, both cruel and kind, on 'man's best friend.'

My family have been phenomenal. Many thanks, to Lesley, my sister, who edited the first drafts of my entire novel and never let me down. My brother, William said, 'Why not you? It has to happen to someone. Keep it up!' A special thanks to my Mum who always said, 'Aim for the stars and maybe you'll hit the chimney pots!' With her help, I aimed beyond that. I would like to thank my dear Dad, a true gentleman, who was kind and compassionate throughout his life. His respect for animals, the smallest insect to the largest of God's creatures, made me acutely aware of the suffering around me. He is in that 'better place' for which we all yearn. Thank you also to Magda, my sister-in-law and niece Michelle who provide a new perspective on life and the importance of family.

My dear friend, Kevin read my very first chapter and encouraged me to 'Go the distance,' and his amazing generosity helped make my book a reality.

A heartfelt thanks to Michelle, Suzi, Patricia, Rose, Shevaun, Rachel, Roisin, Breda, Brenda, Wayne, Maria and Princess who remind me that laughter is what life is all about.

Thank you, Mother, and all the Sisters in the Poor Clares in Simmonscourt, Dublin 4 who keep me in their constant prayers. For Niall and Lisa, Ellie, Mollie and Millie who share their Sunday's on the beach and make 'three brides for three brothers' extra special.

A very special thank you to Garrett Bonner and Steven Weekes of Original Writing, whose patience, expertise and thorough professionalism has transformed this difficult journey to one of total joy. Thank you so much.

In an effort to combat animal abuse and raise its awareness, 25% of the royalties of this book will be shared amongst the following seven charities:

ASH ANIMAL SANCTUARY
DONKEY SANCTUARY IRELAND
IRISH BLUE CROSS
IRISH HORSE AND WELFARE TRUST
IRISH RETRIEVER RESCUE UK
IRISH SOCIETY FOR THE PREVENTION OF CRUELTY TO ANIMALS (I.S.P.C.A.)
PAWS

   With all my love to Daniel, Agnes, Emily and David.

Contents

Chapter One   1

Chapter Two   15

Chapter Three   32

Chapter Four   49

Chapter Five   61

Chapter Six   79

Chapter Seven   94

Chapter Eight	114
Chapter Nine	134
Chapter Ten	147
Chapter Eleven	157
Chapter Twelve	169
Chapter Thirteen	178
Chapter Fourteen	191

Chapter One

Dunshaughlin, 1983

The farm was small: a few cattle, pigs, hens, geese, cats, a horse, and not much else except a tri-coloured English Shepherd bitch called Jassie. Joe Myers was a middle-aged man in his late fifties but looked as though he were into his early sixties. He was bent down with years of working on a farm that had never really given back all he had put into it. He pulled down his farmer's cap over his Roman nose and weather-beaten face to keep the bitter cold wind from whipping round him as he shuffled his way across one of the thirty or so acres known to the locals as Myers Ditch. His wellies squelched in the muck as he beat the grass with a long *shillelagh* to herd his few cattle into the barn. He didn't hold with the idea that cattle should be left out in all weathers; perhaps he had just a bit of a soft heart, and maybe some thought him a little daft in the head, but he was a kind man. He spoke with a soft Welsh accent, warm and lilting. A gentle-hearted *oul'divil*, he almost sang when he talked. It isn't that he was an easy touch or hadn't any business sense; he had, but he just never had the right breaks to really make the farm a success.

Joe had been married for more than thirty years to a fine woman; homely, some would have described her, with her hair in curlers every day of the week except Sunday. She was in her early fifties, grey-haired, but it was obvious that the bloom in her face hadn't totally gone. Bright ice-blue eyes belied a generous, warm-hearted woman who had time for everyone and everything. She was a good neighbour, but more than that, she took a genuine interest in people and animals alike.

'God put you on earth for a reason; when you go back to Him you better be sure that He won't be disappointed in you,' Mary would say. No one could say that *He* could be disappointed in Mary.

Joe knew that he was one of the luckiest men in the county. Sure, she was no spring chicken, but then again, neither was he, and he loved her, truly loved her. He remembered when he married her all those years before, how apprehensive he was that she wouldn't be able to put up with him and the hard life ahead of them. He needn't have worried; it had been a good life, yes, and a happy one. It wasn't all roses; there were times when money was a might short, and the possibility they could lose the farm because of it sometimes loomed, but they managed in spite of it.

It was quite dark at this stage, and Joe had just managed to put the cattle away when a call came out from the kitchen

'Your tea is ready. Hurry up, or it'll get cold.'

'I'm on my way, just gimme a minute,' was the reply. As he twisted the knob on the outer door into the little hallway, a gush of warm air hit him, and a smile crept over his face.

'Hmm. Nice to be inside. It's bitter out there,' he said as he stamped his feet.

'Don't forget to take off those wellies. I don't want my nice clean floor trampled on.'

'How do I get from the door to the table if I don't trample on it?' he asked, bemused. Mary spun around, a hand on her hips, and looked straight at him sternly, with her wooden spoon in mid air. She thought a moment and then burst out laughing.

'You've got a point! You weren't born with wings. Sit yourself down.'

He hobbled over to the table, his socks soaking wet, with one toe sticking out of the top. He took off his socks and hung them on the rail beside the Aga cooker. It was an old one, but it filled the kitchen with warmth, and though it was well used, it had plenty of life in it yet. He rubbed his feet together to get the dampness out of them and slipped on his warmed slippers.

They sat down to their tea and talked of things on the farm, bills, and general chatter. An hour or so passed, and after tea, they sat beside the Aga cooker warming themselves.

'When do you think the puppies will be born?' Mary asked.

'Oh, not for some time yet. I've missed Jassie lately. She'd nearly bring the cattle in by herself.' he sighed as he lit up his pipe and nodded his head.

'Well, she won't be doing anything like that for a long while yet, not now that she'll be having puppies.'

Joe's eye fell on Jassie, a beautifully marked tri-coloured English Shepherd, gazing on her floppy ears, snow-white chest, and snow-tipped tail. Her body was black with the exception of her face, which was denoted by the crisp clear markings of brown, almost as though she were wearing spectacles. Yes, she was a beauty. She had been his workmate for nearly six years. It didn't seem that long; it had gone in a flash, and now she was to be a mother. She wasn't any different than she had been. He had worried that her gentle nature would change, but it hadn't. Mary and Joe went to bed thinking of the following day and all the preparations to be made.

It was a Saturday in March, bright and crispy cold with a clear blue winter sky. It still felt like winter but was on the cusp of spring, when the farm would come alive with new life. The house was in a tizzy. There were things to do besides the usual washing, ironing, and baking, and spending extra effort in getting the house ready—not that it wasn't always ready, clean as a new pin.

They had longed for children, but children didn't come; years passed, and by the time Mary hit her early thirties, she had given up hope of ever having any. However, life can be strange; Mary did have a child, a daughter, Anne, and now she was coming home. She had been away at university studying law. Mary sighed. 'She's coming home,' though what a prospective solicitor could do on a farm was beyond her. 'Ours is not to wonder why, ours is just to do and die,' she muttered to herself.

Anne was a hard worker, bloody-minded but a hard worker nonetheless. When she got something into her head, no one could get her to change her mind. She got the highest marks in her Leaving Cert. in her school. She wanted to do law, and nothing would change her mind.

Mary gazed out the kitchen window, reliving the moment when Anne had burst into the kitchen with the 'big news.'
'Mam, look! *Look*!'
'Look at what?'
'Look. I've got enough points.'
'Enough points to do what?'
'To do law, to do law in Trinity.'
'Did you fill out the CAO form and ask?'
'Yes, mam. That's what I'm saying, I've got Trinity.'
'Can you believe it? Trinity!'

She had heaved a great sigh and settled into the big, worn sofa chair beside the Aga cooker, thinking of her good fortune and dreaming of how the world would open up for her. She'd dreamed of being a famous solicitor, of going to Trinity, though in truth, until then they had only been pipe dreams. She had only ever heard of Trinity College; she had never been and once she had been accepted, the thought of going seemed quite daunting.

Mary had glanced over at her as Anne leaned into the cooker to warm her hands. She didn't look much like Joe, or herself, for that matter. She was slight in frame, not much more than five feet in height, with green eyes and long, curly, red-gold hair down to her waist, which she wore in a thick single plait. She was pretty, bright, witty, and hard working. She had a tendency to be a little sharp, often snapping at her dad, who was too polite and soft mannered to say anything except, 'one of these days you'll be sorry you said that, Miss.' He couldn't be cross with her for long, though; he was that proud of her, getting the best grades in the school, his daughter. There was an unspoken connection between them. She knew how he felt. If she had been a bit short with him, as soon as he had said, 'one of these days ...' she'd feel uncomfortable, think about it, jump up, hug him, and say, 'I am already. Sorry, dad.'

Mary remembered now how she had felt, how a huge lump had come to her throat and her hand automatically leapt to her mouth as if to stop the lump from popping out. *Where were they going to get the money?* She had thought. She couldn't let

Anne down after she had studied so hard. Anne would have to have fees and a place to stay, food and a bit of money to do her for during the week. Mary had heard students drank a lot, and what they got up to sent shivers up and down her spine. She couldn't stand in her daughter's way. She had the points, after all. She was only just sixteen, good God in heaven; she hadn't been much further than the local pub, which had a bit of a disco at the back on Saturday nights. Even at that, she was only allowed to go a few times and in the company of girls that she had known all her life, girls that were level headed and didn't go off doing God only knew what. Now she wanted to go and live in Dublin, on her own! The thought of it had made Mary positively queasy.

The day it happened seemed like yesterday, though of course it was months before, just after Anne had broken in with the 'big news,' as she continued gazing out the window and peeling the spuds for lunch, dipping the potato and wetting it in icy cold water every few minutes.

'If you peel that spud any more, there won't be anything left to boil,' a voice said cheerily over her right shoulder.

'Oh, Joe, I didn't hear you come in.'

'I thought I'd have a cup of tea and a slice of that lovely buttered orange cake you made yesterday.'

Wiping her hands on her apron, Mary put the kettle on, took out a plate, and cut a thick slab of cake, smothering it with warm butter as the knife glided over it like a skater on ice. Joe smacked his lips as Mary set a mug of steaming hot tea in front of him.

'I never did like lukewarm tea. That looks smashing. Thanks.'

The words washed over her as she smiled, patted him on the shoulder, and went back over to the sink to continue peeling the potatoes. By this stage, she had peeled so many that Joe was really beginning to wonder if there was something wrong, and he glanced over every now and then. She seemed distracted, gazing into nowhere and getting the lunch ready as if she were on autopilot.

Mary's thoughts returned once more to that fateful day when the two letters had arrived at the house. One of them she would leave and think about opening for the moment, determined to open it at a later date, fearful at the prospect. The other, was from the bank telling them the difference between the amount of money Anne would need to complete four years at Trinity and the student grant she would receive from the local authority; naturally, it would help a great deal, but it wouldn't cover everything. The money borrowed from the bank to pay for bills left over would make a decided difference in the mortgage repayments. Perhaps they could go up by another two percent or more. Her mind went into overkill as she thought how in heavens they were going to get the extra cash to make the repayments without losing their farm. Maybe, if she explained her situation to the bank manager. Perhaps there was another solution as she thought of all the possible scenarios. She wouldn't tell Joe, he had a dickey heart and that would be enough to set it off. No, she would have to deal with this situation on her own.

'Something wrong, luv?'

'Oh, no, just thinking, just thinking ....' Her voice trailed off, as she was jolted back to the present. Now she was thinking of the letter that she had never opened.

'Probably, nothing.'

'What is, pet?'

'Oh nothing, nothing'

'Anybody else coming for lunch?'

'No, just Anne.'

''Cause you've peeled enough spuds for the whole neighbourhood.'

Glancing down at the mountain of potatoes, she stopped in mid-potato and sighed. 'Oh blast!'

Mary never swore, so 'blast' was as bad as it could get. She was old-fashioned by normal standards, no dirty jokes, no swearing; grace before meals, and daily Mass or God help you. If anyone did swear in her company, she'd look at them so straight that it put a chill right through them. No one ever did.

Joe pushed the chair back and went over to her. Sliding his arm around her broad waist, he kissed her on the cheek.

'Don't worry about the lunch. We'll manage. Why don't you go up and lie down for half an hour. The roast beef will cook on its own. You're at sixes and sevens. A rest will do you the world of good.'

'Maybe I will. I don't feel the best at the moment.' As if in a daze, she turned round, went out the kitchen door and up the stairs to bed.

'Up you go, Jassie. Keep an eye on her.'

Jassie looked at him, head tilted as though he had just asked her to go to the moon!

She tilted her head again, as though questioning the command; she never went upstairs.

'Up you go, Jassie, there's a good girl.'

She did as she was bid, climbing with difficulty out of her basket, waddling up the stairs after her mistress, her tail flicking from side to side as she went. Joe nodded, wondering what was going on. It had to be something, but no doubt, Mary wouldn't keep it to herself for long. He upturned his collar, pulled down his cap to brave the outdoors once more, shivered as he thought of it, and ventured back out, closing the door behind him. It never really closed properly, and the lock had a habit of not sticking, taking only a small nudge for it to blow wide open again; another thing to be added to the long repair list.

The weather seemed to have improved a little, and it didn't seem quite as cold as Joe's eyes scanned the horizon, taking in his little farm. It wasn't much, but it was all his—well, the bank's, like everyone else thereabouts. Myer's Ditch was bordered on three sides by greenery. The front side leading to the main road was a granite wall with a small, squeaky gate, which welcomed them all in. There was a fair distance from the wall to the house by way of an unpaved path, but the grass was worn down on both sides by feet endlessly trundling to and fro.

The barn stood off on its own to the right-hand side of the house, with a couple of open stalls for the cattle and two mare and foal stables further down. It was quite extensive. At the entrance to the barn rested bales of hay, straw, and silage, all neatly divided to avoid confusion. They only had one horse, a sixteen-year-old bay called Mr. Magoo. When Anne was asked what to call the horse when he arrived as a two-year-old, she simply said 'goo' and patted his leg with her little hand.

Joe was a little hard of hearing and exclaimed, 'What a great idea! Mr. Magoo,' and the name stuck. Any hopes for a second horse disappeared when Anne had announced the 'big news' about Trinity, but the mare and foal stable would come in handy when Bessie, their sow, had her piglets. Joe had a small pigsty adjacent to the barn so that everything was within easy reach. It wasn't designed that way, but more or less, took on a life of its own. At the far end were the General and his Harem, as Mary used to call them. It was something that she had read when on a visit to the local library. If she had known what a harem really alluded to, she would have gone bright red from head to foot. The General was their gander, and the Harem members were—of course—the geese.

Some thought it odd that a farmer would give names to his animals, but maybe it was because Joe and Mary only had the one daughter and she was now away at university. Perhaps it made them feel less isolated, as though the farm were really like a large family. The hens, the few they had—six in all—had their own pen and henhouse, like royalty clucking around, scratching about looking for something to eat, with their cockerel in full command, darting back and forth to make sure no one got above herself, with not a care in the world.

That was it, the farm, except for a very young lady cat called Millie, white with blotches of tan and black and the most gorgeous tabby tail. She held her own, scared n' all as she was, for she was in the company of three much bigger tomcats who were all brothers. Tiddles was a very timid, bullied ginger with a ringed tail and a snow-white chest, Pirate, a fearless black-and-white patched fellah with a black patch over his eye to support his name, and Jacob, a beautiful, terrified, but affectionate ebony cat. He had a terrible habit of rubbing himself against hard surfaces on each side, which led to a furrow down the middle of his back and hair shorn on both sides reminding one of a Mohawk Indian ready to go on the rampage anytime he peeped out of the barn.

As Joe thought of the individuals that made up his happy family, he took out his pipe, lit it, shook his head, and felt satisfied with his lot. He chuckled to himself as he made his way over to the henhouse. Suddenly, all hell broke loose and Joe was rooted to the spot, as a hedgehog caught in the headlights of an oncoming car. He glared at Tiddles as the tomcat streaked across the yard with a *yowwwl*, and the General and his Harem in a V shape gunning for him in hot pursuit.

Whatever had upset the General, he was intent on having Tiddles; there was nothing for it but for Joe to make a beeline for the door, open it just in the nick of time so that Tiddles could dart into the corner, where he cowered underneath the kitchen chair.

Diverting his attention to the General, Joe roared at him, 'What's all this, then? What the *blazes* do you think you're doing?' He half expected an answer.

The General stopped dead—he wasn't going to take on Joe—and waddled furiously over to the other side of the yard with his Harem in tow. Joe nodded his head from side to side, as he made his way over to the hens to check on them and then went into the barn to muck out the stalls, fork in hand and wheelbarrow at the ready. By the time he had finished getting the stalls ready for the animals for the coming evening, it was almost two thirty. His stomach rumbled, reminding him of the roast beef that had been put on earlier. He washed his hands at the outside tap, shook them, and wiped them on the front of his trousers. He headed for the side door of the house, opened it, and saw that the previously cowering cat was now snoozing in front of the warm Aga cooker. He pulled off his wellies and slipped up the stairwell to the front bedroom above the kitchen. The smell of freshly ironed linen met him as he slowly opened the door. Mary was sound asleep; he nudged her, and as he did so, she opened her eyes sleepily.

'What time is it?' She yawned.

'Half past two.'

'She'll be home soon. I'd better get up. I needed that, didn't realise I was as tired as I was.'

He looked around the room for Jassie, and there she was in the corner, snoozing soundly. The room was small, a double bed made of pine with a matching dresser and a little lace thing-a-majig on the top of it, under which Mary had placed the unopened letter, upon which stood a few small wild flowers in a tiny vase. The framed Pope's blessing on their twenty-fifth wedding anniversary took pride of place above it, given to her by her mother years before. Joe crept out the door and started down the stairs as quietly as he could, as he didn't want Jassie to come down just yet. He was too late; she opened her eyes and darted for the door, but he gave a half turn and told her to go back in and he would call her later.

'Back to bed Jassie, there's a good girl,' and back she went to the corner of the room and resumed her snooze.

He heard the bus pull up on the main road and peeped out the window to see a small figure bobbing up and down as she made her way towards the squeaky gate. His eyes weren't as good as they once were, and he squinted to make out the features, but of course, it was Anne.

A sports bag crammed with dirty washing was her gift, along with a smile and a peck on the cheek for her dad as he opened the door.

'Hi, dad. How's she cuttin'?'

A broad grin filled his face. She was only home two minutes, and she was already trying to get a rise out of him!

'Not too bad. How's she cuttin' yourself?'

An even broader grin was on the receiving end. Breezing through the door, she plonked her grubby sports bag on the ground in the corner.

'Where's mam?'

'Oh, she'll be down in a minute. Set the table, will you, Annie?'

Mary pushed the small door at the end of the stairs that led to the kitchen and beamed as she met her daughter. Jassie followed, trundling down the stairs; her belly made it difficult to manoeuvre. Mary turned to the picture, kissed her hand, placed it on the picture for a moment, and turned to Anne.

'So what's the news? How do you like it? Are you working hard?'

'I've brought you a gift.'

'A gift? For me?' she exclaimed. 'That?' as she pointed to the grubby sports bag, smiling. 'Do you know that's what I've wanted to be all my life? You've made my day. I've just been made washerwoman of the year, but where's me trophy?'

'May I present you with your trophy?' Anne asked as she made a deep bow and handed her mam a pair of stinky socks. They burst out laughing.

Anne and her dad sat beside the cooker warming themselves, chatting forty to the dozen about Trinity, her dad quizzing her as if he were part of the Spanish Inquisition. Then, when everything was ready, they said grace and sat down to eat.

It was a memorable afternoon, and Mary was hoping that Anne would stay in and chat about the new flat and the friends she had made, but Anne had other ideas; she wanted to meet up with old friends and go out for a bit with the girls.

Mary and Anne had gone up to Dublin on the bus the previous September to look for a place to stay. They stayed in a B & B guesthouse at the lower end of Gardiner Street. They weren't sure where to look first and so got a map of Dublin and marked out the closest locations. It had to be central, but safe. They bought the *Irish Independent* and *Irish Times* and started scouring the ads for student digs for the coming year. They circled a few places with a biro, all pretty close but unsuitable for one reason or another. Then Mary saw it: what about Ely Place? *Studio Flat, one double bedroom, bathroom, and small kitchenette/sitting area.* It sounded perfect, but the price wasn't mentioned. *Ring 634521 for interview. References are essential.*

'You mean they interview you?' Mary asked Anne.

'Maaam, we aren't in Dunshaughlin now where everything is taken on trust! Welcome to Dublin.'

They rang the number, and a woman answered, brusque but polite.

'No, I'm sorry. You have to have a reference.'

'Would it be possible to see the flat at least? If we're acceptable, we could get one from the parish priest. Would that do?'

'Hmm, well, it's not the norm, but all right.'

She said she would meet them outside the property at half past two sharp the following afternoon. Promptly at half past two, she showed up. Anne and Mary were turning the corner into Ely Place at twenty-five to three as the woman looked up and down the street, tapping her shoe on the ground. She was the most business-like woman they had ever seen, polite but to the point, a no-nonsense sort. She was small and thin, with black hair tied at the back, dressed in a smart grey business suit—not at all what they expected.

'I'm sorry about being a few minutes late. We couldn't find the place.'

The usual pleasantries were exchanged as they followed her into 27 Ely Place. It was the studio flat at the top of the house; after three flights of stairs, they were almost out of breath.

'If this goes on much further, I'll have to get Scotty from *Star Trek* to "beam me up",' whispered her mother under her breath.

'Sssh, she'll hear you.'

'Now, Mrs. Myers, this is a clean, respectable house, no drinking or carousing until the late hours, no loud music, no smoking ....' The list was endless. 'I take it that those conditions are acceptable?'

'Yes,' Mary said half-heartedly.

'Of course, you will have to sign a lease from now until the end of June.'

'Naturally,' said Anne, trying to sound sophisticated but not pulling it off, and the woman peered at her, wondering as to whether she was being impertinent or not.

'The rent is paid at the end of every month, with two months in advance, all right?'

She started rummaging in her bag for a handkerchief as she could feel a sneeze coming on.

'How ... how... how much is the rent?' said Mary with an apologetic, wry smile.

The landlady looked at her as if to say, if you're asking, you can't afford it.

'£400.00 a month,' was the reply. Mary half smiled at her again as the landlady went over to the window to point out the various advantages of being so central and went from the bedroom to the bathroom to the kitchenette/sitting area as though she were a sergeant major on parade.

'Heavens above, Anne, we only want to rent the place, not buy the whole bloomin' house.'

'Sssh, she'll hear you,' Anne replied.

'Would you like to think it over? Though I *am* obliged to tell you that I have two other prospective people looking at it later this evening, and I am sure that they will take it, that is, if it is still available. So have you decided?'

Anne nudged her mother in the ribs.

'Yes,' said Mary as she cleared her throat, 'we'll take it'.

'*Provided*, of course, that your parish priest, Father—?'

' —O'Brien,' was the reply.

'Provided, of course, Father O'Brien is prepared to furnish you with a proper reference.'

'Of course.'

They shook hands on the deal and parted ways. Anne and her mother scurried down Ely Place towards Trinity College. Turning the corner, they went down Grafton Street towards Suffolk Street in the hope of getting a bus to O'Connell Street. They would pack their few belongings back at the B & B and head down towards Busarus. The bus for Dunshaughlin was at four o'clock, so they hadn't time to hang around.

When they arrived at the B & B, the woman who ran it was as different from the woman they had just encountered as night is from day. She was a short, plump woman in her fifties with a well-worn overall apron and soft slippers and the warmest Dublin accent ever encountered. She reminded guests of an aunt they always wanted to visit. A broad smile greeted Mary and Anne, which delighted them after the frosty reception they had just received.

'Yer back, then. How did ya' get on, Mary?' she asked. 'I know yer goin' at half past three, so I did yez' a bite to eat. I knew ya' wouldn' have tie'um.'

'Oh, Mrs. O'Brien thanks very much.'

Anne ran up to their room, packed up their few bits, had a quick look around to make sure they hadn't left anything behind, and hurried down the stairs. Mary was in the kitchen having a cup of tea and a slice of barm brack, after having had a small fry up. A photograph of a young priest taken thirty or so years before took pride of place in the kitchen right beside the picture of the Sacred Heart.

'Here's yours, luv,' Mrs. O'Brien said as she handed Anne a hot plate with sausage, egg, chips, and a few rashers.

'Oh, Mrs. O'Brien, that looks just great.'

Mrs. O'Brien stood back, smiled more broadly than before, as if she had been given an Oscar for the best fry up in Gardiner Street, and sat down with them as they finished their tea.

'Let me know how you get on, won't cha'? Keep in touch.'

They both agreed and thanked Mrs. O'Brien again as they hurried down Gardiner Street, turning to wave goodbye.

'Don't forget to keep in touch.'

They arrived at five to four and had just enough time to be on the bus before the engine roared to get underway.

Chapter Two

They got off the bus after spending the whole ride discussing how kind Mrs. O'Brien was and how lucky they had been to find her. Anne spent packing and repacking over the next few days, thinking of Trinity and wondered how Fresher's week would go.

'Well now, have you got everything?' Joe asked.

'Yes, dad.'

The landlady had said that Anne could buy any pots, pans, and bits n' pieces in the local supermarket in Baggot Street, and what she couldn't find there, she would be able to get in the hardware store next to it, close to the bank.

The journey up to Dublin was one of regret and excitement. The first few days were spent trying to find suitable pots and pans, dishes, and a food supply for the week. When Anne had finally settled into her new studio apartment, she thought herself quite independent and infallible. She would soon learn that it wasn't true in either case.

Fresher's week, as it is known, is the first week for a Junior Freshman at Trinity. Freshmen start a week earlier to help them get their orientation of the university. The first day was an eye-opener; walking wide-eyed through the Arts Block, Anne felt that she had finally attained her dream. She made her way through the short, dark corridor before emerging into the sunlight, where the campus was filled to bursting with new students, like bees around a honey pot. She walked a little further on, past the bell tower, or campanile, and there they were in Front Square, like apple sellers in Moore Street, enticing one to buy their merchandise. Each society had his own stall, all the various clubs, which, for a small fee, would let one become part of their illustrious little world: fencing clubs, chess clubs, debating teams, equestrian clubs, philosophical societies, so many—where would she start? First was registration.

Oh, God in heaven, the very prospect was like climbing Mount Everest. Anne made her way to the end of the queue of a long line of young people, all with their appropriate documentation, each looking excited but rather dumbfounded, checking and rechecking their documents to make sure that everything was in order. The exam hall, where registration took place, was huge, filled with people, students, and staff alike. By the time registration was over, Anne didn't feel much like being part of any society or club but felt rather alone amongst all the chattering students who looked a lot more 'tuned in' than she was. She felt apprehensive about the future. She wondered whether it was such a good idea after all, away from everyone who loved her, from her friends, some of whom had already started working and earning a wage.

She sat at the side step with her hands cupping her face, off in a world of her own. A voice from behind her said, 'It's a lot to take in, isn't it?'

She turned, transfixed by a pair of intensely green eyes peering at her, until she realised that they belonged to a young man about eighteen, with tousled brown hair and wearing a blue shirt and jeans. She burst into a smile.

'Yes, an awful lot.'

Don't worry; everyone feels the same. Some show it, some don't. You're not from Dublin, are you?'

'No. No, I'm not.'

'Where are you from?'

'I'm from Dunshaughlin.'

'Dun where?'

'Dunshaughlin. Where are you from?'

'Blackrock.'

'Is that far?'

'Oh, about twenty minutes by bus.'

'What are you doing?' Anne asked.

'French and Spanish. How about you?'

'Law,' she said, struggling against disappointment. *That's just great! I meet someone who could be a friend, and he turns out to be studying something totally different. Well done, Anne!*

He almost read her mind, as he replied, 'Never mind. Let's go and get a bite to eat in the Buttery.'

'The Buttery? What's the Buttery?'

'Your home for the next four years! My name's Brian. What's yours?'

'Anne.'

'Okay, now that we know who *we* are, let's find out what *they* have for lunch.'

She smiled as he led her from the hall, and they marched over to the Buttery Bar, stumbling on the cobbled stones as they went.

'You got your student card, then?'

'Yes.' She showed it to him.

'You're under eighteen?'

'How did you know?'

'Oh, it's a red line that appears on your student card to let the guys know so they won't serve you any booze in the bar.'

'I don't mind about that. I don't drink.'

'Just as well!'

'Do you know who your tutor is?'

'Oh ... a Professor John Bartholomew Higgins at the Russian Department.'

'Hmm, Professor Higgins, like Professor Higgins of *My Fair Lady*.'

'God, I certainly hope not! How 'bout you?'

'Dr. James Masterson, French Department.'

'What do you think they'll be like?'

'Beats me. They have to be okay, though. They're like a buffer between you and the lecturer you have a problem with.'

She looked at him, puzzled.

'Know what I mean?'

'No, I don't, to be honest.'

'Well, he's like a referee at a boxing match. You and the other contender are going at it, hell for leather, blood spattering everywhere.' Brian was revelling in the graphic account of his imagined fight, hopping from one foot to the other, jabbing at thin air, ducking and diving. Anne, always fainted at the sight of blood, was feeling quite queasy, her mouth agape as she was drawn into his imaginary fight.

'You and your lecturer don't see eye to eye on something, see? Well, the tutor's the one who rings the bell and calls time out.' He stopped jabbing, hopping, ducking, and diving as unexpectedly as he had started.

'God, I don't know whether I want one of those. They sound desperate.'

'Which? The lecturer or the tutor?'

'Both ... I mean either.'

'Nah, Godsend, really, especially if you get into trouble. Don't worry. I don't expect you will be in any hot water at all.'

'I hope not,' she said worriedly as she imagined the boxing match. Brian started to egg her on as he bounced and jabbed at thin air again. Laughing, he patted her on the shoulder.

'Only kidding. Come on. Let's have some lunch.'

Trinity wasn't so daunting after all. Maybe they could still be friends, who knew? Life didn't seem so bleak, and she was beginning to look forward to her new life at university.

The next few weeks passed quickly as Anne found her feet and started to enjoy Dublin—enjoying it a little too much, as her grades started to suffer. It was true she was a bright girl, but she had to work: the stuff couldn't be injected into her. By the time the end of November came, her previously promising grades had deteriorated greatly. She never went to the library, preferring to chat with other students in the Arts Block, friends of Brian. It was inevitable when her head of department called her in to find out why she had failed in two different term essays. She knocked on the door of the department office, and the secretary cheerily called, 'Come in.'

'I'm Anne Myers. I was told to come to see you.'

'Oh, yes, you have an appointment to see your tutor, Professor Higgins, at two thirty on Wednesday.'

'Do you know what it's about?'

'I'm afraid that's confidential. That's between you and your tutor.'

'Oh, God!' She went deathly pale.

'Don't worry, dear. You're very lucky. He's been a tutor for a long time. I know him quite well, and he's extremely nice.'

Anne couldn't sleep for two days, worrying about her upcoming bout with her tutor as she remembered the conversation she had had with Brian the first day. 'Don't worry. I don't expect you will be in any hot water at all,' echoed in her ears and she relived the boxing bout that Brian had so enthusiastically relayed to her two months before.

Wednesday, twenty past two came, and she made sure she was early. She had never been in trouble in her life. She had always been a source of pride to her parents and teachers alike, winning medals for everything from swimming to language competitions. She found herself suddenly in unfamiliar territory, and she started to feel uneasy. She promised herself that if she came out of this situation, she would work like a demon possessed. She had to have another chance. She knocked on the door of the small office.

'Come in,' bellowed from inside.

She turned the handle, feeling sick as she did so, imagining a boxer in red silk shorts inside ready to knock her block off.

'Professor Higgins, I'm Anne Myers, you … you … wanted to see me?'

'Oh yes, Anne,' he bellowed. 'Come in.'

He looked to be about six feet tall as he stood up to welcome her in, not at all like the Professor Higgins of *My Fair Lady*: mid forties, short dark brown hair, with a beard and brown eyes hidden behind the most awful black-rimmed glasses. They were ghastly. When he took them off and smiled at her, he didn't seem so terrible.

He appeared to be a kind but stern man. He asked her why her last two papers had produced such dire marks. Was there something wrong? Did she need help? That was what he was there for, to help her in whatever way he could. She had to do better if she wanted a chance of passing her exams in May. He said he had looked at the papers and was quite surprised that the level was so poor. Did she understand the subject matter in hand? If things continued this way, she would fail her exams in May.

Anne didn't respond to any of the questions but just bowed her head and nodded in agreement, as he kept trying to get an answer from her. Hot tears welled up inside her, and she felt a lump come to her throat; before she could stop them, the tears ran down her face like a flood. She sobbed and sobbed.

'Now, now, don't get yourself in a state. You haven't failed yet, you know.'

She explained what happened and was truthful about all her socialising and lack of study. Professor Higgins seemed quite impressed by her honesty and lack of excuses. She bowed her head again, gritted her teeth, and scrunched her eyes tight. She imagined herself once more in the boxing ring with Professor Higgins, his red silk shorts fluttering as he started bouncing around with two enormous boxing gloves heading right for her, ducking, diving, bobbing left and right. Camera bulbs flashed on every side. She felt frozen to the spot; her head started to swim. *Oh, God, here it comes.* She imagined one glove undercut her and the other heading for the right side of her face for the ultimate knockout. 'Make it quick and painless,' she muttered.

'What's that?'

'Oh nothing, Professor.' She was brought back to the reality of her tutor's office.

'I will make you a deal. I want you to submit two new term essays to replace the ones you did on tort law and constitutional law 1, *and* in addition, I want you to do another two essays on these titles. You have only a short time to prepare. They have to be typed in double-line spacing as before, and you have to follow the guidelines outlined by the department. I spoke to Dr. Rutledge and Dr. Hanson before our meeting, and we decided that if I felt that the situation warranted it, you could resubmit. Remember: they will be *very* tough on you. Few people get a second chance. You will not be resubmitting the same titles as before, so you will have to work very hard to do the research. Are you prepared for that? Will you submit them in time? If they are done properly and are of an acceptable standard, they will be taken as replacements. However, I want to make this crystal clear. This is to be a "once off". Is that clear?' Professor Higgins was clearly adamant about this.

'Yes, I'll do my best. Thank you for this chance, Professor Higgins.' Anne nodded and smiled. She wouldn't be home for Christmas or New Year. She would have to do all the research before the term break and resubmit the first day of the new term. Perhaps, if she worked like a maniac, she might get home for Christmas, only time would tell.

Anne worked like never before, staying at the law library until the last minute. The Berkeley, as it was known, closed at ten o'clock at night, as did the Lecky Library in the Arts Block. She thought how blessed she was living so close to Trinity. She didn't have to pay for any public transport as everything was within easy walking distance. Initially, Anne had thought the studio flat expensive and the landlady too gruff, but taking into account the proximity, she could understand that it had many advantages, especially after coming home late from the library.

The last day of Trinity term came sooner than Anne had anticipated, and Brian didn't see Anne for the next month or more. Christmas came; Christmas trees were seen being bundled onto cars, and people rushed to and fro for last minute Christmas shopping. The lights in Grafton Street and carol singing made everything very festive, but Anne didn't feel like celebrating. She had brought this on herself. She walked down to the Pro-Cathedral for Christmas Eve Mass and lit a candle, hoping that things would turn out okay. She felt lonelier than she had ever felt before as she saw families, with children filled with anticipation, arrive and later leave after the Christmas celebration. Soon her thoughts turned to home and she rang her mother to explain that she was studying and had a heavy workload. Although Mary was disappointed, she understood. She would see her in March.

Computers were only in their infancy, but Trinity prided itself in keeping abreast of the times. Anne had access to a computer on campus where she was allowed to type up her essays, often staying until very late. Finally, the first day of Michaelmas Term began; it was a new start. She submitted the essays and felt a sense of achievement and relief as she walked away. Well, that was it. Come what may, she could say that she had done her best.

A week after submission, Anne was sticking to what had become a very methodical and tiring timetable. She went out at the weekends, but during the week, she studied in the Berkeley every night until ten o'clock. Professor Higgins left a note at the law department to tell her that he wanted to see her Tuesday afternoon at four o'clock. The results were in.

'Professor Higgins?'

'Come in, Anne. Well, now, about those results.'

'Did I pass?'

'Hmm, now, let me see. Your first essay was on tort law with Dr. Hanson, 2.2.' He peered up at her over his spectacles. 'Hmm, and the second one, the replacement, D.'

'Oh, I thought that it would have been better than that, all that hard work.'

'Don't despair.' A smirk crept over his face, peering down over his spectacles. 'Now, let's see what Dr. Rutledge says, your first essay was on constitutional law 1. Hmm, 2.1.'

'That's better, isn't it?' She asked enthusiastically.

'Now, the replacement essay. D.' He peered at her again.

'Oh, God, I shouldn't be here. I'm not clever enough. I'll never be clever enough.'

'Sit down, Anne,' Professor Higgins replied sternly.

'That means I've failed. That means I won't pass. D. God, I worked so hard on those essays and they gave me a D. They could have given me a C!'

Professor Higgins took off his spectacles and looked straight at Anne.

'D is distinction. D is a First. You cannot get higher! Now let's see about the comments on the D paper on constitutional law 1: *"Anne shows an in-depth aptitude for this subject. The research carried out is far beyond that expected of a Junior*

Freshman. No less will be accepted from this student in any future assignments."

'What do they say about the tort law replacement essay? I wonder. Ah, yes. Here we are; *"Anne has produced balanced and fair observations. Her knowledge of tort law for a Junior Freshman is quite outstanding. I will be keeping a close eye on this student and should work of this calibre be submitted at the exam in May, I would expect her to attain a 2.1, however, extra work will be allocated to ensure Anne does not fall into relapse."'*

'You should be happy with that, Anne.'

'Yes, thank you. I'm very grateful to you, Professor Higgins. I don't mean any disrespect, but I hope I won't be seeing you again.'

Professor Higgins smiled and chuckled. 'No, Anne. I don't suppose you will.'

Anne continued working hard, and Easter was there before she knew it. The break came, and she finally went home, weighed down with her sports bag filled with dirty washing. She was looking forward to going home. When she arrived, her mother had just come down the stairs from the bedroom with Jassie following her, her belly making it difficult for her to move with any dexterity.

'So, it's goin' all right, then?'

'Yes, it's going fine.'

'Jassie is due soon.'

'Yes, I can see. Dad, will you ring me when they arrive?'

'Sure thing, luv, as soon as they do.'

Anne went off that evening with the girls she had known all her life, and though Mary wanted to chat with her, she was pleased that she was able to go. A couple of weeks staying at home were enough to recharge the batteries.

Mary had made a few culinary delights for her during her first week back to start the final term properly: a steak and kidney pie, roasted chicken legs, a quiche, some sultana tea buns, a brown bread soda, soft cheese, and homemade butter. The washing was done, ironed, and packed back into her sports bag. She was laden down with all the stuff her mother had made for her with the admonition that she didn't eat properly and was losing weight like a freight train going downhill. Anne went back to Dublin that night and wondered about Jassie and how many puppies she would have this time. She was half-asleep by the time the bus pulled into Busarus.

'Time to get off, dearie.' The driver rocked her to and fro.
'Oh, thanks, thanks.'
'Need a hand?'
'No, thanks. I can manage.'

Anne got back to her studio flat and put her things away, the smell of fresh clothes reminding her of home as they were released from the sports bag. Her goodies were put away, and she put on the kettle for a cup of tea and relaxed for the rest of the evening. That night at about one o'clock, the phone in the hall rang out. The phone box was just outside her door.

'Anne? Is that you, Anne?'
'Yes, dad. Is everything all right?'
'You told me to tell you when Jassie had her puppies. Well, she has just had them, three beauties. They came earlier than we thought, but they're all fine.'
'Oh, I am glad, dad. I was worried about her. See you at the weekend, okay? Thanks, for calling. Tell Jassie I love her.'
'See you then, luv. Bye.'

Joe had spent the night in the kitchen helping Jassie have her puppies. He was tired but thrilled beyond words. She sat in her basket, licking them constantly. Happy as could be, every now and then she glanced up at Joe for confirmation on her ability as a mother.

'You're a grand girl, the best in the world, and that's a fact,' he said as he patted her on her head.

Anne would see them at the weekend; she couldn't wait. The week dragged as she waited until the last Friday lecture finished and then grabbed her stuff and ran down to Busarus to catch the bus home. She often thought of Mrs. O'Brien, how kind she had been to her when she had first arrived in Dublin. Maybe she'd call in to see how she was and bring her a barm brack from her mam. *That's a good idea. I think I'll do that*, she said to herself. Anne couldn't wait to get home. It seemed as though the bus dragged along. She was so anxious that she counted almost every tree in sight.

As she got in and breezed through the door, she said, 'Jassie. Oh, Jassie, I *have* missed you.' There was Jassie in her basket with her three beautiful puppies.

'Well, lass, choose one.'

'I can keep one, can't I, dad?'

'They're all fine looking, two bitches, and a dog. Which is it to be?'

'Oh, dad, can I have the dog?'

'What are you going to call him?'

'Bob.'

'Someone I know? Or ought to know?'

'No, it just popped into my head.'

'Bob it is, then.'

Anne played gently with Jassie and the puppies, stroking them and spending most of the weekend telling Jassie how great she was and that they would spend every day together. Jassie, a little older and wiser than she, wagged her tail and paid no attention except to her little brood.

The last term, Hilary Term, of which remained only six weeks, went by relatively briskly. Endless hours of study meant that Brian and Anne rarely saw each other during the week, but on the weekends she was in Dublin, they went to *The Duke* pub in South Anne Street or *The Bailey* and had a few drinks and had a bit of a laugh. They told each other about what had gone on in their week. They had become close friends, and it was something that was going to be sorely needed.

Exam time came, and it was as tense as ever as she was trying to cram in as much as possible the night before. Anne had worked solidly throughout the year except for the short period at the beginning, which turned out to be a Godsend in getting her back on track, though it didn't seem so at the time. When the exams were over, they went on the tear and had a whale of a time. They hadn't attended Trinity Ball earlier in May as it had started smack in the middle of their exams and they weren't taking any chances. Whilst everyone else was enjoying themselves to the hilt, Brian was at home cramming, as was Anne, in her studio flat in Ely Place.

Soon it was time to go home and pack up all her belongings. Mrs. McLoughlin, the landlady, said that she could store her things in the basement if she had intended on returning.

She went home on a high, glad everything was over, and that she would be returning in September as a Senior Freshman. First, she had to get the results. The results were posted at six o'clock outside the exam hall on 27th June for French and Spanish and on 28th for law in the law faculty. Anne travelled up on the 27th for moral support, so that should anything go wrong for Brian, she would be there to console him. Everyone gathered together, pushing and shoving once the results had been posted. Anne stood off to the side, waiting nervously.

Unlike now, each student's name was printed alongside the student number. Anonymity was not part of the package, so whether you failed or passed, everyone knew. Brian went up to see the results, waiting until the row of people at the front had already seen their results. Student No: 5366425; Student Name: Brian Maguire, Junior Freshman. Two Subject Moderatorship: French 2.1, Spanish 2.1, Overall 2.1. He read it slowly again, taking in every syllable. He had achieved a 2.1. A 2.1! He couldn't believe it. He hung his head, repeating everything he had read and turned to walk slowly down the steps. Anne stopped him as he feigned failure, and he burst out. 'Ha! ha! A 2.1!' He was elated as he grabbed her and spun her around. 'Can you believe it?'

She was so happy for him as he went home on cloud nine to tell his parents.

Anne stayed with Mrs. O'Brien in Gardiner Street and brought her a barm brack from home from her mother. She explained that she was getting her results the following day.

Mrs. O'Brien looked very seriously at her. 'Do you think you'll do all right?'

'I hope so.'

'I tell ya what, luv. I'm going to ten o'clock Mass tomorrow mornin' and I'll light a candle at the Sacred Heart. Great man, the Sacred Heart, great man.'

'I'd be very grateful,' Anne said sincerely, needing any miracle, large or small.

The following day after breakfast, Anne left to do a few things in town, telling Mrs. O'Brien she would call back later to tell her whether her prayers had been heard.

Mrs. O'Brien was as good as her word, donning her scarf with a few coppers in her purse, her well-used rosary beads, and a coat that had seen many a day. She turned into the Pro-Cathedral and went to Mass, stopping at the Sacred Heart statue, lighting a candle, and asking the good Lord to help her friend in need. She blessed herself, but not before thanking Him, for having heard her and answering her prayer. She suffered from arthritis, which prevented her from bending, but she always made a special effort to genuflect before leaving. She had a belief that would shift mountains; she was not someone who was showy or hypocritical, but a quiet, gentle soul who had good manners and believed that you should always thank a giver, *especially* if you don't know if he's going to give you something. Then that would make him feel obliged to do as you had asked, a mental elbow in the ribs so to speak, a type of blackmailing with politeness. Whatever she believed, it worked every time, without fail.

The results were to be posted in the law faculty by half past two, and Anne made her way up to the faculty office notice board at three o'clock. She didn't want to be the first there in case things hadn't worked out and she was disappointed. Brian was sitting on a large red felt box outside the department waiting for her. He didn't say anything but just pointed to the notice board. A rush of dread ran through her body.

'Oh, please, God. Please don't say I've failed,' she exclaimed. Student No 3659925: Junior Freshman. Student Name: Anne

Myers. Results: Constitutional Law 1: 2.1, Criminal Law: 2.1, Torts: 2.1, Legal Systems & Methods: 2.2: Overall Result: 2.1. She shrieked, not believing what she had just seen: 2.1. Brian gave her a pat on the shoulder.'Well done.'

'Well done yourself,' she replied.

'Going out tonight, are you?' He was hoping she would go out for a quick drink, even though she didn't actually 'drink.'

'I can't. I have to get the four o'clock bus home—first weekend of the new term. Okay?'

'Fair enough.'

They walked outside the main arch; he turned left to get the 7A home, and she turned right to go down the quays and up Gardiner Street to collect her rucksack before going home. She arrived at the B & B and feigned defeat, and Mrs. O'Brien exclaimed, 'But ya must 'ave passed! The Sacred Heart has never let me down, never!'

I didn't pass! I got a 2.1.'

'What's a 2.1?'

'Like a B.'

'Good girl yourself, good on ya.' Mrs. O'Brien patted Anne on her back.

'Don't forget to bring this to yer mam. It's an apple tart, baked when I came back after me little visit to see "Himself".' She pointed back to the Sacred Heart picture.

'Who's that beside him?'

'Oh, that's me brother-in-law. I haven't seen him for yeeears, I keep meaning to go and see him, and especially after me dear Billie passed away. It'll be twenty-two years this August, Lord, rest him.'

Gesturing towards the picture, she continued. 'He's a parish priest in Our Lady of—eeh, eeh—what's the name? —eeh —now I remember. Yeah, that's it, Our Lady of the Holy Rosary Church, somewhere in Dun somethin' or other in Meath.' Delighted that she had remembered the name after so many years, Mrs. O'Brien nodded her head.

'What's his name?'

'O'Brien.'

'No, no. No, his *first* name.'

'Francis Mary Aloysius. His mother was very partial to Aloysius.'

'But he can't be.'

'I'm sorry, luv.' I was never really partial to the name meself, but there you have it.' 'But ... but that's *our* parish priest,' she said, pointing to the picture.

'Whaaaat? Jesus, Mary, and Holy St. Joseph ... save us all from an early grave.' She blessed herself rapidly. 'Well, it looks like I'll have to pay a visit on Father Francis, long overdue, I'd say.' She flopped down in the kitchen chair.

'Stay at our house. Dad and mam will be really pleased. They'll be delighted to return your kindness.'

'Not at all, luv. Not at all.' She looked at the clock and got up as quickly as she could. 'Fair enough. Ask your mam first, though. Off ya go now or you'll miss yer bus.'

Anne ran down the street with her rucksack over her shoulder and the apple tart under her arm and was just in the nick of time before the doors of the bus swished closed on the way home.

In her first days at home for the summer, Anne spent some time checking out summer jobs in and around Dunshaughlin—nothing doing. Then she saw a notice in the local paper about a pub needing a barmaid. Her father wouldn't hear of it; she had only turned seventeen. She was underage to work in a bar anyway. He told her that the hours were unpredictable and he wouldn't be able to go and collect her. Well, could she go and work waiting tables and the only late night would be clearing up after the disco. He said he would think about it.

The bar disco was his local, O'Neill's. He had beaten a path to the door on more than one occasion, though he wasn't a hard drinker. He liked the banter of the farmers who would talk about local prices. He hadn't been out for a good while because Jassie always accompanied him from the time she was quite young. It had been nearly three months since the puppies had been born, and the two little bitches had been sold after eight weeks. Only, the little dog, Bob, remained with his mother. Although Jassie had been upset at first, looking for her lost puppies, she soon abandoned the idea that they were lost. They had gone to good people, local farmers, who had known the family for years. Bob wasn't yet old enough to venture outside but remained with Mary as Joe went out to bring the cattle in from the field. Then Jassie was sent off to collect Anne from O'Neill's pub/disco.

The disco had finished and the last remnants of people were leaving as Jassie crept in the side entrance and lay down, waiting for Anne. After about twenty minutes, as Anne stood chatting to some young man, Jassie sat up and barked at her, reminding her politely that it was time to go home and her parents would be worried. She said goodbye and patted Jassie. 'Come on, pet. Your little fellah will be waiting for you.'

The young man approached her, asking to walk her home, but Jassie growled a little, and the young man quickly abandoned the idea as he realised that she was adequately protected. Any other ideas that might have gone through his head quickly took flight, and he wished her goodnight and left.

Anne saved a fair amount of money, not a fortune, but it would help with her weekly expenses at university. She helped her mother at home and had done so, from the time she was knee high to a grasshopper. She knew how to make beds, scrub floors, wash windows, and do the bathroom and toilet from the time she was about nine years old. Her culinary skills hadn't been hewn until she was about eleven, when her mother taught her everything she knew, with the exception of skinning a rabbit and gutting fish. Those skills were shown to her when she was older, when had acquired a steady hand with a knife. This early training would prove to be very useful later on.

She wasn't able to help her mother while at university but tried to help her when she was home during the summer. She was a good girl, something of a daydreamer but a good girl just the same. It may have seemed strange to some that a little girl would be shown so much and given such responsibility, but her parents relied on her to do her share. No one shirked duty, though it would never interfere with her schoolwork.

They were different times back then, not better, just different. If she saw anybody of her own age out playing, she would look at her mother and start.

'Look at—. She's been playing all afternoon and look at me. I'm—.'

'We can't run the farm by ourselves, and I haven't seen any elves or fairies put in a job application, so I'm afraid you'll have to pull your weight.'

If she protested, a firm, 'It's your duty. You're not doing me any favours. It's your duty,' was the reply.

That didn't happen too often; more often than not, Anne did what she was told. Once, when she protested too much, her mother sent her off to the local shop a mile or so down the road to buy a few necessities.

'Now, Anne, mind as you go, and go to the Spar shop and ask Mrs. Mulligan for the following: soap, deodorant, toothpaste, elbow grease, and Pears' shampoo, and ask her to put it on account. Here's the list. Mind you don't lose it.'

On her arrival, Mrs. Mulligan looked at the list and smirked.

'Now, Anne, soap, deodorant, toothpaste, and Pears' shampoo.'

'But you've forgotten the elbow grease, Mrs. Mulligan,' she piped up.

'Well, Anne, you better tell your mother that the only elbow grease available, is when you pull up your socks and do a bit of hard work instead of lolling about all day like lady muck!' Anne nodded her head and went home, repeating to her mother exactly what Mrs. Mulligan had said. Her mother roared with laughter at the seriousness with which she delivered the message. She never complained about doing 'too much work' again. It was a lesson that she never forgot.

Chapter Three

The end of the summer had arrived, and Anne would be going into second year in Trinity. She had made a fair few friends, but her best pal had been Brian from the time he introduced himself on the first day of registration. She had thought that perhaps after she graduated she would move to Dublin permanently. There was nothing in Dunshaughlin, really; yes, her mam and dad were there and the farm, but she never really thought of living there for good. It was nice to see old friends when she went home, but she had made a new life in Dublin and had moved on, just as they had moved on with their lives. She loved Dublin, but she loved Trinity more. It was more than she had expected, and the thought of failing her exams and having it all snatched away from her made her realise just how much she really did love it.

When she moved to Dublin after the summer holidays, she stayed in the same studio apartment in Ely Place, and that seemed to suit Mrs. McLoughlin, as she seemed satisfied that Anne had complied with her rules. Anne had never warmed to the woman; there was something too aloof about her. She had hardly anything to do with her. She might meet her on the stairs as she collected her rent from other tenants or was checking that the rubbish had been left out, and dealing with little repairs that needed attention. Anne often thought that she would be just the ticket to get her dad to do the 'long list of repairs' that never got done. She was efficient and reminded Anne of a robot. She rarely smiled, and when she did, it was forced.

The public telephone outside the door of her apartment was a Godsend and meant that she didn't have to go outside at night to ring her parents to see how everything was. At the same time, if she wasn't going home at the weekend, they would prearrange a time to ring her. Brian did the same, and it was during one of these conversations that he told her that he was heading off to the Sorbonne in Paris for an Erasmus exchange. He didn't tell her when university broke up before the summer, as he didn't know if he would be awarded the place. He paid the tuition fees as normal as though he were attending Trinity, and the other student in the Sorbonne would do the same. They literally swapped places.

'How long is it going to be for?' Anne asked, a little deflated.

'Oh, not long at all. It'll do my French the power of good.'

'How long?'

'Just a year.'

'Oh that's great. I hope it goes really well for you. I really do.' she tried to sound animated but wasn't. 'A whole year ... in France ... that's wonderful.' She tried even harder to sound animated.

'I can't wait. Imagine the Sorbonne. Paris.'

'Yes, I *am* imagining it.'

God, he was the only friend that she had, but she didn't want to put him off. He went. She didn't know that it was probably the best thing for both of them. It would make her more assertive, less shy, and worried about what other people thought of her. It would help him, too. He would miss her and realise that friendship was a two-way stretch; that in itself would make both of them very aware of how lucky they were to have each other as friends. It wasn't going to be 'wonderful' for either of them; it would have its ups and downs, but it was necessary.

Efflam d'Avennes was Brian's substitute. She didn't know he existed except for a letter that Brian had written to her shortly after he arrived in France. Brian had given him her address and told him to look her up.

Université de Paris III: Sorbonne

Hi Anne,

Thought I'd drop you a quick line, between lectures to tell you about the university and life here in Paris. My French is improving. That needed doing, I can tell you. At first, it was difficult because they speak so fast, but I seem to be getting the hang of it.

I hope you don't mind but I've given your details to the exchange student who is now studying in Trinity but I forgot to leave your telephone number. He's called Efflam d'Avennes, he's a real charmer, very French, and he's looking forward to seeing you. I told him to leave a note outside the law notice board for you so you can meet him. He did the same for me and I'm going out with some of his friends now. I always thought Parisians thought they were too good for anyone else. Was I wrong! They're really dead on; you just have to give them a little time to get to know you.

Well I'm going to do all the tourist things, like taking walks down the Champs-Élysées past the Arc de Triomphe seeing the wonderful Eiffel Tower and the Palais Bourbon. Next week I intend visiting the Palais et Jardin du Luxembourg and Notre Dame Cathedral. It will be a while before I make my way to see Sacré Coeur Cathedral in the Moulin Rouge District, but I'll get there. I also plan to visit the Palais de Versailles soon but as it's outside Paris and will involve a 30 minute train trip I might have to postpone seeing that beauty for now. Don't worry I'll take some photos of that too when I get there.

I live in a small apartment not far from the university. It's very handy. I hope you'll write to me.

Miss you already.

Brian

Fair enough, Anne thought. *Since this d'Avennes fellah's friends are doing their best to make Brian feel so welcome in Paris, the least I can do is make him feel at home at Trinity. After all, last year I felt out of my depth and Brian came to the rescue.* Anne wrote a message on the notice board, leaving her telephone number and explaining who she was to the d'Avennes fellah. *God*, she thought, *he's either the typical suave, French fellah with gel in his hair and has an answer for everything and can sweep you off your feet with luv' n' stuff or he's un-suave and a hippy. One's as bad as the other. What have I let myself in for? Brian I could just kill you!*

That night at about ten thirty, the phone rang.

'Allo? a heavy French accent said. 'Cood I speak to Anne pleeeze?'

'Yes, this is Anne.'

'My name is Efflam, I sink mon ami Brian told you of me.'

'Oh, yes,' She was unimpressed by his French purring.

'I was wonderhing if you would like to miit.. tomit?'

'What do you mean tomit? 'to miit ... tomitt?'

'Oh, riiight. To *meeet*? All right then, when and where?'

'D tree at zee Arts Block tomorrow at one?'

'Fair enough' and they said goodnight.

Anne thought, *Brian, you owe me big time.*

The following day came quicker than anticipated, and Anne went to *the tree* at the Arts Block entrance. Whoever planted the tree there made way for the most perfect place to meet. Anyone at Trinity knew *the tree*. It was as famous as Midas! Anne waited at five to one at the tree and five past one came and went. She started tapping her toe, wondering if this French fellah was ever going to turn up. *Why was he so late?*

'I thought French fellahs were supposed to be sophisticated and *on time*,' she blurted out.

He was there on the other side of the tree, immersed in a book.

'God, trust me! I choose to meet some French fellah, and he doesn't even have the decency to turn up on time,' Anne said, annoyed, in a loud voice.

Efflam looked up from his book and realised that the annoyed person was probably Anne.

'Are you Anne?'

'Yes, I am. Why?' she retorted.

He apologized profusely and explained that he was the French fellah. Anne's face fell forty feet. Her mouth agape, she said, 'But you can't be. You don't even look French. You're not at all as I imagined.'

The d'Avennes fellah turned out to be blonde, with blue eyes that reminded her of a young Robert Redford, and was a good six-foot-three to boot. She was only five feet so, as he stood up, her eyes went from his knees to the top of his head.

'You're quite tall, aren't you?' she exclaimed as though she were gazing at a tall cedar tree. He beamed back at her. She'd need a ladder just to be able to hear him, she thought.

'Are you *sure* you're French? She said questioningly.

'I can assure yuuu, mademoiselle, I am French from head to tuu.'

'All right, then, let's go, and get a cup of coffee' she added, not waiting for an answer.

Anne spent the rest of the afternoon talking to Efflam and found him really quite interesting once she got over the heavy French accent. She had imagined a guy with dark eyes, a swarthy complexion, and black hair immersed in gel, who had a quick answer for everything. He was as different from that as he could possibly be. He listened, and he didn't charge into a situation with all guns blazing like she did. Now she understood what Brian meant by charming; she had confused smarmy with charming, not that dark-haired, dark-eyed guys couldn't also be charming. He was polite and well mannered. When they got to the door, he held it open for her and then pulled out a chair for her to sit down, that impressed her. *God, I really think Irish guys could learn a thing or two from you*, she thought. As though he had read her mind, he smiled and continued to chat away.

A farm in Brittany was home until he was about fourteen, and then the whole family moved to Paris. He had grown up in Brittany, and his maternal grandmother was Irish and his mother Scots, born in Edinburgh; hence the blue eyes and blonde hair. His father, both grandfathers, and his paternal grandmother were as French as the French Resistance and so, he said, he was a mongrel but didn't know if there was a name for an Irish-Scots-French fellah who had lived in Brittany.

'Well, you have a distinct advantage,' she continued sounding extremely well knowledgeable on the subject. 'When in Ireland, you're Irish, when in Scotland, you're Scots, and when you're in France, you're French. If you ever go back to Brittany, it'll be a real conundrum as you will be all three, since Brittany is Celtic. It's distinctly illogically logical, don't you think?'

He nodded in agreement even though he couldn't quite work out how he could be three distinct nationalities in three different locations and possibly all three at once in the fourth, but she sounded as if she knew what she was talking about, so she must be right.

It became custom that every Tuesday and Thursday afternoon at about five o'clock, they would meet outside the Berkeley, then go and have something to eat in the Buttery. It gave them a chance to catch up on any news. He was enjoying his time in Trinity. The weeks flew by, and although they weren't firm friends, they had a lot in common. They started going out and soon found themselves in the enviable position of being completely besotted with each other.

Anne didn't make the mistake of letting her study get in the way of her goal. She knew that it was possible that the year would end and Efflam would return to Paris and forget all about his Irish girlfriend. She was very levelheaded, almost clinical in her surmise of the situation in which she had found herself. Efflam, on the other hand, did not intend to let her go, and even though they still had a further two years ahead of them in different universities, he was going to stick with her—at least that was what he intended.

She hadn't heard from Brian for a long time and was wondering what had happened to him, when she received a letter from him inviting her to spend Christmas with him. He wasn't going back to Dublin for Christmas that year. Efflam thought it a great idea; he was going to go back home to Paris and they could both come to spend Christmas Eve with his family. She was almost carried away with the idea. She came down with a bump when she realised that her dad would not approve at all and her mother would just say no. Perhaps, it mightn't be all that bad; she knew that her parents trusted her, but did they trust her enough?

Anne thought about the possibility of travelling to Paris, dreamt of the Champs-Élysées, of seeing the Palais de Versailles, and sighed to herself. Some chance, she thought. She wasn't sure what to do. Then it popped into her head: Mrs. O'Brien. I'll speak to her, and maybe she'll have a word with the Main Man. At this stage, Mrs. O'Brien had become like an aunt, a long lost relative from Tasmania, so to speak. She was part of the family. So, unusually for Anne, she left the library early and rang her.

'Mrs. O'Brien?'

'Yes.'

'It's Anne. I need your help. I mean I really need your help.'

'Sure, luv, come up and stay for tea, and we'll have a chat.'

Anne knocked on the door, and Mrs. O'Brien, friendly as ever, opened it. This time, however, she was worried.

'What's wrong, Anne?'

'Well, it's like this ….' Anne started to explain about the d'Avennes fellah who by this stage was her fellah and Brian and the wonderful chance to see Paris, her parents and their reaction to her possible trip. What was she going to do? She really wanted to go. It was all blurted out in a moment, and Mrs. O'Brien, thinking something completely different, crossed herself, heaved a great sigh of relief, and thanked the good Lord that Anne had far more common sense than she had given her credit for.

'Not to worry. It's simple.'

Anne was perplexed. 'What do you mean, simple?'

'Well, speak to your mammy and say that you have a friend in Trinity who is away from home and could he come and stay for the weekend. It'd be nice for him to have a nice home-cooked meal for a change and feel part of a family since he is so far from home. If he's as nice n' polite as you say he is, he will win her round, never fear. As long as there's no hanky panky, if you know what I mean.' She wagged her finger at Anne, giving her due warning,

'I don't want to be party to anything that Himself there wouldn't approve of.' She gestured back to the Sacred Heart.

'I give you my solemn word, cross my heart and hope to die. I won't do anything that you wouldn't be happy with.'

She meant it, too. Anne never said, 'I give you my solemn word,' unless she meant exactly what she said and intended to keep it.

'You're a wonder, Mrs. O'Brien, a true wonder. Do you think it will work?'

'I'll have a wee word with Himself, provided you keep yer word. Agreed?'

'You've got an iron clad deal, Mrs. O'Brien. Iron clad.'

Mrs. O'Brien smiled at Anne as she ate her tea, and they chatted about Father O'Brien, whom Mrs. O'Brien still hadn't had a chance to visit, and the B & B and how things were going. Before they knew it, it was half past seven and she had to go home. Anne was glad she had had a chat with Mrs. O'Brien and would do precisely what she had suggested. *Roll on the weekend*, she thought to herself.

Anne rang her mother the following afternoon, assured of Mrs. O'Brien's influence and confident that her mam and dad would agree, given the circumstances. She wouldn't say anything about Paris until she had got an idea about whether her parents liked Efflam or not. She explained the situation as Mrs. O'Brien had put it, and her mother was only too delighted to have one of Anne's friends home from university for the weekend. Anne's dad wasn't enamoured of the situation, but Mary won Joe over by telling him that they couldn't stand in the way of progress. Anne was growing up, going to university, and discovering new things and ideas. She was meeting new people, and they had to be one hundred percent behind her. He had to understand that. Finally, Joe relented, knowing that Mary wouldn't ever agree to something that she didn't think was right.

'All right honey, all right,' and that was settled.

Friday afternoon came, and Efflam, a little daunted at the prospect of meeting Anne's parents, imagined that he was going to go through questioning like the Spanish Inquisition. *What were his designs on their daughter and all that sort of stuff?* He was apprehensive about going, but Anne wasn't going to be budged; he had to go if he wanted her to go to Paris for Christmas. She had already said to him that she had missed Christmas the previous year due to a hectic work schedule. She didn't elaborate. She thought, *He doesn't need to know everything.* She hadn't even told her parents about the meeting with her tutor and the events, which ensued. Well, that was the past and this was the present.

The trip home was a quiet one. Normally, they chatted ninety to the dozen, or rather, Anne chatted and poor Efflam nodded and listened. He seemed to understand her; he listened, and when he thought she was babbling too much, he would simply draw her close and kiss her gently. It was an unspoken sign for her to shut up. He did so now, and after once or twice she snuggled up to him and fell asleep on the bus home.

Finally, the bus arrived in Dunshaughlin. It had been delayed by the endless heavy Friday traffic, and the normal hour-and-a-half had turned into more than two hours due to the new road works. It was easy to see that the winter had set in; it was only quarter past six and already pitch-black. Anne's dad was out in the field getting the cattle in; her mother opened the door.

'Mam, this is Efflam. Efflam, this is my mam.'

'Enchanté, Madame. Enchanté.'

Mary was not easily gob-smacked, but this was one occasion when she surely was. Her mouth agape like a freshly caught cod, she wasn't sure what to say. He certainly was not what she was expecting; he was like a film star. He had to bend his head to get in the doorway, not built for six-foot-three fellahs.

'Mind your head,' she said.

Joe followed a couple of minutes later and took him in his stride, and they shook hands.

They sat down to a lovely supper of shepherd's pie with carrots, followed by steaming hot tea and lashings of hotly buttered drop scones with warmed homemade strawberry jam. They were obviously impressed by his manners and could see that he was very respectful. He was shown to the top bedroom at the back of the house that looked out over lush green fields. It wasn't big but roomy enough with a pine suite, a wardrobe, chest of drawers, and double bed. Clean towels lay folded on the chair, and the room was fresh and airy. As he switched on the light, he could see carefully polished floorboards with a large rug in beige with dark green, red, and gold swirls in a Celtic design. The curtains matched the bedcover in beige with dark green ties. It was modest but comfortable.

Efflam set down his bag and unpacked the few belongings he had brought with him, including a large box of chocolates that he had bought to thank Anne's mother. As he made his way out the door, he nearly tripped over something, not looking where he was going. It was Bob, whose curiosity had the better of him as usual. Who was the new person that had come to stay with the family?

Bob was identical to his mother, a beautiful, tri-coloured English Shepherd who had inherited his mother's placid temperament. Poor Efflam wasn't expecting a visitor and nearly jumped out of his skin.

'Zut!'

There was Bob, his tail wagging from side to side, wondering what all the fuss was about. Efflam patted him, and they went downstairs.

'See you've met Bob, then,' said Joe.

'Ah, yes, Bub. We will become good friends, I sink.'

'Well, I have to go out and check on Bessie and see how she's doing with her new brood. You missed all the fun, Anne. Bessie had her piglets last week.'

'Dad, can we come out and see them? It's not too cold, is it?'

'Not at all. We had a problem with one of the little fellahs. He seemed as if he wasn't going to make it, until I put a bit of poitín into him. Then the poor fellah looked a little drunk but perked up no end. Now he's grand.'

'Poitín! Dad, you didn't!'

'It's an oul' farmer's trick, honey. There are things that you won't learn in university, except in the University of Life. I didn't give him a glass of it, just a little mixed with a little milk, and he drank it in a baby's bottle with a larger teat. More to your oul' dad than you think there is, Miss.'

'I never doubted your ingenuity for a moment, dad, not even for a moment.' Jassie introduced herself by looking over at Bessie, her head turned and tail wagging as though she recalled how she felt when she had her own little brood, and she nestled in beside Joe. Bob pushed through Anne's legs so that he could be on the other side of Joe as they both peered over at Bessie, their tails wagging in unison. Efflam was formally introduced to everyone on the farm, each of the cats, the General and his Harem, the cockerel and the hens, Mr. Magoo, Bessie, and the cows.

Over the following day or so, Efflam helped Joe with work on the farm and enjoyed it immensely. He threw himself into it and impressed Mary so much that she felt guilty that he was working so hard.

'Anne, that poor fellah will think God only knows what, he's working so hard.'

'He's glad to help, mam. He wouldn't do it if he didn't want to.'

Joe was going to O'Neill's with Jassie and asked if Efflam wanted to come with him for an hour or so while Anne had a bath and washed her hair. You could see that Joe heartily approved of him. What an honour! No one ever went to O'Neill's with Joe except Jassie. Now for the first time, Bob would go, too.

They chatted, or rather, Joe chatted, and Efflam stroked Bob beside the fire in O'Neill's bar. It was a bar with no frills, just the bare pub, and a roaring fire with a few tables and a cosy spot beside it where Joe liked to sit, smoking his pipe, and staring into the flames. Sometimes he would banter with a few of the locals; other times he would be on his own. This time

Efflam was with him, and they sat down to a couple of pints of 'the black stuff' and an Irish whiskey chaser. They walked home, followed by the dogs, after having spent a very enjoyable hour. Anne was just ready when they came in. Anne and Efflam went off to meet a few of her friends for the evening.

'He's a nice lad, Mary, a very nice lad.'

'Yeah, she could do worse, a lot worse.' Mary nodded in agreement.

Mary and Joe went to bed shortly afterwards. At about two o'clock, Joe woke up with terrible pains in his chest. He couldn't breathe and started to have a panic attack. Mary ran in to call Anne, but she hadn't returned. She ran down the stairs and phoned for an ambulance. Poor Joe, he was petrified, scared to death. Mary rarely got flustered, but this time panic set in. She rang the ambulance once. Ten minutes passed by as she ran up and down the stairs with cold compresses. It still hadn't arrived. She rang again.

'Which service, please?'

'Ambulance.'

'One moment, please.'

'Ambulance service. How can I help you?' the operator said calmly.

'Look, my husband is having a heart attack and the ambulance isn't here yet. That's ten or fifteen minutes ago, and it still hasn't arrived yet.'

'Your name? Your address?'

'I've already given those details,' Mary said curtly.

'The ambulance will arrive when it arrives. It's on the way.'

'It may be, but so is Christmas,' snapped Mary. 'Can you find out where in God's name it is?'

'It'll be there shortly. Thank you for calling emergency services,' and the phone went dead.

Mary was terrified. All sorts of terrible scenarios went through her mind, and she nodded, discounting each one in turn. The ambulance had come from Beaumont Hospital. Why that hospital? Maybe it was on call and the closest at the time. No wonder the ambulance took so long. It had left Beaumont, going through the Phoenix Park like the very devil himself were in hot pursuit. By the time the ambulance had arrived, the pains had subsided a little, but Mary's mind still went into overdrive. Mary was just climbing into the back of the ambulance, which took some doing as she was told that she couldn't go with Joe.

'Look here, young man. I've been married so long that I can't remember a life without my husband. If he is going to meet his Maker, I want to be able to hold his hand before he leaves this world, rules, or no rules. Have you got that?'

'Well, I'm sorry, but you can't—'

'You'll be an awful lot more sorry if you don't let me go with my husband, I can tell you.'

Looking at her face, red with anger, the ambulance paramedic wasn't going to take any chances. She looked so angry that he thought she would have knocked him sideways without a second thought.

'You're a force to be reckoned with, missus.'

'You'd better believe it!'

Mary climbed into the back of the ambulance just as Anne and Efflam were walking up the road, and they saw it speed away, with the sirens going full blast. They could see just enough to realize that her father was on the stretcher.

Anne was beside herself. What was going on? Efflam comforted her. They wouldn't go back to Dublin but would wait for her mother to ring her and tell her what had happened. The cows would have to be milked, and she hadn't an iota how to use the machinery to do it. She was shaking as she went into the kitchen, and Efflam held her close to comfort her.

'We will wait until your maman rings you. Everything will be all right.'

He rocked her to and fro and kissed her on her head as Anne started to sob uncontrollably.

'Oh, Efflam, what am I going to do? What am I going to do?'

'Don't worry, *mon petit chou (my little cabbage)*. Don't worry. I will help you.' Anne went to bed and sobbed herself to sleep.

It was almost four o'clock and time for the cows to be milked. Thank God, there were only a few or they would have been goosed. The farm still had to be worked. Efflam's memories of working on his parents' farm in Brittany would stand him in good stead. He wasn't exactly sure how the machinery worked, so he decided that rather than break anything he would go to the closest farmhouse to ask for advice. He pulled out an old bicycle that was leaning against the wall of the barn and went on his way.

Mr. McCloskey, the neighbouring farmer, knew Mary and Joe Myers well. They often helped each other out. Of course, the idea of a total stranger with a deep French accent knocking on the door at four o'clock in the morning was a little unusual, to say the least. He opened the door, a shotgun by his side, and said, 'Yes?'

Efflam spoke hurriedly. 'So sorry to disturb you, seer, but Mr. and Mrs. Meyeers have gone off in an ambulance. I am Anne's friend. The cows need milking, and I am noot sure how zee makchinery wuurks.'

Don't worry, I'll come up and bring the cows down, and keep an eye on them on my farm until things work out.'

'Oh, I would be very grateful, seer.'

Mr. McCloskey arrived just after five o'clock to collect the cows for milking. He would keep them on his land until something more suitable could be worked out. Then Efflam went out and fed the hens, geese, horse, Jassie, Bob, and the cats. He let out Mr. Magoo to graze after breakfast and fed Bessie and her brood. He realised that they would be missed in classes, so he rang Trinity and explained to the law department what had happened and then rang the French and Spanish departments and let them know the situation. He worked as quickly as he could, and it was nearly ten o'clock before he decided to lie down and take a snooze; before he knew it, it was three o'clock.

Anne awoke to a continuous ringing sound. It was her mother to tell her what had happened. Mary was anxious about the farm and who would be able to look after it. Anne explained that everything was all right and Mr. McCloskey was looking after the cows. Efflam had looked after everything else, so she could relax. Her mother told her that her dad would be kept in for a week or so to run tests and make sure that he was fully recovered. It had been a heart attack, a mild one, but it was enough to alert them to the fact that he was no longer young and had to start taking it easy.

The idea of Christmas in Paris was no longer on the cards, and although she was disappointed, she was glad that she hadn't mentioned it to her parents in case they might have felt guilty. Efflam knew it too and was equally disappointed. Who would look after the farm; after all, the Christmas break was only ten days away. Her father couldn't start working straight after the hospital. What would they do? Efflam thought to himself and suggested that perhaps it might be an idea for him to stay with them over the Christmas holidays and help out on the farm until her dad could get back on his feet. He felt that he was being a little forward in his suggestion but thought it was the only solution. He spoke to Anne about it and explained that he thought it would be for the best. She looked up into his face; her eyes filled with tears, and for the first time in a long time, she was lost for words.

'Oh, Efflam, Efflam,' and she hugged him. She was so touched by his unselfishness. She spoke to her mother when she came home and told her the plan. Her mother felt bad that Efflam would miss the chance to see his family at such a special time of the year. Was she sure, he wouldn't mind? What about his family? It was no time to be proud. Mary said that she would be very grateful if he helped out in some way. It would be great to have him for Christmas, and it would give them the chance to get to know him a little better.

Mary and Joe had read Efflam right. He was a decent lad. By the time, Joe returned home from hospital, he was surprised to see that Efflam was still there.

'I thought you were only staying the weekend?'

'I'm afraid, monsieur, I have invited myself to stay for Christmas. I hope you don't mind.'

'Not at all. The more the merrier!'

Joe had a very good inkling of why Efflam was going to stay, as Mary had already given him an idea. He was grateful, and the family would do their best to make sure that he had a wonderful Christmas. It would be a great Christmas, more memorable than any of them anticipated.

Efflam helped on the farm, and the relationship that he had forged with the family was now rock solid. Anne was in seventh heaven and had put to the back of her mind the idea that Efflam would go back to Paris in June. Brian would be home then. She missed Brian, but she would miss Efflam even more. Only six months, she thought to herself. Efflam contacted his parents and explained the situation. They were very understanding. They hoped that they would see him at the Easter break.

By the time Christmas was over, Joe was well on the road to recovery. Efflam would only allow him do the absolute minimum amount of work as he had to get his strength back.

There was a possibility that Anne would have to forego her studies if Joe got worse. Anne and Efflam made a pact to go home to Dunshaughlin every weekend, if possible. That way, she could keep a close eye on her dad and it wouldn't get too much for him. This arrangement suited everyone. Efflam experienced life with an Irish family; Anne saw as much of Efflam as she could, and at the same time she didn't need to worry about her parents coping on their own.

The months flew by, and before they knew it, Easter was upon them. Efflam had to go home, if only for a short time, to see his family. This he did and stayed a week. Anne was with her family in Dunshaughlin, and she felt that it was the longest week of her life.

The previous arrangement of checking every weekend still stood by the time the summer exams came and Anne knew that Efflam had to go home for good. She threw herself into her work and retained the 2.1 average that she had done the previous year. She gave out to herself for getting so involved. She knew it was going to be difficult but didn't imagine how difficult. The day came for them to say goodbye, and no words came to either of them. They just hugged each other, afraid of letting go. He would be back sooner than either of them had planned. It was the end of another year at Trinity. Bags had to be packed, and the bus journey down to Dunshaughlin had to be undertaken. It was the end of Senior Freshman and the beginning of Junior Sophister, a new year and a fresh beginning.

Chapter Four

The summer wasn't as daunting as Anne had thought. Efflam had gone back to Paris, but he wrote every week, and she looked forward to his letters with great anticipation. He phoned once a month and intended on travelling to see them all before term started in the Sorbonne.

It had been a strange year, certainly one of ups and downs. She hoped that their relationship would stand the test of time, but then again, only time would tell. Anne got an overall 2.1 in her exams and was thrilled by the result; however, it was marred by the fact that neither Efflam nor Brian were there to share in her happiness. Anne didn't get a job during the summer but opted to help out at home instead. Joe wasn't getting younger but seemed to be almost back to his old self again. Mary and Anne would keep a close eye on him so that he wouldn't relapse.

By the time Anne moved her stuff back up to Dublin, she wasn't sure if Mrs. McLoughlin would remember that she would take the studio apartment again that year. However, she was blessed that Mrs. McLoughlin had warmed to her and seemed to trust her completely. She had retained Anne's studio apartment in Ely Place, and she said she had been hoping to have Anne as a tenant the following year. The façade that Mrs. McLoughlin put on fooled everyone. She was brusque and 'all business' to the tenants, but the truth of the matter was that once a person spent any time with her, he or she could have seen her (that is if she *let* a person see) the way she *really* was, which was a real eye-opener. Sometimes, Mrs. McLoughlin would find herself offering to help someone out of a situation into which they had found themselves through no fault of their own. Then her true colours shone through. She would ask that the tenant or whoever she was helping to 'observe the rules of discretion' and keep her name out of it, if asked.

'To be honest, I don't care if you say it was a six-foot rabbit with blue hair as long as my name isn't mentioned.'

Senior Freshman year was over and the beginning of Junior Sophister, a new year and a fresh beginning was about to start. It was wonderful to see Brian again and bring him up to speed on all the news. Anne settled back into student life, retaining the same timetable in the Berkeley library as before. She never forgot her second chance. She wasn't going to let anything or anyone stand in the way of getting her degree, no matter what happened. She continued working as hard as ever. At the weekends, before her dad had the heart attack, they used to go out. Now she went home every weekend.

Mary was glad to see her daughter at the weekends. She looked forward to it. She didn't seem so afraid that something would go wrong, as she knew that she could last the week as long as Anne was home by the weekend. In a fit of energy, she decided to turn the house upside down and do a real clean out. It was always clean as a new pin as Mary was always very particular. She would leave her bedroom to the last. She started on the Monday and had finished by Thursday. Everything was spotless, and she nodded to herself. A few fresh wild flowers and the rooms all aired. Just as she was about to close the door of the bedroom, she gave a quick glance round and thought that she might put a fresh thing–a-majig on the top of the chest of drawers. She exchanged it for a fresh one and noticed that underneath was the letter that she had left unopened. She cast her mind back and remembered that she had been planning to open it the week after receiving it and then weeks had run into months and she had completely forgotten about it. She looked at the postmark. It was dated 14 October 1982. This was now October 1984. She sat down on the side of the bed, her hands shaking a little. *Probably nothing, probably nothing, Oh, Mary, you are silly. Get a grip, girl.* She opened the letter and it read.

DUNSHAUGHLIN CLINIC
14 MAIN STREET, DUNSHAUGHLIN, CO. MEATH

Dr. James Dundale   Dr. David McIntyre
Dr. Timothy Maguire   Dr. Patrick Hughes
Dr. Maria McCarthy   Dr. Catherine Robinson
Surgery Hours:
Mon-Fri: nine a.m.— one p.m. and three p.m.—six p.m.

Mrs. Mary Myers,
Hazelhurst Farm,
Dunshaughlin,
Co. Meath.

14th October 1982

Dear Mrs. Myers,

Following tests carried out, I strongly suggest that you make an appointment to see Mr. James Brady, in St. Vincent's Hospital, Ballsbridge, Dublin 4, as soon as possible. I will forward the test results to him, advise him that I have seen you, and suggest that further examination is warranted. I believe that the matter requires immediate attention.
    Please do not hesitate to contact me should you have any questions on this issue.
                    Yours sincerely,

                          James Dundale

'That further examination is warranted ... that further examination is warranted, immediate attention?' she repeated to herself. 'What on earth does that mean? Is it good or bad? It probably just means that they want to be sure that I'm as fit as a fiddle. Yes, that's what it means. Yes, I'm sure that's what it means.' Mary picked up the phone.

'Hello, operator. Could you give me the number for St. Vincent's Hospital?'
'Hold for the number, please. Yes, it's 01694533.'
'St. Vincent's Hospital?'
'Good morning. I would like to speak to the secretary of Mr. James Brady.' 'One moment and I will connect you with Outpatients.'
'Thank you.'
'Outpatients. Good Morning.'
'Good Morning. I would like to make an appointment to see Mr. James Brady. My referral letter has already been sent up to him.'
'I see. Name, address, and date of birth, please?'
'Mary Myers, Hazelhurst Farm, Dunshaughlin, Co. Meath. I was born on 3rd October 1930.'
'One moment and I'll check the records ... Ah yes, Mrs. Myers, here we are. Your G.P. is Dr. James Dundale in 14 Main Street, Dunshaughlin, Co. Meath. Is that correct?'
'That's it.'
'Mrs. Myers, Dr. Dundale sent up this referral letter in October 1982. Are you aware of that?'
'Yes, I'm terribly sorry, but I completely forgot about the letter and only opened it this morning.'
'Well, hold on, and I'll see if I can disturb Mr. Brady as such a long time has lapsed. Would you mind waiting a moment?'
'No, not at all,' was the reply.
'Mr. Brady, it's Louise I'm terribly sorry to disturb you.'
'It's all right, Louise. I've just finished with a patient. What's the matter?'
'Mr. Brady, I have a lady on the phone here, Mrs. Myers. She's ringing about a possible appointment, and her G.P., Dr. Dundale, sent up a letter in October 1982 about her condition.'
'October 1982? God! Bring me in the letter straight away, and I'll ring Dr. Dundale. Take her telephone number and tell her you'll ring her back. Tell her I'm with a patient.' 'All right, Mr. Brady. I'll do that.'

'Hello, Mrs. Myers? I'm sorry for holding you so long. Could I get your telephone number and I will ring you back? Mr. Brady is with someone at the moment.'

'Surely it's 835236.'

Mary put down the phone. *The receptionist didn't sound worried. It's probably my imagination.*

Mr. Brady rang Dr. Dundale as soon as Louise brought in the letter. Dr. Dundale didn't sound hopeful. He was afraid that the length of time would be detrimental. He still wanted her to see Mr. Brady. Mr. Brady rang Louise and told her that she was to make an appointment for Mrs. Myers—the first possible appointment.

'Well, Mr. Brady, the first appointment is ten o'clock on Monday.'

'Ring Mrs. Myers straight away and tell her to come in at nine o'clock on Monday and tell her to fast from midnight, not even a drop of water.'

'I'll do that immediately, Mr. Brady.'

'Mrs. Myers?'

'Yes.'

'This is Louise at Mr. James Brady's office at Outpatients in St. Vincent's Hospital. Could you come in on Monday morning at nine? Mr. Brady says you are to fast from midnight, not even a drop of water.'

Mr. Brady followed Louise and overheard the conversation.

'I didn't expect it so soon,' Mary replied.

Louise put her hand over the phone as Mr. Brady whispered, 'Tell her you had a last-minute cancellation. Don't give her any cause for concern.'

Louise returned to Mrs. Myers. 'Well as it happens, Mrs. Myers, you're in luck as we just had a last-minute cancellation.'

'Oh, that was lucky, wasn't it? Well I'll be there on Monday at nine, then.'

The whole weekend Mary didn't know what she was about. She was 'all thumbs,' dropping dishes left, right, and centre. She was clearly out of sorts. She was worried. Joe noticed that something was definitely amiss.

'Something wrong, luv?'

'No. No. Just wondering if I have enough beef to make a shepherd's pie.'

'Oh, that's okay then. We can always have something else. Don't go to too much trouble.'

'Yes, silly, isn't it. I suppose we can.'

She smiled at him. She would have to make up some excuse for her to go to Dublin. It was so out of the ordinary; she wasn't used to lying to her own husband.

She blushed. 'Joe, I know money isn't exactly flush at the moment, but do you think that I'd be able to go to Dublin to have a look at a few dresses. The ones I have are so worn, and I would like to look in on Mrs. O'Brien again, maybe take up a barm brack and a dozen freshly laid eggs to her. What do you think?'

'I think it's a great idea. There's always enough money for my girl.'

He beamed back at her as he puffed on his pipe, rocking to and fro on the rocking chair with Jassie and Bob beside him.

Joe mentioned to Anne that Mary was going to Dublin on Monday to look at a few dresses and maybe they could meet up.

'Funny, she never mentioned it to me. Are you sure, dad?'

'Positive.'

Anne asked Mary if she was going to Dublin, and she seemed a little uneasy at the question.

'Oh. I'm not sure yet. I mightn't,' and she left it at that.

Anne went back on the bus on Sunday evening to university and never thought any more about it.

Monday came. Mary couldn't sleep and got up at five o'clock in the morning. She got washed, dressed, and decided to bake an apple pie to keep her mind off things. She got her money together in a small battered brown purse and made sure that she brought her rosary, a set of small brown beads. They were the ones her mother had given to her as a child, and she taught her how to use them. She relied on them to get her through every possible situation.

She got on the bus at seven o'clock and waved goodbye to Joe as he stood at the bus stop. It took over an hour and twenty minutes to get into Dublin. Unlike now, the terminus for the number 7 or 8 bus was on the quays opposite Stanley's Newsagent, just up from Busarus. After a few initial enquiries, she found it. It was already eight thirty and she didn't know if she would make it in time. The bus pulled up, and she asked for St. Vincent's Hospital and inquired how long it would take to get there.

'About fifteen minutes, no more,' was the reply.

The bus left her opposite St. Vincent's Hospital, and she walked across the road, clutching her weather-beaten brown handbag. When she got to the Outpatients Department, she said that she had an appointment to see Mr. Brady.

'Mr. Brady doesn't start before ten o'clock, you must be mistaken. What's the name?'

'Mary Myers.'

'You aren't on the list. Are you sure it was Mr. Brady you were to see today?'

'Yes, I'm certain I was told nine o'clock.'

'I'll just check, then.'

Mr. Brady was phoned.

'Mr. Brady, Louise is sick today.'

'Oh, I see.'

'There's a Mrs. Myers to see you at nine o'clock I told her that you don't start before ten o'clock but she's sure that the appointment is for nine o'clock'

'It is for nine o'clock. Ask her to come straight in.'

Mr. Brady stood up to welcome her in. 'Mrs. Myers,' please do come in.'

'Thank you, doctor, or is it mister?'

'Don't worry about the title. Sit down and make yourself comfortable.'

Mr. Brady was a handsome man in his late fifties, with light grey hair and steel grey eyes. He was tall and had a stately comportment. He carried himself so well that the first person he reminded her of was the father of Sean Connery in *Marnie*.

'Do please sit down,' he repeated.

He was suave, gentle, and sophisticated, a real gentleman who was beautifully spoken. He explained the letter and why he was concerned. He said that she must have tests, to make sure everything was as it should be. Mary spent the most of that day getting one test or another.

Unbeknown to Mary, Mr. Brady rang the Blackrock Clinic to see if they could do an MRI scan that day. It was an emergency. He wanted to be completely sure of all the facts. Mary went out with the referral letter from Mr. Brady in hand and made her way to the X-ray Department in the Blackrock Clinic. The MRI was done, and she was told that Mr. Brady would be given the results. The Blackrock Clinic told her to tell Mr. Brady that it would be a couple of days before the full results came through. She went back to St. Vincent's Hospital and told Mr. Brady's secretary in Outpatients what she had been told in the Blackrock Clinic. Mr. Brady told her that he wanted to see her on Thursday at two o'clock so that he could go through everything with her.

She walked to the bus stop and made her way back into town, none the wiser on her condition. She went to see Mrs. O'Brien, gave her a barm brack and a dozen eggs, and stayed for a cup of tea and a chat. She didn't relay anything to her, passed an hour chatting about Anne, and thanked her for being so good to her. By half past three, she got up to go.

'Mind yourself now, Mary. Don't do too much; you look a little tired. One of these days I have to pay a visit on my brother-in-law, Father Francis.'

'Yes, please do and stay with us, won't you?'

Mary said goodbye and made her way down to Busarus for the four o'clock bus. When the bus pulled into Dunshaughlin, Joe was on his way in from the field and waved to her. She waved back.

'Didn't you buy anythin'?'

'No, I didn't, but I might go up again on Thursday, just to make certain.'

'Sure, luv. Not something worrying you, is there?'

'Me? No, not at all,' she said confidently.

Tuesday and Wednesday dragged. Finally, Thursday arrived and she went up to Dublin again. She made her way to Outpatients for her appointment with Mr. Brady at two o'clock. He called her in.

'Mrs. Myers, please do come in and sit down. Is your husband or family with you?'

'No. No, why?'

'Well, I'm afraid I have some bad news.'

Mary's heart began to race, and suddenly she felt queasy and she wanted to get out. 'Oh, what's that then? Serious is it?'

'I'm afraid so. I'm very sorry. It's ... it's...'

Mary echoed. 'It's ... it's ...' as she leaned forward.

'It's ... cancer.'

'There's no hope, then?' She asked.

'It's gone too far. I'm really sorry.'

Resigned, Mary looked him straight in the eye and said, 'I'm very grateful for all you've done. I know that you must've arranged that scan in the Blackrock Clinic because they said they had people waiting weeks and that I must have been a real V.I.P. to get it done that day. I'm very grateful. After all, when the good Lord calls you home to a big shindig, you should accept the invitation with gratitude.'

A lump came to her throat, and a forced wry smile came over her in an almost apologetic way because Mr. Brady had to be put to the trouble of telling her the sad news. Then Mr. Brady, seeing the great faith in her, said something quite out of the ordinary.

'Say a prayer for me when you're next in church.'

'You won't be out of my prayers, I promise. What do I owe you, Mr. Brady?' 'Don't worry about that now. We'll manage something. Now, here's a prescription. Get it filled straight away.'

'I don't want my husband or daughter to know.'

'Get it filled in town. They're strong painkillers that will alleviate any suffering or discomfort. They're very effective in cancer patients.'

'Thank you, doctor. Thank you very much. Oh, how long do you think I have?'

'That's always difficult to gauge. I would think from four to six months. Keep in touch with me. Tell Louise to make an appointment three weeks from today.'

'I'll do that, Mr. Brady. Thank you again.'

They shook hands, and Mary left his office. She made the appointment as instructed and left the Outpatients Department. She left the hospital a little worse for wear. She walked down to make her way to the bus stop as though in a total daze. She saw a pharmacy as she got off the bus stop across at the beginning of O'Connell Street on the corner, and she filled the prescription.

'Are these for yourself, Mrs. Myers?' the pharmacist enquired.

'Yes. Yes, I'm afraid so.'

The pharmacist smiled, handed them to her, and told her how much it was. If the pharmacist had said it was twice as much, Mary wouldn't have questioned it.

She walked down to Busarus and got on the four o'clock bus as though in a dream. The tears welled up and trickled down her face as the bus trundled along. She pulled out her handkerchief from her pocket, and her beads came with it. She recited ten decades of the rosary and didn't stop praying until the bus had almost pulled into Dunshaughlin. She prayed for Joe and Anne and that she would have the courage to face this on her own. She couldn't tell them until the very last stages. It wouldn't do any good and wouldn't achieve anything. She would have to make sure her Will was in order, and she would have to have a chat with Father O'Brien about funeral arrangements. It sounded morbid, but she wasn't going to leave that to Joe or Anne; she would have to deal with that herself, and it was something she couldn't put off. As she got off the bus, Joe was waiting.

'No dresses then, Mary? What's wrong? Don't they make dresses in Dublin anymore?' Mary smiled. 'No dresses that'd suit me, I suppose.'

'You won't be going back to have another look, then?'

'No, Joe, I won't be going back, but I might pop up to see Mrs. O'Brien in a few weeks' time.' She continued 'Do you know we are a really lucky pair? Do you know that? We've been blessed, being happily married for so long!'

'I sure do. I thank the good Lord every day. Do you know I didn't even know if you'd marry me, an outsider from Wales or if you'd be happy with a man like me. After all, you *were* ... hmm, I mean ...hmm, *are*... the belle of the county. Your dad was so proud of you.' 'Would ya' go on with yer oul guff. Ha! ha! Well, I *am* happy and I always will be, for however long ... *always* ... is,' she replied.

Joe looked at her strangely, but she grabbed his hand and smiled as they walked towards the house.

'A nice cuppa' tea, that'll fix everything,' said Joe.

'You're dead right, it sure will. It'll fix everything,' she said cheerily. 'Well, *almost* everything,' she muttered.

'What's that?'

'Oh nothin', nothin'. Nothin' of any importance.'

As they went into the house and the bedlam of dogs, cats, and everything else helped her forget the immense sadness that had engulfed her, she recalled what she had said so courageously to Mr. Brady: 'After all, when the good Lord calls you home to a big shindig you should accept the invitation with gratitude.'

She didn't feel very grateful. She felt terrible; she felt cheated. Why her? What had she done? She didn't deserve this! Why couldn't this invitation be given to someone else? Why? Why? You always think it's going to happen to someone else, that you're immune, or not on the list for things like that. Those sort of things only happened to *other* people.

Yet, she shouldn't feel that way, she argued with herself. Look what she had, a lovely daughter, their pride, and joy, the apple of their eye, she had never gave them an ounce of trouble her whole life. She had a wonderful farm and a great home, a loyal, kind, and gentle husband who worked very hard. He never so much as blinked at another woman; he didn't drink to excess, only a pint of 'the black stuff' on occasion. He never shouted, cursed, or hit her.

In all the years of married life and the small trials and tribulations that she thought of, the good Lord had spared her some trials that others had known frequently. Yes, she did have a lot to be grateful for. Religion and faith had always been a major part of the Myers household.

When she went to bed, she still knelt down like a little child to say her prayers. She knew that He would get her through this, too. The good Lord, as she called Him, had already given her the tools, her faith. She nodded to herself and smiled. Now it was time for someone else to be given those gifts. The wonderful gifts that she had been given throughout her lifetime were only 'on loan' after all. She smiled again and said, 'Thank the Lord,' as she cut the ham for the tea.

'What's that, pet?'

'Oh, just thanking the good Lord for all His blessings. We've a lot to be grateful for.'

Joe rocked to and fro on the rocker. He was tired after such a long day. He napped a little. Mary had done a nice spread of ham with pickles, potatoes, peas, and nice white sauce. She took out the baked apple tart that she had done earlier that morning before going to Dublin, and she put it in the Aga to warm it a little.

Bob and Jassie knew it was suppertime. Jassie nudged Joe to waken him softly by pushing her head underneath his arm.

'What? What's all this?'

'Supper's ready.'

'I better get the cattle in first.'

'You'll sit down and have your supper first. The cows can wait a few minutes.' 'All right Mary. You're right, as always.'

After that, they both had their tea. Everyone else—cats, dogs, and the whole menagerie—was safely tucked up in bed after being fed. Joe went out to bring in the cattle. Mary went to bed early that night. She tucked the pills that she had bought in the Dublin behind the chest of drawers so that Joe wouldn't find them.

She knelt down. 'Please, Lord, help me get through this. Help us all get through this.'

She got into bed as she heard Joe follow her up the stairs.

'Goodnight, Mary luv.'

'Goodnight, pet, goodnight. Sleep well.'

Chapter Five

The following morning, Mary woke early; Joe had already been up to milk the cows at half past four and decided to return to bed as he had an almighty headache. It was six o'clock in the morning and still dark; she went downstairs and got breakfast ready: boiled eggs, hot buttered toast, and tea. She shouted up the stairs, and Joe came down, a little bleary-eyed. After breakfast, he went upstairs and was washed and dressed to be ready for the day ahead. Mary did the same and started on the daily chores. The animals were first. She went around like a looney, mentally ticking off everything to be done. She collected the eggs and then fed and watered the chickens and the geese, put Bessie and her now-abundant brood in the pigsty and fed them. She made her way towards the house and called Jassie and Bob.

'Breakfast. Breakfast,' she said almost impatiently, and, 'Sshwsheshe here, kitty kitty,' alerting the cats that it was time for breakfast.

The barn was home to the four cats, who yawned, stretched, and headed for the house, a couple of them, hungry enough, ran, bobbing along, and the others strolled in, as if to say, 'I'm coming, keep yer hair on. I'll be there when I'm there. No rush.'

Joe had already watered and fed Mr. Magoo and was in the process of bringing out the cows to the field.

Mary started on the house, and by the time she looked at the clock it was already ten past seven, almost the middle of the day for the Myers household. October reminded her that winter was hot on its heels, and Mary was sad at the prospect that this might, or rather would, be her last Christmas. Next year ... well, there would be no next year. She had always liked October; many people didn't, but it was one of her favourites. Animals got ready for the onslaught of winter by making sure they had ample stocks of nuts. It was a time of preparation, and this was no exception for her, either. In fact, it was vital for

Mary. Time to put her life in order, to pay any debts and to get everything squared away with 'the Man above.' Nothing could be left to chance.

She stood thinking for a long time about what lay ahead, and then she donned her scarf and coat and left the house. Normally the house would be all a bustle and fuss, but today she decided that more important things needed to be done. Joe was surprised as Mary always went to a later Mass.

'Off to Mass are you, luv?'

'Yes, Joe. I might be a little late.'

'Not to worry. I'll see you when you get back.'

Mary marched a mile or two down the road to the local church. The bell was peeling for eight o'clock Mass when she got there. The Church of Our Lady of the Holy Rosary was a small quaint country church, but it fulfilled the needs of the community. It had been there a long time and was the centre of village life.

Father Francis Aloysius O'Brien was the parish priest, a small quiet, bespectacled man in his early sixties. He was a Dubliner, born and bred. He never lost his accent; it was as though he wanted to hold onto his identity and that was an intrinsic part of it. At first, people treated him rather warily, always respectful, but never as one of the 'real village community.' It took some time before they realised that they had struck gold when Father O'Brien had come to live among them. He always had time for people and looked after them. He was wise, and he listened, asking the community what he could do to improve attendance at Mass; he got himself involved in social issues that both mattered and affected them. When Mass was over, Mary went up to the sacristy door, knocked, and asked if he had a moment. He was still in his altar vestments and asked her to wait a few minutes outside. The altar boy was standing beside Father O'Brien, head bowed as he was told off.

'Now, Ruari, I know it's difficult because you have a lot to do, but *trry* to remember to ring the bell after the consecration. I'm not as young as you, you know.'

'Yes, Father, sorry, Father ... '

'Never mind. Besides that, you did very well. You're a credit to your parents.'

The young boy of nine or ten with bright blue eyes and a mop of unruly brown curly hair looked up at the priest.

'Do you *really* mean that?' His eyes narrowed questioningly.

'Yes, I most certainly do!' and the little boy beamed back at him and marched 'on a high' out of the church. Father O'Brien followed him out and stopped outside the sacristy door.

'Hmm.'

The boy glanced back and remembered.

'Sorry, Father.' He blessed himself, genuflected, and left the church, heading towards the local national school he attended.

Father O'Brien saw Mrs. Myers and apologised for keeping her waiting.

'Sorry to bother you, Father O'Brien, but I need to speak to you.'

'Of course, Mary. What is it?'

'Well, it's like this, Father .... ' Mary pulled out her handkerchief, and tears started to well up in her eyes. They spilled down her cheeks, and she blew her nose.

'What's wrong? There, there now, it can't be all that bad.'

'I'm afraid it is.' Mary blurted out everything that had happened, the unopened letter, St. Vincent's Hospital, Mr. Brady, and how kind he had been, and finally that she wasn't going to live too long. She wanted to sort out her funeral arrangements.

'I see. I see,' was the reply. 'Joe, does he know?'

'No, and I don't want him to until he really has to.'

'He will want to help you. He's your husband.'

'I know that Father, but whatever life I have left, I want it to have some sense of normality. I don't want one where people are running around after you like headless chickens and you aren't allowed to do anything for yourself. Know what I mean?'

'I suppose I do.'

'I want to be in charge of my own life for as long as I can. I'm not afraid of meeting my Maker. I'm worried about Joe and Anne and how they will cope—sounds a little proud, I suppose—I'm sure they'll manage just fine without me. I'm going to miss them more than they know. I don't want to leave them, I don't *want* to go.'

The priest stood there, nodding his head, listening attentively. 'I understand.'

Mary checked herself for feeling so sorry for herself and her situation and then switched into organizational mode. Mary wanted to speak to Father O'Brien about the floral arrangements, the hymns, and the Mass sheet. It was almost as though she were orchestrating it for someone else as she rabbited on ninety to the dozen.

'Oh, Father O'Brien, I know it's a little unusual, but you know at the "removal," a decade of the rosary is said for the deceased. Could you say it for The Holy Souls instead?'

'It will be said for both,' he said, and he patted her on her shoulder.

She continued. 'I'm going to ring Branigan's and arrange as much as I can, but I don't want to arouse any suspicions.'

'Branigan's, hmm,' replied Father Francis. 'Good people, very approachable. They're in the business for as long as I can remember. Leave it to them; they will sort out the flowers, hymns, etc. You needn't have worried about that, you know. Go and have a chat with Michael. He's very understanding. Tell him I sent you.'

Changing the subject, Mary asked if he had seen Mrs. O'Brien.

'Mrs. O'Brien? Lord have mercy on her, my mother's long since dead.'

'No, Mrs. O'Brien, your sister-in-law that lives in Dublin?'

'Oh, Maggie, no, I haven't seen her in a long time … a very long time. I always keep meaning to go and see her, but something always seems to crop up. I really should make the effort. I will, one of these days.'

'Well, Father, before you know it, five years turns into twenty-five and that promise that you made yourself never gets done.'

'But how do you know Maggie?'

Mary smiled at him and started to tell him the whole story, how kind Maggie had been when Anne and Mary had gone up to Dublin to look for a place for Anne to stay during university and the subsequent visits.

'Come into the house, and we can have a nice little visit.'
'Thank you, Father.'
She followed Father O'Brien to the little house adjacent to the church. Mrs. McGonigle, the housekeeper, answered the door 'Oh, Father, I'd quite given you up.'
'Mrs. McGonigle, could you put on a pot of tea and maybe we could have a scone or two?'
'Of course, Father.'
He went into the parlour, followed by Mary. A small fire in the grate flickered and crackled as if adding to their conversation, and they sat down to their chat. A knock at the parlour door followed a few minutes later.
'Oh, you're kindness itself. Thanks, Mrs. McGonigle. Nine o'clock maybe a bit early for most people to have scones, but after Mass it's nice to half a couple of Mrs. McGonigle's famous scones and warmed strawberry jam—they're just the ticket.'
'Not at all, Father.' Mrs. McGonigle blushed, became a little flustered, and left the room, embarrassed but delighted with the compliment.
'Now then, where were we? Oh, yes,' and they continued to chat for the next hour. Mary felt a lot more relaxed by the time they had finished their chat.
Father O'Brien said, 'Come and see me often, and we can have a chat and a cuppa tea. I enjoyed that.'
Mary thanked him and left.
She didn't feel that it was the end of the world. A new chapter, a different chapter in her life had already begun. Mary walked home, feeling decidedly better than when she had left home that morning. She felt more at peace with herself. She was grateful that she could rely on Father O'Brien to keep her confidence, and he had promised to help her in whatever way he could.
'Americans have analysts—the Irish have priests. I'm sure analysts are all very well,' she thought, 'but they can only do so much. Priests have experience in this world and in the next, sort of like analysts of body and soul, so when you are going into the unknown, it's better to have an idea of what to expect.' She nodded to herself, certain that she had arrived at the right conclusion.

The following day, Mary decided that she was going to ring Branigan's funeral home. She got the number from directory enquiries and dialled, her hands shaking as she did so.

'Branigan's. Good afternoon.'

'Good afternoon.'

'How may I assist you?'

'I would like to arrange a funeral.'

'I understand. I'm sorry for your loss. When did the deceased pass away?'

'Pass away? Oh, well, I'm not sure. I mean, it hasn't exactly happened yet.'

'Not happened?'

'I mean, it's a bit difficult to explain over the phone, you see. It's for me. I'm arranging my own.'

'Of course, now I see what you mean. Would you be able to come and see us and sort out the small details?'

'Oh, yes. What about Monday afternoon, and would it be possible to see Mr. Michael Branigan?'

'Monday at half past two with Mr. Michael Branigan. Fine.'

'Could you give me your address, please?'

'Yes, of course. It's 109 Dame Street, Dublin 2.'

'Thank you very much.' She hung up.

As it happened, Monday was perfect. Joe had arranged to see Mr. McCloskey, their friendly neighbour (who had helped them out when Joe had had his heart attack), to discuss a few things about the farm and ask his advice. In turn, Mr. McCloskey had a lovely clutch of hens and wanted Joe to see what he thought of them. At the same time, he was hoping to barter a piglet or two in exchange, but whether he was successful or not remained to be seen. If she told Joe beforehand, the chances were that he would have lunch with Mr. McCloskey, and so that would give her at least three hours to get to Dublin and back. She decided to tell Joe that she wanted to go for a walk an hour or so beforehand; that would give her enough time to go to Dublin and be back before Joe. She didn't like being deceitful, but it was necessary in the circumstances.

Mary was a Meath woman through and through, born and bred in Dunshaughlin. She used to be wary of Dublin and Dubliners. She finally came to the fair assumption that they were like people everywhere, with their own quirks and ideas, the same as people in Dunshaughlin. She caught the bus to Busarus and asked directions to Dame Street. As she had put a good foot under her, she got there in plenty of time, stopping and asking people on the way to make sure she was on the right track. She stepped back, looked outside the building, and read repeatedly to herself; 'Branigan's Funeral Directors.' It seemed big, overly somber, a place that she didn't want to be in, but it had to be done. She swallowed hard and marched right into 'the Lions Den.'

A young gentleman wearing a navy pinstriped suit approached her, and in a polite respectful tone asked, 'Good afternoon. May I help you?'

'Yes. Yes, please. I have an appointment to see Mr. Michael Branigan at half past two.'

'Please take a seat—and the name?'

'Mary Myers.'

'Just a moment, please.'

He went out of the room, and a moment or so later another gentleman, in his mid-forties, with short brown hair and a distinguished air about him came out of the office. He walked straight over to her, confidently shook her hand, and introduced himself, ushering her quietly into the office for more privacy.

'Father O'Brien of Our Lady of the Holy Rosary Church in Dunshaughlin suggested that I talk to you,' she explained. He offered her a cup of tea, and they spoke of the arrangements.

Mary wanted to be buried in St. Mary's Cemetery, County Meath. She was shown a brochure of the various coffins, and after some deliberation, she decided on the elm veneer coffin. Mary gave Mr. Branigan the list of hymns.

'I would like "Ave Maria" and "Abide with Me" at the removal,' she said, and Mr. Branigan wrote it down.

'Now as far as the funeral is concerned, I would like "St. Patrick's Breastplate" to start, "Soul of My Saviour" at the

Communion, and "When the Saints Go Marching In" to finish.'

'"When the Saints Go Marching In"?' Mr. Branigan repeated what she had said as if he had misheard her.

'Exactly.' A broad smile crept across her face. '"When the Saints Go Marching In."'

She thought she didn't want to leave Joe, Anne, or her friends, but she came into this world happy, she was happy all through her life, and she was going to go out the same way—happy—and she was going to make sure everyone knew it too.

'One spray of white lilies and white roses should be placed at the statues of the Sacred Heart, Our Lady of the Holy Rosary, and St. Joseph, and one on the coffin. The newspaper obituary should read, "Myers, (née Powers): Mary, devoted wife of Joseph and beloved mother of Anne. Sadly missed. Removal from Sts. Francis and Clare Mortuary to the Church of Our Lady of the Holy Rosary, Dunshaughlin. Funeral at ...... followed by burial at St. Mary's Cemetery, County Meath. Family flowers only. All floral donations to The Poor Clares. May she rest in peace."'

She explained that she had a life assurance policy with Canadian Life Ltd., and that it would cover all the expenses on her death. Mr. Daniel Smith was her assurance advisor. She would make sure that her solicitor, Mr. Anthony McMahon, would deal with everything. Mr. Branigan asked his address, and she gave it: McMahon, Lynch & Whelan at 17 Main Street, Dunshaughlin, Co. Meath. Mr. Branigan assured her that when the time came, everything would go exactly to plan. She was relieved as she left, as though a great weight had been lifted off her shoulders. It was done. Now all she had to tackle was the solicitor, and she would do that first thing in the morning. There was no time like the present to get things going.

Mary contacted Mr. McMahon of McMahon, Lynch & Whelan and arranged for an appointment. It was to be the following day at three o'clock. She went to see him at his office, a small, unassuming place, quite the contrary of Branigans, she thought. The secretary knocked on the door to tell Mr. Mc-

Mahon that Mrs. Myers had arrived. Mary went in, closed the door behind her, and discussed her Will, amongst other confidential matters. After about forty minutes, she emerged from the meeting, opening the door, leaving it slightly ajar, as the secretary overheard.

'Naturally, Mr. McMahon, all that I have told you must remain confidential. I don't even want Joe to know that we met.'

'Of course, Mrs. Myers. We are bound by oath to be confidential in all matters concerning our clients.'

'Provision of course has been made for the fee as you understand.'

'Thank you. Goodbye.'

Mrs. Myers left the office, relieved that everything had been dealt with in a very professional manner.

The next couple of weeks followed without much ado, and Mary went up to see Mr. Brady in St. Vincent's Hospital once more. As usual, he was polite and reassuring. He gave her a prescription for the pain that she had been experiencing lately and told her to rest as much as she could. She explained that she didn't want to give Joe any cause for concern and it was important to try to keep the family together as much as she could. Strong painkillers were prescribed if the pain became unbearable, but she wanted to avoid taking these as long as possible.

This would be the last Christmas they would spend together as a family, and she wanted it to be a memorable one. Mr. Brady understood but was insistent that she take it as easy as possible. Mary had decided to call on Mrs. O'Brien in Gardiner Street on her way back to Dunshaughlin and brought her up the usual barm brack and dozen freshly laid eggs. It had been a few weeks since she had seen her, and Mary was delighted to have a chat with someone outside Dunshaughlin. They had become close friends over the last few years. Anne was in her third year in university, and the couple of years had flown by since they first came to know each other.

Mary told Mrs. O'Brien that she had had a chat with her brother-in-law and that they had spoken about her. She told her how Father Francis always intended going up to see her in Dublin but things got in the way.

'It happens to me, too. I always mean to go and see him but never get around to it.' Then Mary told her the news—Mrs. O'Brien was flabbergasted, lost for words, which in itself was a minor miracle. Mary asked Mrs. O'Brien to keep an eye on Anne, as she had no aunts or uncles. Mary had been an only child, and Joe's brother, Andrew, had died years before from a heart attack. Mrs. O'Brien assured her that she would and that she intended on visiting Father Francis very soon indeed.

The following few months became increasingly difficult for Mary, and she was constantly tired, especially during the day. The pain was increasing, and she had experienced many listless nights. Mary knew that the time was coming when she would have to tell Joe. She didn't know how to broach the subject but hoped that it would be easier than she anticipated. On occasion, he would look at her strangely, asking her if everything was all right! *Did he suspect?* she wondered.

Mary decided to tell him one Wednesday morning; her stomach was filled with butterflies. Joe came in for his usual cup of tea at about eleven o'clock after being in the field. He put his cap on the door hook. She decided *this* was the time.

'Joe,' she said as she was putting a pot of freshly brewed tea on the table. He stirred his tea, not listening, and started his own conversation with her.

'Do you know, Mary, I think I'll start a herb patch, maybe. I'll put it close to the kitchen so you don't have too far to walk to it. You seem so tired lately. What do you think?'

'Joe,' she insisted.

He continued. 'We must decide on what vegetables to do next year, marrows, maybe and some French runner beans. Yes, that's it.'

'Joe,' and then she lost her rag. 'Joe, are you listening to me? I've something to tell you. Are you listening? Forget about the garden, for crying out loud.'

Joe was gob-smacked. 'What ... what's the matter, luv?'

'What's the matter? I've been trying to get a word in for the last five minutes. Will you stop blabbering about the garden?'

He stopped and stared hard at her. Never in his whole life could he remember her getting so riled up.

'What's wrong, pet?' he exclaimed.

She pulled out a chair and sat down. 'I need you to listen. I have something to tell you.'

'What is it? What's wrong?' Joe replied, alarmed.

'Remember when I went to Dublin? And all the times I went since?'

The colour drained from Joe's face.

She continued, shaking. 'Well, the truth of the matter is I ... I wasn't in Dublin looking at dresses. I—'

Joe leaned forward as if to try to help her get the words, which seemed stuck in her throat. 'I ... I was ... yes, I did see Mrs. O'Brien,' she continued disjointedly, 'but I went .... for another reason and ... I think ... I think I had better tell you before ... it goes much further.'

His mouth opened wide. 'Mother of mercy, it's another man. I always thought that you would regret marrying me, I was so lucky. You're the belle of the county and someone is taking you away from me. I'll kill him! God give me strength, I'll kill him!'

He ranted on.

'Remember how I couldn't believe my luck and how happy we were. Good God in heaven. You're going to leave me aren't you? Mary, we can fix whatever's wrong, can't we? Do it together like we always did, can't we? Don't leave. You can't leave. I won't let you! Mary, please don't leave!' he pleaded.

He didn't know whether to lose his temper or cry, but the latter seemed to overtake him. He felt a lump come to his throat as he swallowed hard.

'I just don't know how I'd cope.'

'Joe,' she exclaimed exasperated.

He put his hand up to stop her saying any more. He got up. 'Thirty odd years! Do you know how long that is?' he asked her as if she were an observer in the conversation instead of a participant, and he shook his head. She looked at him, nodding no and then nodding yes. He had her so confused that she didn't know what she was doing.

'Joseph Myers, sit down!' She slammed her hand on the table. He stared at her as if Scotty from the Starship Enterprise had just beamed her down. 'I'm not leaving you.' After a long pause, she continued. 'I'm leaving everyone and everything.'

Joe quizzed her. 'I don't understand, Mary. What do you mean?'

'I've cancer,' she replied.

'What?' He couldn't believe it. Joe's large hands cupped his face. 'God in heaven, woman. Why, why didn't you tell me?' he stuttered.

It was Mary who got up to comfort Joe. 'I mean, when you think about it, it's kinda funny.'

Joe looked up at her. 'I don't see what's so funny about it.'

'Well, not funny exactly, but ironic. You thinking that I would go off with another man—are you mad? I remember before we went courtin' when I saw you, that first time, *all* those years ago helping old Mr. Maher cut his wheat with that long scythe. Do you remember my dad used to help Mr. Maher because that mechanical thing-a-majig was forever breaking down? You were there, and I used to go and bring him his lunch, remember?'

Joe nodded, and she continued. 'You'd just come over from Wales and were new to everything. You were plonked in the middle of all the Dunshaughlin lads. You held your own, though. Strong as an ox, you were and the August sun blistering down on you, you were brown as a berry! You were cutting the wheat as though it were butter and the rest of the lads had one heck of a time melting in the sun trying to keep up with you. They soon stopped trying to get a rise out of you about your accent and whether a lad from a Welsh mining town could "cut it" in the fields in Dunshaughlin when they saw how fast you could shift that wheat! That really shut them up, I can tell you.'

She threw her head back and laughed. 'I think I fell in love with that lilting accent of yours long before I clapped eyes on you. I thought, *Interesting, but what's he* really *like?* It was as though the good Lord let me in on one of his best-kept secrets. I saw this tiny kitten hiding in the long wheat. It must have got away from its mother. All the rest of the men continued cutting away and you saw that helpless little creature. You picked him up, put him out of harm's way, and took off your shirt to keep him from getting cold. You tipped your cap as you walked right past me as you stroked and talked to your new little friend. I thought, *I'm going to marry that man. He's the one for me. There will never be another.*

Joe smiled. 'Well, I always did think you were too good for the likes of me. After all, you could have any of the lads in the county and didn't have to settle for an outsider like me.'

Mary interrupted. 'I will never love another man nor look at one with such gratitude to the good Lord for so many happy years together. Anyway, you were never an outsider. You became a local that day as soon as you put a stopper in their blithering and blathering and all that blarney they were forever going on with.'

He smiled. 'So long ago and yet it went so fast. How long do we have left?' He asked as though he had had the disease too. Joe never thought of 'I', it was always 'we.'

'Mr. Brady, the doctor, says a couple of months, probably. February.'

Joe said, 'It's such a short time. We will have to tell Anne. It won't be easy.'

Mary sighed. 'I know, but at least we will have Christmas together.'

When Anne came home that weekend, both Joe and Mary sat down and told her the sad news. Anne couldn't believe it. Were they sure that there hadn't been a mix up? Anne had heard of hospitals, even consultants, making errors.

'Everyone is human. We all make mistakes,' Anne exclaimed.

Mary assured her that there *was* no mistake ... no mistake at all.

Anne was in total shock; she felt her whole world was falling apart. When she went to bed on Saturday night, she asked God,

'Why her? Why did it have to happen to her? Why did it have to happen to my mam?'

No answers came in the darkness as the tears trickled down her face, and she kept repeating to herself. 'It's not fair, why her, why her?' By the time she had fallen asleep, the pillow was soaked through. Dawn was breaking by the time she had dozed off. Joe didn't wake her and let Mary sleep a little late, too. Christmas was almost upon them. Another few weeks and it would be there.

Anne went back to Trinity that weekend and finished up for the Christmas break. She dropped into her tutor's office and told him what was happening. He sympathized with her and gave her his home telephone number should she need him. She went home and tried to sound perky. Efflam had rung from Paris and wished everyone a Happy Christmas. He was told what was happening and told Anne that he was thinking of them all.

Mary vowed to make it a Christmas to remember. Joe brought her downstairs, and Anne cooked the dinner. It ended up with paper hats and streamers and whistles and a commotion that would wake the dead, the four cats beside the Aga cooker and Jassie and Bob barking and joining in all the fun, with Christmas carols being belted out and rotten jokes being read from inside the crackers with boos and laughter. Father O'Brien called in and brought an old friend with him: Maggie, his sister-in-law.

'You were going to stay with me, remember?' Mary scolded her.

'Next time, maybe,' Mrs. O'Brien replied.

Joe looked at Anne and agreed. 'Yes, Mary, next time.'

They didn't stay long, just a short spell to have a whiskey and wish everyone a Happy Christmas.

Anne decided to ring her tutor, Professor Higgins, and explain the seriousness of the situation.

The following few weeks dragged. It was as though everything were going to sleep. The flowers had died, and the grass was cold and crunchy underfoot. It was as though the world were saying goodbye to her mam. The Home Help Cancer Association sent someone twice a week to help out. Mary hadn't been able to attend morning Mass for some time, due to the aggressiveness of the cancer, and that distressed her terribly, especially on a Sunday. However, Father O'Brien dropped in every morning with the Sacred Host and had a chat with her, allaying whatever fears she might have.

Mary was now on a relatively high dose of painkillers; the pain increased so much without them that she could hardly breathe. She still insisted that she didn't want to take any morphine. She wanted to stay at home and didn't want to die in a hospice or a hospital amongst strangers, however kind they might be. Mrs. McCloskey, the wife of one their closest neighbours, popped in every afternoon with a meal for Joe and Anne. Anne made lunch, but she was hopping up and down every five minutes looking after her mother, who was mainly on fluids. It just wasn't possible for Anne to make an evening meal as well as do everything else. Anne read to Mary in the afternoons; a romance novel was her favourite. The time dragged and dragged. Somehow, Anne wanted it to be all over. She wanted her mam to be relieved of all her pain. Then she felt guilty for having wished it. She knew that what she was feeling was the most natural thing in the world but couldn't shake the guilt.

'God, when will it all end?' she asked one evening as she washed the dishes.

An hour or so later, Anne heard a cup fall off the bedside table, smashing to smithereens. She ran up the stairs, and there was Mary, propped up by so many pillows, the remainder of the tea swirling on the polished floor mingling amongst the broken pieces of cup and her arm extended downwards. It was over. She was gone.

Anne knew that Mary had contacted Branigan's. She rang them and spoke to Michael Branigan. She was told that her mother had already organized everything. The local G.P. issued a death certificate following his inspection of her remains; Branigan's then came and took her away. Anne rang Efflam in Paris and told him what had happened. He asked when the funeral was going to be. Saturday, was the reply. He would arrange for the next possible flight to Dublin. He rang her back and told her that it would be the following day; arrival time would be two o'clock He still cared about her. He still loved her.

Anne went up to meet him at Dublin Airport. She looked up the monitor: Dublin to Paris ... flight AF552, arrival at 14.00. That had to be it. She waited nervously at the arrivals hall. Passengers, one after the other, were met by loved ones. Where was he? Her eyes searched the crowd of descending passengers; then, there he was. As tall as ever, blond, piercing blue eyes, exactly the same as she had remembered him. He saw her as she waved frantically. He hurried over, weighed down by his bag. He grabbed her and held her close for a few moments. They would get through it all together.

The house wasn't the same. The heart of it had died. Joe was broken. It was Efflam who persuaded him to go to O'Neill's with Jassie and Bob. They sat in the same spot as before. Joe didn't talk; he just puffed on his pipe and shook his head. Sometimes he would make a comment about how they had met years before, expecting Efflam to know what he was talking about, and he chuckled to himself as though living the moment all over again. That's all that remained. Memories, fragments of a life together, a look Mary gave or a tone in her voice, fingerprints on a glass and a worn photograph. That was all that was left—no perhaps not all: that and ... grief.

The day after Efflam's arrival, the obituary was printed. It appeared in the small local paper, the *Dunshaughlin Gazette*, which dealt with local issues, as well as in the *Irish Times* and the *Irish Independent*.

Myers, (née Powers) Mary, devoted wife of Joseph and beloved mother of Anne. Sadly missed. Family flowers only. All floral donations to The Poor Clares. Removal from Sts. Francis and Clare Mortuary at five o'clock on Friday to the Church of the Our Lady of the Holy Rosary, Dunshaughlin. Funeral on Saturday at ten o'clock followed by burial St. Mary's Cemetery, Co. Meath. May she rest in peace.

Friday evening came. The little church was full almost to bursting. People were even outside the church because there was no room inside. The dark winter evening closed in as the rain drizzled down coats and upturned collars and dozens of umbrellas. Joe, Anne, and Efflam had arrived early and were at the top pew. Jassie and Bob were there, too, beside Joe. It was as though the dogs knew what was happening and didn't move a muscle, just lay down in the aisle, quiet as church mice. Father O' Brien had made an exception provided the dogs behaved themselves. 'Abide with Me' was sung, and as soon as it started, the dogs decided that they wanted to sing too. They sat up, Jassie starting off and Bob taking his cue from his mother. They sang in unison, and every few minutes they would pipe up with a howl or a bark. Joe patted Jassie and Bob. They were saying goodbye in their own way.

As Mary had requested, the rosary was recited both for her and for The Holy Souls. She would be buried with her rosary beads, the ones her mother had given her years before. Everything was beautiful, but Anne couldn't remember one face as people streamed up to the top pew to console them in their grief. Anne thought that it seemed as though it were happening to someone else, as though she were watching a film in slow motion. When the drizzle had died down and the removal was over, the thoughts of the following day, of burying her mam, became too much for her and she broke down. Efflam put his arm around her to comfort her the best way he could as they made their way home.

The funeral the following morning was a real ordeal. Again, the church was full to bursting and after it was over, the main car followed the hearse with Joe, Efflam, and Anne as it went all the way to St. Mary's Cemetery. The cars followed one after the other, looking like a long multicoloured snake as they made their way to the cemetery. Anyone who didn't go to the cemetery stood in the street, and as it was custom, crossed themselves as the hearse passed by. After the burial, the group went back to the Dunshaughlin Arms Hotel, where soup, rolls, and tea were laid on for guests of the family.

When the day was over, it was about four o'clock. Mr. and Mrs. McCloskey had kept an eye on the farm in the morning, just going to the Mass, and they later saw Joe at the Dunshaughlin Arms Hotel, shook his hand, and spoke in a low, hushed, respectful voice of how fine a woman Mary was. When Joe got back to the house on his own, the dogs met him. They had been fed earlier, together with the rest of the menagerie. Mr. Magoo and the cows were on Mr. McCloskey's land for the interim period. Anne and Efflam had gone to O'Neill's to have a chat and try to get away from the depressive atmosphere of the house. They wanted Joe to go with them, but he wanted to get back to Jassie, Bob, and the house, to everything old and familiar, and where he could still feel Mary's presence.

Joe walked in the hall door, half expecting Mary to spin around, her hand on her hip, telling him not to track mud on her clean new floor, but she didn't. Everything was dark. He turned on the light, and the realisation that she would never come back set in. He made himself a cup of tea and sat with his back to the window. Directly in front of him was the picture of the Sacred Heart that had been a part of the family for so long.

She shouldn't have died like that; with so much pain ... not her ... it wasn't fair. She didn't deserve all that. Why her? She was a good woman ... a very good woman.

He wagged his finger giving out to the Sacred Heart picture half expecting the good Lord to explain why, but the Sacred Heart just looked right back at him, as if to say that He understood the way Joe felt; then, clear as a bell he could hear Mary saying,'Ours is not to reason why. Ours is just to do and die.'

It was one of Mary's constant sayings. Whether he really heard her or not, was irrelevant; grief makes us all prisoners of misconceptions. He smiled to himself and shook his head.

'You were always right, Mary pet. No point in arguing; you were always right.' His chin trembled, and the hot tears rolled down his cheeks.

'It's all over now,' he sighed, resigned to what had happened. 'It's all over now.'

Chapter Six

The solicitor from McMahon, Lynch & Whelan rang Joe a couple of days later.
'Mr. Myers?'
'Yes, this is Joe Myers.'
'Please accept my sincere condolences on the loss of your wife. I'm Michael McMahon, your wife's solicitor.'
'Oh, thank you. Her solicitor? What the devil are you on about?'
'I wonder if you would be able to come to the office?'
'For what?'
'For the reading of your wife's Will.'
'Will?' I never knew she had a Will. What would she be able to leave anyway? We're not exactly Lord and Lady Astor ... I mean, hmm ... I'm ... not exactly living the high life.'
'Nevertheless, it's necessary so that funeral expenses can be paid.'
'Oh yes, sorry. I see what you mean. When?'
'Would ten o'clock tomorrow morning suit? It's 17 Main Street, Dunshaughlin. Will that be all right?'
'Oh, yes, yes, that's fine.'
'Your daughter, Anne, and an Efflam d'Avvenes are also requested to attend.'
'Oh, that's Anne's young man. Fair enough. We will all be there at ten o'clock.' Joe hung up.

Joe couldn't think what on earth Mary could have to leave in a Will, and the thought rather niggled at him a little. He mentioned it to Anne and Efflam. Anne was equally perplexed.
'What on earth would mam have to leave anyone? I mean we're not really poor, but we aren't up there with the Rothschild's or whatever you call them, are we?'
'That's what I told the solicitor, but he insisted,' Joe replied.

The following morning came, and after breakfast, all three turned up at McMahon, Lynch & Whelan Solicitors. The secretary stopped filing her nails as they came through the door and greeted them with a bright, breezy smile.

'Good morning, how can I help you?'

'Good morning,' Joe replied. 'We have a meeting with Mr. Michael McMahon.'

'Oh, yes, one moment please.' The secretary knocked on the door and popped her head around it.

'Mr. McMahon, the others from your ten o'clock appointment are here.'

'Oh, yes. Show them in, please.'

'The rest have already arrived,' the secretary said to Joe.

'The rest?' Joe replied.

Joe, Anne, and Efflam went into the office.

'Thank you for coming. I understand that you were unaware of a Will being made.' The solicitor addressed Joe.

'Yes, that's right.'

'Your wife was very organized. She left nothing to chance.'

Joe turned to shut the door and saw Father O'Brien and Maggie seated in the office. He was even more gob-smacked when he saw Mr. and Mrs. McCloskey.

'What's all this, Joe?' Mr. McCloskey whispered to him.

Joe shrugged his shoulders. 'Beats me. I never even knew Mary *had* a Will.'

'Now that we are all here, I suggest we begin.' The solicitor addressed everyone as he said this. Clearing his throat, he read the following:

McMahon, Lynch & Whelan Solicitors
17 Main Street, Dunshaughlin, Co. Meath

This is the Last Will and testament dated the 27th October 1984, of Mary Myers, residing at Hazelhurst Farm, Dunshaughlin, being of sound mind, hereby revoking all former Wills and Testamentary Dispositions made by me, the aforesaid Mary Myers.

If my husband, Joseph Myers, survives me by thirty days, I give, devise and bequeath the following part of my estate to him and appoint him my executor.

£60,000 Punts

I bequeath to my beloved daughter Anne Myers, £25,000 and the sum of £5,000 to Mr. Efflam d'Avennes. I bequeath £1,000 to The Poor Clare enclosed monastery, St. Clare's Park., Dublin 4, and £1,000 to the Franciscans, located at The Church of Sts. Francis and Clare, Fisherman's Quay, Dublin 1. The sum of £500 is to be left to Father Francis Aloysius O'Brien, Parish Priest of Our Lady of the Holy Rosary Church, Dunshaughlin, and £500 to his sister-in-law, Maggie O'Brien of Lower Gardiner Street, Dublin 2. I bequeath the sum of £2,000 to my friends and good neighbours, Mr. Tom and Mrs. Teresa McCloskey, to whom I am especially indebted.

The funeral expenses and solicitor's fees are to be deducted from the remainder of my estate, and should any monies remain, they are to be added to the estate of my husband, Joseph Myers.

If my husband does not survive me by thirty days, the following provisions shall apply:

1. I appoint my daughter, Anne Myers (herein after called 'my trustee,') to be executrix and trustee and appoint

her trustee for the purposes of the Settled Land Acts, Conveyance Acts and Section 57 of the Succession Act.

2. I appoint her, Anne Myers, the said trustee, to carry out my aforesaid requests heretofore mentioned.

Dated:
27ᵗʰ October 1984
Signed: Mary Myers:
Mary Myers
Witnessed: Michael McMahon:
Michael McMahon
Solicitor
Witnessed: Siobhan McNally:
Siobhan McNally
Secretary

'Mr. McMahon.' Joe peered at him. 'Are you sure you are talking about the *same* Mary Myers?'

'Yes, Mr. Myers. It should be said that she thought that you would be a little bit surprised.'

'Surprised! I'm shocked. All told, you're talking the guts of £100,000!'

'Actually, £110,000 is the exact amount.'

'Are you absolutely certain?'

'Positive,' was the answer the solicitor gave him.

'But, how? We never had two brass farthings to rub together.'

'Mr. Myers, your wife was a very shrewd and capable woman. She took out a life insurance policy with Canadian Life Ltd., more than thirty years ago. Unfortunately, she didn't take out any serious illness cover. If she had, she would have been able to enjoy a little of her money when she was diagnosed with cancer.'

'But how did she pay for it?'

'Funny, you mention that. She thought you might be curious. She used to work a few afternoons a week at the retirement home helping with dinners and cleaning.'

'I knew that she used to do couple of hours for a few bob, but it never crossed my mind that she got an insurance policy, not even for a moment. I always said to her that whatever she earned she should use on herself.'

'Mrs. Myers saved week in and week out to pay for her policy. She said that nothing could interfere with it. It went into her account every week, and Canadian Life Ltd., deducted it from her account every month. She knew that she was dying, and she contacted her Canadian Life consultant, telling him that in the event of her death Canadian Life was to deposit the cheque with me. Well, Mr. Myers, I know this has been a little shocking, but a pleasant surprise nonetheless. Don't you think?'

He turned to Mr. and Mrs. McCloskey, who were equally shocked. 'But anything we did, we did because Mary and Joe are good friends and neighbours.'

The solicitor interrupted. 'Mr. and Mrs. McCloskey, Mrs. Myers was extremely grateful for your kindness and she wanted to reciprocate in a small way.'

'Very kind, very kind indeed,' was the reply.

Father O'Brien had put his arm around Maggie, who was now crying her eyes out, blowing her nose to beat the band. 'There, there now, Maggie, don't upset yourself.'

Joe interrupted. 'Maggie, Mary was very fond of you, very fond. She was always saying how kind you had been and how Father Francis always had time to chat and pop around. He made time even when he didn't have it. You both did, and we are all grateful.'

'Yes. Yes, we are,' Anne piped up.

Efflam just sat there dumbfounded. He couldn't understand why in the world he would be remembered.

'Well, lad.' Joe patted him on the back. 'Let's go home.'

Efflam looked at him questioningly. 'But seer, I am not of any importonsse. Why deed Mrs. Myeers ...'

Joe looked at him squarely. 'Because you're family, lad ... because you're family.'

Joe left the office feeling sad and happy at the same time. He was glad about not having to worry too much about money anymore and grateful to Mary but wishing that she were here to enjoy it with him.

Efflam had to start making arrangements to get back to Paris, and Anne had to return to Dublin. It was heart aching. Neither one wanted to leave the other.

'Only one more year and we will both be finished,' Anne said to Efflam as he was about to board the plane for Paris.

'Only one more year. You say it as though it's nussing at all, a year is toooo lung, far too lung, but we will get through it *'mon chou, mon petit chou'* (*my cabbage, my little cabbage*).

Anne had decided that she would make a dedicated effort to go to Mass during the coming Lent. She had once been in the habit of going on Sundays, but like her dad, she said a few prayers when she needed something, but when things were going well, like most people, she forgot.

Anne went back to Trinity, returning at the weekends to make sure her dad was all right. She worried about him and often rang Mrs. McCloskey to ask if he was all right. Mrs. McCloskey took Joe under her wing like a brood hen with an injured chick. She was aware that he had to have his independence and didn't wish to make him feel like a total invalid.

It was agreed that Joe would have lunch at their farmhouse. 'After all, it makes sense. One more person will make no difference, and it will be nice for Tom having someone to pass the time with. You would be doing him a favour. As for dinner, I will drop over something at about five o'clock for your tea, in case you want to listen to the radio or watch that new television you have.'

Joe agreed, thankful for her thoughtfulness. He thought it was too much, but she wouldn't be persuaded to do otherwise. Mrs. McGonigle, the parish priest's housekeeper, popped in to do a little tidying up. She wanted to do it without payment, but Joe wouldn't hear of it. She settled on a price, and it meant that Joe didn't have to worry about laundry, ironing, or anything else.

Mrs. McGonigle popped in for two hours three times a week. She did the laundry and ironing. She tidied the house, baked bread, fruit scones, and a homemade apple tart or gooseberry crumble so that Joe felt comfortable about inviting a friend or two for a cup of tea. He felt that he could cope—just about. Mrs. McGonigle saved the couple of bob that she got from Joe to see her sister, Úna, whom she hadn't seen for nearly forty years and who married a young lobster fisherman and had gone to live in Maine, New England. Úna said all the houses looked similar and the people were akin to the Irish, so she felt right at home. A fine strapping young Yank, he was, with a crewed cut who thought her sister was 'a great gal' and who thought her accent quaint. Mrs. McGonigle had always intended to go and see them but was never able to, as she never had the money. This was her opportunity, her big chance.

By the time, the third year exams were over Anne had attained, yet again, her 2.1 average; she decided that she would spend at least a month of the summer with Efflam in Paris. She was worried about her dad but was assured by Mr. and Mrs. McCloskey that they would keep an eye on him and no harm would come to him.

As soon as her exams were finished, Anne packed up as usual and returned home. It wasn't the same. She was a bit cross that life hadn't stopped when her mam had died. She thought that life owed it to her.

'Ours is not to wonder why. Ours is just to do and die,' her dad piped up behind her.

'Mam used to say that. I suppose it's true. We're just travellers on the way to somewhere else. A better place. This is just a resting place until we start on our journey again, I suppose. Nevertheless, I wish she were here.'

'Yeah, I do too. Still, chin up. She's where she is supposed to be ... up there in the Heavenly Club.'

'Heavenly Club? You make it sound that you have to pay to get admitted.'

'Well, you do. You have to say your prayers and be kind to people, animals, and the Holy Souls. Nobody knew that better than your mam.'

'Do you really think that she is there?'

'Annie, I remember going to see a film with your mam, years ago it was; what was it called now? Oh, yes. *Song of Bernadette*, about St. Bernadette's life, and one of the lines in the film captured that very thought. "For those who believe, no explanation is necessary; for those who do not, no explanation will suffice." I've never forgotten it, ever. Don't forget, there are no atheists in a sinking ship or a plane hurtling to the ground'.

For the solicitor to be, this took the wind out of her sails. *Well said, dad*, she thought. He was right. Sometimes people frown on those with faith; it's not fashionable. Nevertheless, when you have no one to turn to, it's great to be able to have a chat with the 'Man Above' and know that he knows you better than you know yourself.

August had come, when Anne was to travel to Paris. She was having second thoughts.

'Annie, don't worry. There's the county fair and the August markets. Don't worry about me. I'm going to be so busy that I won't know you're gone ... and then you'll be back.'

'Well, I'm not so sure. Maybe I'll ask Efflam to come here.'

'You will not. You need a break, and I need to be alone with my thoughts.'

'All right, dad, if you're really sure.'

'I am. Go on, enjoy yourself.'

Anne booked her flight and left a couple of days later. Efflam met her at Charles de Gaulle Airport and said that he had wanted her to meet his whole extended family.

'That's nice, but, you know, my French isn't very good.'

'That's all right. Don't worry. Remember my maternal grandmuzzer is Irish and my muzzer is Scots. They will make you feel at home, even if you don't have a wurd.'

When Anne and Efflam arrived in Paris, she was captivated by the *joie de vivre* of the French. They were cosmopolitan and efficient but loved life. They loved to watch life pass by at the cafés, drinking coffee and smoking while sitting on the terraces outside. She drank coffee but didn't smoke. The brew was too strong, and she ended up having more milk than coffee.

Paris in August—wonderful. Efflam wanted to show Anne around Paris, taking her through the obscure narrow winding streets and the wonderful Cathedral of Notre Dame. The Eiffel Tower and the famous museums filled their days. They walked forever, it would seem, stopping at cafés for a coffee or a sandwich. She wanted to try everything French except escargots and frogs legs; wonderful as they might be, her stomach couldn't manage it.

'Parisian food is excellent, no doubt, but Breton food is the best,' she was assured.

Life in Paris was a feast. Tall apartment blocks with cafés and great nightlife. Couples strolling hand in hand, kissing on corners and embracing. Yes, it surely was the city of romance. It was a thousand miles away from Dunshaughlin, her dad, Jassie and Bob, and from all she loved. This wasn't for her. Nice for a holiday, but she knew she couldn't make it her home. She went out onto the terrace balcony of Efflam's parents' apartment. They had been so warm and inviting. She felt that she had imposed but was constantly assured that she was family.

It was on one of those balmy nights when Efflam asked her, '*Mon petit chou*, (*my little cabbage*) I ... I dunt know, I min I am trying to say, emm.'

'What is it, Efflam?'

'I imagined zees to be quite differen'. Anne ... wud you marry me? Would you make me so 'appy that I can't wait to wake in zee morning knowing that you are zere to share my life ... will you?'

'I ... Oh, Efflam. I will. I do love you.'

Since Efflam had returned to Paris, his English had reverted to its heavy accent. She smiled to herself, imagining 'Inspector Closeau' was going to pop out from his hiding place.

That night, alone, she thought of what marrying Efflam would mean. Perhaps she hadn't thought it through and the emotion of the moment had caught her unawares. She would have to leave her dad and everyone behind. All of a sudden, she felt clammy and scared; she felt as though she were claustrophobic and needed to get out. She went out to the balcony in the moonlight. She was in her pyjamas and fuzzy slippers. Efflam couldn't sleep, either, and felt that perhaps she might change her mind. He heard her get up as her bedroom was next to his. Anne opened the French windows to the balcony and seeing her standing in the moonlight made him wonder why it took him so long to ask her. He moved; she heard something but didn't think anything of it. She couldn't see him as he watched her from the window. She unplaited her long, curly, rich titan hair and shook her head from side to side to loosen it as she brushed it upside down and threw her head back. It reminded Efflam of a waterfall of red-gold sunshine as it cascaded down her back. Anne took in Paris as though it were a breath of air and inhaled it deeply. Somehow, by doing that she could take this memory and all the others with her when she went home. Soon, she would be going home. Soon, she would see and be with everyone she loved ... everyone except Efflam. He promised her that he would make a reservation in the Latin Quarter where some of the best restaurants in Paris were. She still had ten days left, though, just ten days. Efflam wanted to show her around Paris, the Paris known to the locals.

Anne asked him to keep their engagement a secret. She wanted to tell her dad face to face. Everyone was unaware except his maternal grandmother. It was she to whom Efflam turned when he was about to make a decision that affected him deeply. It was she, in whom he confided. She promised to keep his secret as she handed over her own engagement ring.

'It is very old. I've had it a long time. I hope you both have as much happiness as we have had.'

It was a quaint ring, three diamonds with an emerald on either end, but the filigree work was outstanding. A family heirloom had been passed onto her husband by his grandmother.

'Perhaps, it will be your son's or grandson's engagement ring, one day, please God.'

She pressed it into his hand and closed it. Efflam started to protest, but she patted him on the shoulder and put her finger to her mouth to tell him to be quiet.

'What will grandfazer say?'

'I won't tell him until Anne has spoken to her father, and then he will be happy. I think he always hoped that this family would have an Irish addition.'

'You never said that before, Méme!'

'I don't have to tell you all my secrets, do I?' She smiled as she left the room; he could hear his grandfather calling her.

Joe felt Anne's absence, and she hadn't been gone long when he was already looking forward to having her back home. Mr. and Mrs. McCloskey had been great. They looked after him like an addition to their own family. He was grateful for the company, but it wasn't the same as before. However, Anne would be home at the end of the month. Joe had indeed been as busy as he had anticipated. The August fairs were in full swing. The main fair took place 5th—9th August. It covered everything. One of the farmers on the edge of town let the organizing committee use a couple of acres of grazing land so that tents could be pitched. The only stipulations were that only locally produced items could be sold and that they would leave the field the way they found it, clean and tidy.

Joe decided to make his way down to the fair, taking the dogs with him. Jassie and Bob knew something was up once they heard Joe whistling as he went about his daily routine. He did everything in record time and took two packed lunches with him. He made ham and salad sandwiches and included two large pieces of Mrs. McGonigle's apple pie and a large flask of tea. He called into Mr. McCloskey and told him that he was heading to the fair and asked him if he would like to join him. As it happened, Mr. McCloskey was on his way, too. His wife wanted to catch up on her ironing and appreciated being left on her own for a bit.

They both headed off. They could hear the music and bustle long before they got to it. The dogs trailed alongside as Mr.

McCloskey, or Tom, as he was known, chatted away. It was a tonic. Joe forgot about Mary and Anne and enjoyed the company. When they arrived, they found tents pitched all over the field and vendors selling everything from locally produced pottery to homemade jams, biscuits, and cakes. There were woollens, arts and crafts, everything local, for the locals. Competitions and races took pride of place. Egg and spoon races, potato-sack races, three-legged races, all were part of the fair's curriculum. The idea was to get everyone involved, young and old alike. The organizers took it into their heads to pair people rather than allow people to choose their own partners. This caused no end of fun. Young people paired with old age pensioners made it positively hilarious. It also made great sense as it tied the community, often quite literally, together. Competitions ranged from tug o' war to testing how many times the hammer hit the strong man's bell. There were vegetable prizes, too. The biggest didn't always win the prize; the tastiest did.

By the time the day was over, Joe was tuckered out. It was five o'clock or so by the time the men strolled home, Joe puffing his pipe. The dogs were fed, and they all had dinner at McCloskey's. Joe thanked Mrs. McCloskey and made his way home.

He ran around like a looney finishing everything. He fed the menagerie and brought in Mr. Magoo, milked the cattle and brought them in. It was a good day. It was one of the first that he could remember feeling completely happy. It was a great feeling. He sat down in the rocking chair and puffed on his pipe for a little while. He thought to himself of the day and everything that had happened since the funeral. The dogs would follow him upstairs now. It was the custom since Mary had died. Jassie wouldn't leave Joe, and Bob wouldn't leave Jassie. He put out his pipe as he opened the door leading upstairs. He thought to himself that he should feel guilty about not thinking about Mary but reassured himself. *Mary would understand. Whether we like it or not, life goes on.* Jassie barked at him as though she understood. He made his way up the stairs to bed, followed by Jassie and Bob, both tired out and ready for sleep.

Days turned into weeks, and soon Anne was making her way home. She packed her bags and brought a little Eiffel Tower for her father, small boxes of chocolates for Mrs. McCloskey and Mrs. O'Brien, and a book about Paris for Mr. McCloskey. When she had gone to visit the Cathedral of Notre Dame, she had bought a little statue of Our Lady with some Holy Water for Father O'Brien and a box of French pastries for Mrs. McGonigle in the nearby patisserie. She packed her bags, wondering would she ever return. *Sure she would*, she assured herself.

Efflam knocked on the door to bring out the bags. He hardly said a word. He asked that they leave earlier than necessary as he had something to talk to her about. The car was packed, and they walked to the nearby patisserie, which also sold coffee. They sat outside for a while as he stirred his coffee absentmindedly.

Suddenly, he stopped. 'Anne, this is for you. It belonged to my grandmozer.'

Efflam took out the engagement ring as Anne's eyes grew large and wide.

'Do you think it would do for an engagement ring?'

'Do? It's beautiful.'

He slipped the ring onto her finger, and she did what most young girls do; she stretched out her hand, admiring the beautiful simplicity of the heirloom as the sun's rays glinted and the light danced on the stones.

'It's breathtaking.'

'I hope the only day you ever take it uff is the day of our wedding.'

'You can bet on it,' Anne chirped up.

The last parting was bittersweet. It was bitter for the parting and sweet for the wedding, which would take place in July; however, she still had to tell her dad.

The plane journey seemed to take forever. She couldn't wait to see her dad, Jassie, Bob, and Mr. Magoo and the whole menagerie. She couldn't wait to see Ireland. As the plane bumped down into Dublin Airport, she could see green fields stretched out like an emerald velvet cloak. She liked going away, but she loved coming home. She got a trolley, put her bags on it as she made her way through the customs, and finally emerged into the arrivals hall.

She was on her way to see if she could get a bus when a frantic wave and 'Annie, Annie,' drew her attention. There was her dad with Tom. He had driven up in his van. Mrs. McCloskey, or rather Teresa, had lunch all ready at home.

'What a homecoming!' Anne piped up as she hugged her dad. She gave Tom a hug, too. They both helped carry her bags to the van.

'I have another surprise,' her dad said.

He opened the door of the van, and the two dogs barked and wagged their tails as she put her things in the back. They wouldn't leave her be. She was licked from head to toe, it would seem, when she sat in the back. Jassie and Bob lay down on the back seat with their heads on either side of her lap, delighted that she had finally come home.

Teresa was as good as her word, and a smashing roast beef with all the trimmings awaited her. She told them of Paris and the sights she had seen, of Efflam's family and the wonderful evenings, of the Parisian custom of 'people watching' from cafés. She told them everything except for one thing. In order for them not to notice the ring, she wrapped an Elastoplast around her finger, carefully putting a little paper over the stones so as not to damage them.

'You cut your hand, dearie,' Teresa remarked.

Anne ignored the remark and complimented her on her cooking.

By the time they had finished, it was nearly four o'clock, time to feed the livestock and get things sorted. Anne and Joe made their way home, and as they went into the house, Anne suggested a cup of tea. She wanted to talk to him about something. She sat down and cut a piece of gooseberry pie, topped it with a dollop of cream, and gave it to her dad.

Anne poured herself a cup of tea and kept stirring it.

'Dad?'

Joe looked at her as she continued stirring her tea, not looking at him.

'Something wrong?'
'Dad?'
'Yeah, Annie. What is it?'
'Efflam has asked me to marry him, and I've said yes.'
Joe looked straight at her. He got up and hugged her as though he were going to crush her.
'He's a fine lad, Annie, a very fine lad. When will it be?'
'We thought July.'
'You're mam would be that proud of you, but you will finish university first, won't you?'
'Oh, yes, dad. Don't worry.'
Joe felt a sense of deep happiness. He was glad that his daughter would experience the kind of love that he had felt throughout his married life. He felt a little sense of loss that perhaps Anne would go and live in France, but he would cross that bridge when he came to it.
Anne took the Elastoplast off her finger and turned the ring around to show her father.
Joe whistled. 'That's some beauty.'
'It's an heirloom,' Anne proudly interjected. 'It belonged to Efflam's grandmother. His mother was given her engagement ring from her husband's grandmother. It must be a tradition in their family.'
'I'll have to call and congratulate Efflam.'
Joe rang and expressed his delight to Efflam at the prospect of having him as part of his family. Now Efflam could let his own family know. They were equally thrilled.
'Life is strange, isn't it, dad? I saw only darkness around me after mam died. I thought my life was over.'
'I know what you mean, Annie. I know what you mean.'
'It doesn't seem dark any more. I still really miss her, but I know that she is happy where she is.'
'That's right, luv. Don't feel guilty. Happiness is a gift. Life goes on.'

Chapter Seven

October came sooner than Anne had expected. Efflam rang her twice a week to get the news. She had to start studying hard for her final exams in June, she knew. In a way it was better that Efflam wasn't there; it meant that Anne could concentrate more on her studies without fear of offending him. Efflam had told her that French law was based on Napoleonic law and not the common law that she had studied in Trinity. This meant that she would have to look for something different to do if they were going to live in France. That didn't put Anne off, though; she still studied like a maniac.

Anne continued to go home every weekend to see her dad and make sure that everything was all right. She had lost touch with Brian. She had been too busy, and he had made other friends. Efflam had come between them. Brian and Anne had grown apart and moved on with their lives. Nevertheless, whenever Anne saw Brian in the Arts Block, she would make an extra effort to have a coffee with him to chat about what was going on and his future plans. It wasn't the same, though; that seemingly indestructible thread between them had been severed. Anne thought it a shame; they had been good friends. *Friendship is as fragile as a flower*, she thought. *You have to water it or it will die.* That was exactly what had happened.

It was Christmas before she knew it, the first Christmas without her mother. Efflam travelled from Paris, and Father O'Brien and Maggie came for Christmas lunch with Mrs. McGonigle. Tom and Teresa McCloskey also joined them. Christmas was as far from the dreary one that she had previously anticipated as black is from white. Everyone brought something. Tom and Teresa brought the turkey, Mrs. McGonigle the ham. Father O'Brien brought Christmas cake, and Maggie arrived over laden with a Christmas pudding, brandy butter, a bottle of whiskey, and more than a couple of bottles of 'the black stuff.' Efflam was in charge of the rest. Paper hats, streamers, Christmas crackers were the order of the day, and it seemed as though every noise-making contraption ever invented was employed.

When everyone sat down to eat, it was a feast to behold. Father O'Brien said grace and added, 'Thank you, Lord, for bringing us together and for Mary who is with us in spirit. Thank you for good friends and for this great celebration.'

After the meal, everything was cleared away for a real good Irish *hoolie*. The bodrán was brought out on which Father O'Brien had played throughout his life. Mr. McCloskey brought his accordion and Joe his tin whistle. Everyone clapped and sang traditional songs. Even the dogs joined in, howling every now and then. A space had been made in the middle of the floor where Anne danced a reel and a jig and more music was played. It went on into late afternoon, a wonderful Christmas, and certainly one to remember.

Efflam went back to Paris for his last couple of terms as Anne returned to Trinity. He would graduate in early June, and Anne was upset that she wouldn't be able to see him graduate as she would still be doing exams then, but it couldn't be helped. Anne made an even more gruelling study schedule for herself and wanted to try to attain the grade of Distinction that had eluded her for so long, despite her hard work.

The months flew by, and Anne concentrated on her studies. She didn't have enough time to do everything that she wanted. March was upon her more suddenly than she had expected. She had spoken to Efflam about the wedding plans. They would decide everything together as soon as he came to Dunshaughlin for a long weekend.

'Efflam, I would like to get married here in Dunshaughlin and have both Irish and Breton traditions in the ceremony.' With great confidence in herself, she continued, 'I have decided to get a Breton wedding dress made but with some Irish additions. What do you think?'

'*Mon petit chou, (my little cabbage)*that is a great idea. My mother has her own Breton wedding dress. It's not exactly traditional, but you can get ideas from that. It belonged to Méme.'

'Méme?'
'My grandmozer.'
'Oh, that's brilliant, an heirloom!'
When Efflam returned to Paris, he explained the great plan. His mother thought it a very thoughtful thing to do. She did something quite out of the ordinary and posted her beloved wedding dress over to Anne.

On Friday, Joe received a large box addressed to Anne. When she came home from Trinity, he told her and shortly afterwards she ran up to her bedroom and excitedly pushed back the heavy layers of tissue paper. Loeiza had packed each item with exceptional care, so carefully in fact, that she was afraid to touch them. The bonnet came first, a delicate crown of handmade snow-white interlacing lace circles attached to a transparent tuile cap. As she peeled back the paper, Anne's jaw dropped. It was a bodice and skirt of deep heavy burgundy velvet through which threads of gold had been skilfully stitched. Anne put these to one side on the bed as her hand stroked the rich fabric. She then proceeded to remove the thin tissue paper very carefully, only to find no less than five stiff white tuile underskirts. The simple long-sleeved white chiffon blouse went underneath the burgundy velvet bodice, and the cuffs of the blouse were finished in Breton lace. The neckline had a loose ruffle that fell over the neck of the bodice, which was laced up the front with fine gold braid. The hem of the skirt was finished off in thicker version of the same gold braid. The gold silk apron had a thick band that was wrapped around the waist of the bodice and skirt to bring it together. To say that the outfit was stunning was an understatement.

'Dad, dad, you better come up and see this.'
Joe stared; his eyes were wider than Anne's.
'It's Efflam's grandmother's wedding dress, and her mother wore it for her wedding, too. What do you think?'
'It's really beautiful. Look at the workmanship! Do you know your mam has a beautiful wedding shawl that she was given by *her* grandmother that would look lovely with that!'
'Do you think that Efflam's mother would let me wear it?' She put the bodice up against her.

'I'm sure she would, pet. Now let me see where Mary put that shawl.'

He went into his bedroom and rummaged through the enormous trunk where Joe had packed some of Mary's things. He found what he was looking for in a flat, sleek box at the end of the trunk. He lifted the box out as though it were a national treasure. He pushed back the layers of paper in a frenzy and found a pressed flower in between tissue paper. He stopped and thought of his own wedding day for a moment but restrained himself from getting sentimental and peeled back the last sheet.

'Anne, Annie, here it is,' he shouted as he took it out of the box. 'What do you think?'

She came into the bedroom, thinking how wonderful wedding dress had been and that nothing could top it; her eyes nearly popped out of their sockets as she beheld this cascade of snow-white Irish lace icicles.

'Oh, dad.' Her eyes filled with emotion. 'It's perfect. Just look at the detail. What a combination. They're both like brand new.'

'This should be. It's only ever been used twice. It was worn on your grandmother's wedding day, and then your mother's, and now it's yours.'

'Oh, dad.' She hugged him.

'Here, watch now, watch the shawl.'

'Sorry, dad,' and she smiled.

Anne rang Efflam to see if it would be possible for her to wear the dress itself. His mother was thrilled and explained that she had that in mind as she had spent many hours making sure that it was as perfect as the day it was when she had worn it. Anne was petite, a size 10. Efflam's mother was the same when she married, so it was as though the dress had been made for Anne. Anne was smaller in stature so alterations to the skirt and sleeves would have to be made but they could be done without ruining the dress.

Efflam would wear traditional Breton dress.

'What does it look like?' Anne asked.

'You will have to wait and see!' Efflam replied.

Efflam's cousin, who still lived in Brittany, would bring a *carré* and some sprigs of hawthorn with him when he came to the wedding in July. Efflam hadn't had time to explain to Anne what they were for but would do so at the beginning of June when he arrived in Dunshaughlin after his graduation.

Efflam's mother would arrange the wedding bouquet. Each flower represented a gift for the bride and groom. His mother had already decided. Ivy would surround the bouquet, signifying eternal fidelity, camellias for gratitude, cyclamen for modesty and shyness, flowering almonds for hope, forget-me-nots for true love and remembrance, violets for faithfulness, and last, white Irish heather for the luck of the Irish!

The bride's mother and the mother-in-law would normally buy a small gift for both the bride and groom; however, since Anne's mother was dead, Loeiza, Efflam's mother, would buy both and take them with her when she went to Dunshaughlin at the beginning of June with her son to help with the wedding arrangements. She decided to get one of the sets of gifts in Ireland and the other—the other would require a lot of hard work to be extra special.

Loeiza had already asked the family priest in Brittany, Père Benead, to officiate with Father Francis at the wedding so the celebration could be held in English and Breton, with some Irish and French thrown in; that way everyone would feel at home. The date was set. It was to be 27th July. In the latter half of April, the invitations went out to all the guests. They had to be printed in English, French, and Breton. Loeiza took care of the French and Breton and sent them from Paris once she received the original English version to work on.

Mr. & Mrs. Thomas McCloskey
At the wedding of

Miss Anne Myers to Monsieur Efflam D'Arvenes

On Saturday, 27th July 1986 at 11.00 o'clock
At the Church of Our Lady of the Holy Rosary, Dunshaughlin, Co. Meath
Followed by an Irish-Breton reception
in the Church grounds and adjacent meadow.

R.S.V.P. In writing before 7th July
'Hazelhurst Cottage,' Dunshaughlin, Co. Meath

Efflam hadn't called Anne for a week, and she was getting worried. *Is he all right?* she asked herself. *He's probably working like a lunatic for his exams. I don't know why I get so worried. Maybe he's changed his mind!* So many scenarios went through her mind that she was almost ready for the funny farm by the time he did ring.

'Why didn't you ring? I was so worried. Why did you leave it so long?'

'I'm sorry, *mon petit chou,*(*my little cabbage*) but it's only been a week, and I have been studying very hard for my exams.'

'God, you had me worried to death,' she ranted on.

'Nothing is wrong. Don't worry so. I will be in Dunshaughlin in June. It will be only a few more weeks. I will be there before you even finish your exams, and it will be me that will be worried after that.'

'It serves you right for worrying me half to death.' Then Anne laughed nervously.

'Is everything all right?' he asked.

'It will be when I see you at home. How are the exams going?' she enquired.

'I have studied very hard so I think I will be all right.'

'Don't leave it so long before you ring the next time.'

'Don't wuurry; by the time we get married, you will be sick to dess of me.'

'Bye, luv. Talk to you on Wednesday.'

'Bye, ma petite.' He hung up.

It was nerves, a double batch, pre-wedding and pre-exam. Anne didn't have to worry too much about the wedding arrangements, as Efflam's mother would take care of everything. She had no daughter of her own so it was a real treat for her. Loeiza was wondering whether she was getting too involved in the wedding preparations. Perhaps she wasn't giving Anne a chance to decide on the little things herself and would prefer something else. Efflam assured his mother that it was nerves and that Anne would be very grateful for any help. Anne had already stated emphatically that she had wanted an Irish-Breton wedding. Anne relied on her help. After all, Loeiza wasn't just a mother-in-law; she would be a potential mother as well, one, which was sorely needed. Efflam advised her that if Anne expressed a differing opinion not to take it personally. Loeiza agreed.

Efflam finished his exams in mid-May and wanted to take a break to clear his thoughts and see his cousins in Brittany. He wanted to separate himself quite literally from the whirl of wedding arrangements and the bustle they incorporated. He rang Anne and told her of his plans, and she thought it was a good idea. Efflam arrived in Brittany a couple of days later and stayed in his aunt's house in Le Pouldu. Deniel, Efflam's cousin, had taken a few days' holidays to spend with him.

It wasn't until Efflam arrived that he realised how much he had missed Brittany. It was distinctly different from Paris. He loved seafood and the Breton way of cooking. He hadn't tasted lambig, the traditional Breton apple brandy, in a long time. As they toasted his forthcoming marriage, Deniel suggested bringing some Breton cider over to Ireland, as he would need it when they sang 'Ev Ev Chistr Ta, Laou!' Efflam wasn't at all sure that they would sing the Breton drinking song which praised the wonders of cider, or indeed, if he would remember the words.

'You will have to teach Anne to dance the Dans-tro Fisel at your wedding,' Deniel said animatedly.

'I'm not sure *I* even remember how to dance it, never mind teaching someone!'

'Well, then, we had better get some of the guys together to remind you!'

'Deniel, I can just about remember how to dance a simple Rond. I can teach her that. That'll do.'

'*Oh no*, you don't. You will have half of your cousins laughing their heads off at you, saying that you have forgotten your Breton roots and you have become a total Parisian. You are *not* going to make a fool of us. We will start tomorrow night.'

Deniel told his mother of the plan, and she thought it very important that if Efflam was going to do traditional Breton dances at his own wedding, they should be done properly. Deniel then got in touch with various friends and cousins and told them of the little party at his home that evening and the reason behind it. Efflam's aunt spent much of the day preparing seafood, gallettes stuffed with ham and eggs, and other crêpes with savoury fillings. She made two large clafoutis; the sweet prune pudding dessert typical of Brittany would bring Efflam back to the days of his youth. Lots of ice-cold Breton cider accompanied the delicacies.

'Hmm. Smells delicious. You have been working very hard,' Deniel exclaimed enthusiastically to his mother, smacking his lips and trying to slip one of the galletes into his mouth.

She spun around and smacked him on his hand like a little boy.

'Just as well I had another one in my left hand!' He smirked and kissed her on the cheek.

'*Deniel*! No one is going to get a bite until Efflam knows at least some of the steps,' she replied.

'But of course, of course, maman. Efflam will be dancing until his legs fall off, I guarantee you.' He chuckled.

The old barn had a floor 'slick as a whistle' and was perfect for dancing. Efflam's cousins and friends sat in the corner checking their instruments. The celtic harp, the biniou flageolet, and drum all joined to create a unique Breton sound. More friends, cousins, and neighbours came, girls and boys to help remind Efflam of one of the most difficult and taxing of Breton dances.

It was hilarious. Efflam had to start and stop so many times that he almost gave up, but Deniel wouldn't let him.

'Zut! I'll never get the hang of this.'

'Give it a chance. Your head remembers, but your legs have decided that they belong to someone else—a Parisian maybe?' he teased.

Deniel continued. 'Look, you are thinking of each individual step instead of trying to put a couple of them together. You will find it easier that way. Watch this.' Deniel demonstrated the first couple of steps very slowly. 'See? You'll catch on, you'll remember.'

'Remember? You would think that I wasn't even Breton! I'm crucifying this dance. I'm glad that my father isn't here. He would be falling about the place laughing at me. Talk about embarrassing.'

'Patience! Patience! Here, have some cider. It will help.'

His cousins and friends were very persistent. Slowly, the hop-skip-and-a-jump step became more intricate and faster and faster, and finally, after a couple of hours Efflam felt that his legs stopped at his knees.

'No more ... no more.' He begged. 'I can't do it anymore.'

Efflam had finally re-mastered the dance that he had known so well in his youth. He felt a sense of both achievement and exhaustion. He finally sat down, catching his breath. His friends smiled or slapped his back in admiration as he rested.

He became immersed in the soft lilting of Breton songs about the glories of the sea and of lost love, and he felt his misgivings about his previous ineptitude at mastering the Dans-tro Fisel melt away as he swayed to the music and joined in the songs.

The following day, however, his legs felt as though they would give way from underneath him if he tried to walk.

'The best thing you can do is to go swimming. It will loosen the muscles in your legs,' Deniel told him.

'Legs. I don't feel I *have* any legs.'

'Go on,' his aunt urged. 'You will feel fine afterwards.'

He did as his aunt suggested and surprisingly he felt much better. He bought a *carré* and some sprigs of hawthorn. Deniel wouldn't have to bring them since Efflam was in Brittany. He asked his aunt if there were any farms for sale. She said that she would ring a few friends. When Efflam came back with Deniel that evening, she had found two farms. One was too big; almost the equivalent of sixty acres, in Châteaulin, but the other one was only thirty-five acres in Moribhan and might be just what he was looking for. He wasn't sure what to do.

'Why don't you go and see it with Deniel?' his aunt suggested. 'How can you know unless you see it?'

'You're right. A look wouldn't hurt, I suppose.'

Efflam looked at Deniel. 'What do you think?'

'Let's go and see it tomorrow,' Deniel replied.

Efflam's aunt arranged for them to see the little farm. The owners were four or five generation Bretons. The old widow of nearly eighty-four, Madame Brelivet, had lived there all her married life, but now, she was on her own. She had no children, and her husband had passed away some three years back. She had tried to keep the farm going, but it had become increasingly difficult for her. She had decided to sell the farm and move to lodgings that were more modest, closer to the town centre where she could be looked after. The only stipulation she had for selling was that the livestock would go with the farm. She didn't want to turn the animals out, either. After all, this was their home, too.

Efflam looked over the farm: a large barn, a small pond with ducks and geese, a cockerel, a few hens, two donkeys, and a Jersey cow called Lou Lou. The widow wasn't so much in a hurry to sell but was anxious that it be sold to the right person, preferably a local. Efflam explained that he was from Brittany, and she brightened up but tilted her head and narrowed her eyes, noting his distinctive Parisian accent.

'Oh, yes? What part?'

'From Lorient. I left with my parents to live in Paris when I was fourteen.'

'I was wondering. Your accent gave you away.'

'I want to come back to my roots. I want to come back home, to Brittany.'

The widow smiled to herself and seemed well satisfied with the explanation.

Efflam saw that it required a fair amount of work, a new chicken coup, mending fences, clearing away rubble and debris. The house was in a relatively decent state but would need modernisation and repainting. It looked like a monumental task. He told Madame Brelivet that he would have to talk to his parents and his fiancée. The widow agreed to wait until the middle of August before requiring anything to be finalised. Deniel told Efflam that if he did decide to move back to Brittany, his cousins would help him get the farm back into shape. It was a lot to take in, a great deal to think about.

When Efflam got back to Paris, he spoke to his parents about the possibility of returning to live in Brittany. He explained that he had seen a little farm that needed work but might be just what he was looking for. Loieza suggested that he concentrate on his graduation, now that his exams were over, then he could think about his wedding, but now he should just to relax. If the farm wasn't too expensive, his parents and grandparents would pool their resources and put a sizable deposit on it. Efflam would have to talk to Anne. Anne was always sensible. 'Fools rush in where angels fear to tread!' He would have to sit down and see if the project was a viable way to make a living and if Anne would be happy uprooting herself to go and live in Brittany.

Efflam's exam results arrived more quickly than expected. He sat down at the kitchen table and for five minutes stared at the envelope that contained his future. His hands started shaking as he started to open it. Both sets of grandparents and his parents studied him carefully as he opened the envelope.

'I've passed.' He sighed.

'Passed?' Efflam's mother echoed as she looked questioningly at her son.

He handed her the envelope nonchalantly, and she carefully read the results to herself and pressed the open letter and envelope to her chest and smiled, closing her eyes, letting out a great sigh of relief.

'What did he get Loieza? *Loieza*, are you listening to me?' her mother enquired gratingly.

'An overall mark of seventy-five percent. He came the second highest in his class,' Loieza said as she dreamily handed over the wonderful news to her mother. The piece of paper did the rounds, and each of the group contributed congratulations, saying how wonderfully studious he was and how proud of him they all were. It was a very positive end to his university career. Soon he would graduate. He rang Anne to let her know, and she was exuberant in her congratulations. She couldn't wait to see him and expressed her disappointment at not being there in person.

Efflam's graduation day came, and it went off without a hitch. It was long and tiring but most enjoyable. Loieza took so many photographs that Efflam started to get embarrassed, but he sensed that it was better not to say anything as she was so proud of him that she almost floated on air. She was quite simply acting like a queen bee. They all celebrated at a wonderful Breton seafood restaurant just outside Paris, *L'huître Bretonne (The Breton Oyster)*. It was a wonderful day, and Efflam was delighted that the exams and nerves were finally over. He could look forward to getting married, but first he would have to get everything ready, and Anne's graduation would take place in June before the July wedding.

Anne was still doing exams and studying like a nutcase when she heard the wonderful news about Efflam and his results. She started to get jittery about what the future held in store but at the same time calmed herself; in other words, she was a bag of nerves. She was, as it were, like a cat on a hot tin roof.

When the exams finally ended, she packed her bags. She wanted to go home. Tom and Teresa McCloskey came up the morning after her exams in their van to help her move her things back home. She loaded one thing after another until the van was almost full to bursting. Mrs. McLoughlin was upset at saying goodbye to such a good tenant. Anne had scrubbed the flat and cleaned it to perfection, including the windows, so that Mrs. McLoughlin would have nothing to do. She left a small gift on the bed with a thank-you card. Mrs. McLoughlin had already given back the deposit. She was the soul of honesty. It was unlike her to wait to meet a tenant's relatives. Mrs. McLoughlin told Mr and Mrs. McCloskey what a fine woman her mother had been, assuming that they were her aunt and uncle.

They left, waving out of the window and wishing her all the best.

'I left a small thank-you gift on the bed. Thank you for everything. I hope we will have plenty to chat about in July.'

'July? What do you mean July?' was the answer.

'Bye now, see you soon.' Anne waved out the window.

Mrs. McLoughlin went up to the studio apartment to check that all was in order and was wondering if she would be able to get cleaners in quickly to give it a thorough clean. She needn't have worried. She opened the door, and a breeze met her through the open windows. She glanced around; everything was perfect. It was cleaner than clean. She put her hand on her hips and nodded her head, smiling to herself.

She went to the bedroom, and there on the bed was a small box. She opened it. It was a small Lladró angel kneeling down in prayer like a little child. The inscription in the card read:

Dear Mrs. McLoughlin,

You looked after me during my time here in Dublin.
My own private little Angel.
Thank you for being so kind
All my love,

Anne.

Mrs. McLoughlin became overcome with emotion. *Private little angel indeed. What sentimental nonsense*! She picked up the small gift and stroked it, smiled, and very carefully placed it back in the box. She then noticed an additional card. She wondered what it might be. Maybe it's something important. She opened it hurriedly and was more than surprised at what lay inside. As she opened it, she realised what it was. *Me? Oh! How kind, how very kind, Mrs. Clare McLoughlin and Mr. & Mrs. William McLoughlin. Oh, how thoughtful.*

Meticulous as ever, Mrs. McLoughlin wrote to the address and thanked the hosts immediately for the invitation. She wrote that she would love to attend, together with her brother William and sister-in-law Magda. However, she would have visitors, her sister and brother-in-law from Belgium, and she couldn't dessert them so had no alternative but to regret the invitation.

She felt that perhaps her answer was a little cold, so a few days later, she rang to wish Anne the very best and explain the situation. Joe picked up the phone.

'Hello.'

'Mr. Myers, this is Clare McLoughlin from Dublin.'

'Oh, hello, how are you? Anne was very disappointed that you can't come to the wedding, very disappointed.'

'Well, I just rang to explain and to wish her well on her big day. My sister and brother-in-law have lived in Belgium for twenty-odd years, and my brother-in-law is from Brussels. They're over for a short break so I can't exactly leave them stranded. You understand.'

'Bring them along. You and your family are most welcome. I'll ask Anne to send up another invitation. We are very happy to have some French speakers on our side of the family. So, I expect to see you there, then.' He chuckled.

'Oh, that's most kind. Are you sure?'

'Positive. I look forward to seeing you and your family in July,' and with that he hung up.

Joe was as good as his word and the invitation arrived soon afterwards.

'French speakers on our side of the family,' she repeated to herself, 'family, how kind.' She no longer felt uncomfortable, as her relatives had been invited as well. She had a strange sensation that it was going to be a fabulous day.

Anne was tired after all the cleaning and getting everything spic and span before she left. She was glad that she had done the right thing and left the apartment the way she should have. There was so much to think about now. Graduation would take place soon, if she passed her exams. Anne went home and unpacked. Efflam hadn't arrived yet, but it was only the 10th June so she wasn't worried. She threw herself into the work at the farm. Loieza had rung to say there had been delays, and they wouldn't be there for a couple of weeks. Anne didn't mind too much. She wanted to have time with her dad on her own anyway. She would have plenty of time with Efflam later on. She started to worry about her exam results and whether they were going to be good enough. *Would her dad be disappointed in her if they weren't as good as she had wished?* she wondered. Anne asked and answered the question in the same sentence. The idea was that perhaps she would be disappointed in herself, but her dad would never be disappointed in her no matter what results she got because he would know that she had tried her best. No one could ask more than that.

She rang Trinity ten days later to find out when the results would be posted. She was told that they would be out at six o'clock on 23rd June. The days in between dragged, but finally the day of days came. She went up to the law faculty to find they had been delayed by a few minutes and found herself pacing up and down like an expectant father. She started to bite her nails in anticipation.

'They're in!' She heard a faint shout followed by a rush to the faculty board. Then, 'Oh, God. I thought I would have done better than that.'

It wasn't Anne. Anne stayed way over at the corner until the furore had died down and she was on her own except for a few stragglers in the corner laughing and chatting as they had obviously done quite well. Anne nervously looked at the notice board. She started at the bottom name on the list in case she had done badly. Her eyes slowly checked and rechecked, but she had already looked three quarters way up the list and her name wasn't on the list. Had she failed?

Please, God, no. Her eyes quickly scanned the rest of the names and there she was: Student Name: Myers, Anne, Student Number: 3659925, Grade: Distinction. She had come first in her class. She nearly fell out of her standing.

Distinction ... God!

The girl standing beside her said, 'Yeah, some get all the luck! Lucky girl, I only got a 2.2.'

'What did you get?'

'I ... I ... I got a Distinction! Me. A Distinction!'

'God, are you going to be on the tear tonight.'

'Yeah, I'm going home to tell my dad. He'll be *really* pleased.'

'Congrats! Well done!' Her colleague, whom she had never set eyes on before, patted her on her shoulder.

'Thanks!' Anne beamed back at her and turned around, forgetting to congratulate her colleague and shouted after her, 'Well done yourself!'

Her colleague waved back in acknowledgement and disappeared down the passageway. Now Anne really knew the meaning of 'walking on air' or 'being on cloud nine.' She couldn't wait until she got home to tell Joe. She wouldn't ring. She would tell him herself. There were only two buses a day to Dunshaughlin during the week, one at four o'clock, and one at eight o'clock. The bus service from Dunshaughlin to Dublin was somewhat better. The bus trundled along, slower than expected. She felt like one of the Flintstones ready to pick up the bus and run along the road. That way it might go a little faster. It did get home eventually, though in reality it wasn't any slower than usual; it just felt that way. Anne returned home to Dunshaughlin brimming over with joy.

Joe had just brought the cattle in from the field. He left them outside a little later in the summer than in winter to avail of the grass. At this stage, it had turned a little chilly and a light rain had started to set in. The bus screeched to a halt, and she was jolted forward. This time, however, Anne didn't bob along but broke into a full-blown sprint to tell her dad the wonderful news.

Joe hadn't seen Anne at this stage. He had gone into the barn to look after Mr. Magoo.

'Dad, dad... dad? Where are you?'

There was no answer. Anne rushed into the house to see the four cats sprawled out in front of the Aga cooker. Tiddles, the ginger, raised his head to check out the commotion as Anne blustered in the door and then decided it wasn't worth bothering about and dropped his head to the floor to continue his luxurious nap. Anne called around the house, and no answer came. She ran outside and into the barn.

'DAAAAD,' she screeched like a banshee, waving the piece of paper with her results around like a woman deranged.

Joe was brushing down Mr. Magoo when Anne spooked the horse something terrible.

'Easy there, fellah, easy there, take it easy now.' Joe reassured the frightened horse, stroking and patting him on the neck. Joe came out of the stable, not too thrilled for her having caused such a commotion.

'Dad, look. *Look*,' she said as she waved the piece of paper about.

'Hold on a minute. Let me put on my glasses. Now, where *did* I put them?' Joe patted his pocket.

'They're on your head, dad,' Anne declared impatiently.

'Oh yes, so they are. Now what is it you wanted me to have a look at?'

'Look, look.' She thrust the piece of paper into Joe's face. 'See. I did it.'

'What did you do?'

Anne, totally bereft of patience, poked at the piece of paper. 'Read it and weep!' she declared triumphantly, as though she had just fanned out a royal flush in a high-stakes poker game.

'*Distinction*. Is that good?'

'Da-ad! I came first in my class.' She started to strut about like a peacock.

'Well done, Annie luv. I'm proud of you. Your mam would have been twice as proud. I would have been proud of you anyway no matter what the result—you really tried and that's what counts. It's not whether you win or lose, it's how you play the game. It's what you got out of your time in university, not the result, however good it may be.'

She hugged Joe, kissing him on the cheek. 'Thanks, dad.'

'I suppose you will be going out with the girls.'

'Well, to be honest, I have a date?'

'A date? With who?'

'With Mr. Magoo. I thought I'd help you groom him. After all, it's the least I can do after scaring him half out of his wits.'

Joe and Anne spent some time grooming Mr. Magoo. The horse didn't know what was going on, as he hadn't had that type of attention in a long time. They finished the farm duties together and went into the house, talking of the graduation that would take place in ten days time. By that stage, Efflam would be there and they would go together.

The days dragged once again, but finally he was here. There were hugs, kisses, and plenty of welcome.

The graduation day came, and Joe and Efflam accompanied Anne to the ceremony. Only two people were allowed to accompany the graduate. They entered the Exam Hall in Front Square with their invitations. The prospective graduates were already seated closer to the front according to the grade attained and in alphabetical order. A blue leaflet left on each chair showed the subject studied, the grade attained, and the name. The ceremony started as the master of ceremonies entered the hall in procession, followed by the provost, senior lecturers and heads of department. Everyone stood up. It was full of pomp and ceremony, all derived from the Elizabethan Era, of Elizabeth 1, who founded that most esteemed institution of learning. After various speeches from the provost and dignitaries, it was requested that no photographs be taken during the ceremony and then names were called. First was Anne. 'Myers, Anne.' She went up to receive her parchment. The sound of applause could be heard throughout. 'Reading law has attained the grade of First Class honours.' This of course was all in Latin, and no one understood a word except for 'Myers, Anne.' She then took the tassel from her black mortarboard changing its position from right to left, a sign depicting that she was now a graduate, and descended the stairs and was ushered to the right-hand side to sign the book of graduates and returned to her place. After everyone had graduated, they threw their caps in the air and cheered.

This was followed by a reception of wine and canapés in the reception hall at the side of the Dining Hall. Mothers and fathers chatted constantly, smiling and looking decidedly pleased with their sons and daughters. A student then went round asking if anyone wanted a studio photograph of the special moment.

Anne looked at Joe.

'Go on, luv. Get it done. It'll be a nice memento.'

Anne was told where to go and disappeared to get the photograph done. She returned twenty minutes later with the photograph in her hand. They left the reception and walked towards Front Square once more. She stopped a student and asked if someone could take a few photographs. One photograph was taken of Anne and her dad, one of Anne and Efflam, and one of three together.

'Shame yer mam isn't here to see this. She would have been so proud of you.'

'She is, dad. She is.' Anne hugged him.

It was a memorable day. They returned to Dunshaughlin after dropping back the graduation outfit. Efflam took Anne and her dad out to an early dinner in the Dunshaughlin Arms to celebrate. It was a wonderful day.

When Joe got back to the farm that day, Efflam helped him get various jobs done. The whole menagerie was fed and in bed sooner than they could say, 'bob's yer uncle.' Joe decided to go to bed early. The excitement of the day had totally tuckered him out.

Efflam hugged and kissed Anne and told her how proud of her he was. He took her over to the table and said he had to speak to her about something. Anne's heart started beating ten to the dozen.

'What is it, Efflam?'

'Sit down, *mon petit chou*,'(*my little cabbage*) he replied.

'Cloze your eyez and upen your 'andz,' he insisted.

'What is it, Efflam?'

'Shusss.' He pressed a small green box in one hand and a much larger red one in the other. 'Now you can open zem.'

Anne opened her eyes and gazed in admiration at the boxes.

'Oh, Efflam they're beautiful. Thank you.'

'How do you know what zey are? You haven't opened zem yet.'

She smiled and opened the green box first. In it lay a pair of tiny diamond and seed pearl drop earrings. Her eyes opened wide and her mouth was agape. For once, she was speechless!

'They are from my family for your graduation.'

Before she could express her thanks, Efflam insisted that she open the other box. A seed pearl necklace with centre drop pearl with a tiny diamond in a circle together with a matching bracelet completed the set. Words failed come to her. Tears filled her eyes as she threw her arms around his neck.

'But how could you afford anything so magnificent?'

'I saved all year to get you zee best gift I could.'

'Oh, Efflam!' She hugged him again, nearly choking him in the process. It had been a remarkable day. It had been a day of saying goodbye to university, to something old and familiar. It was also a day of possibilities and dreams, as she would shortly be embarking on something new and adventurous—a life with Efflam.

Chapter Eight

The weeks of preparation for the wedding seemed to fly by. Loieza had made it over to help prepare for the wedding. She had decided to stay in the Dunshaughlin Arms Hotel, as she didn't want to impose on Anne's father. At the same time, she could keep an eye on things and make sure that everything was done encompassing both Breton and Irish traditions. Anne had been very emphatic on that point, and Loieza was not going to let her down no matter what.

Loieza often popped into Joe's house late in the morning in case he needed a hand with anything, in that way she would be there to help out. She needn't have worried too much. Mrs. McGonigle still kept the house spic and span, and did her usual gooseberry crumble, apple pie, or rhubarb tart. It was easy to see that Loieza would feel at home, for it was in her nature to make others feel the same. She dropped into Joe's kitchen just when Mrs. McGonigle had set two pies down to cool on wire racks.

'Mmmm. What a wonderful smell. I haven't smelled rhubarb tarts like that since I was a little girl.'

'They're just the plain ones, nothin' special; I'm just an ordinary cook—nothing to write home about.'

'Do you think I might have a little piece?' Loieza enquired.

'Glory, where's ma' manners? Please sit down. I know that you drink coffee, but I only have instant. What about tea?'

'When in Rome, do as the Romans.'

'Oh, I didn't know you were from Rome.' Loieza kept quiet and smiled.

'Some fresh cream might be just the ticket with that.'

'Mmmmm. Oh! Mrs. McGonigle you must give me the recipe. This is just divine. I have a little favour to ask you. Would you help me arrange the food for the wedding and give me your ideas? It would be so helpful.'

Mrs. McGonigle was stunned, shocked, thrilled, and surprised all at the same time. It was difficult to determine which emotion she felt. Much like the Irish weather, you could have all four seasons in one day. She lacked confidence in most areas; she felt that her plain Irish cooking wouldn't do the wedding justice. However, she was often assured that it was a success because she didn't try to gussy it up but instead left it to stand on its own strength, and it was this very point that proved to be its best feature.

There were so many preparations going on, an outsider would have thought that a celebrity was getting married. It was the custom in Brittany for children to place ribbons across the road, and the bride would have to cut them on her way to the church. At the same time, the groom would have to remove briars placed beside the ribbons and pay whoever was responsible for putting them there. This charming Breton custom wasn't possible so Loieza arranged the next best thing by having ribbons and briars across the long windy avenue that led to the country church where they would get married. The multicoloured ribbons fluttered in the breeze and the promise of warm sunshine added to an already magnificent day.

The small country church of Our Lady of the Holy Rosary had Romanesque style architecture but on a very small scale and, like most churches in the county, was made of granite. Most of the villagers had been baptized, married, and buried from that nucleus of the community. As the wedding was going to take place in the morning, in keeping with Breton tradition, tables had been set with small cakes outside the church door. These were covered until the bride and groom filed out of the church after the ceremony and each would take a cake from the table and leave a donation for the poor in its stead.

The meadow adjacent to the church was all a bustle. Two enormous pristine white marquees that stood like glorious pavilions of times long past would be the venue for this illustrious day. The Tricolour and Breton flags stood as a backdrop to the main table. Each additional circular table was covered with a snow-white linen Damask table cloth upon which stood a vase of Irish Heather and Fleur-de-Lis, accompanied by eight napkins in the shape of bishop mitres. There was a section beside the marquees that was cordoned off so that, before the wedding lunch, Efflam and Anne could dance the Dans-tro Fisel together. Anne had mastered the intricate steps almost as well as Efflam. Then everyone would join in and dance together until lunch was announced.

Efflam's cousins had come together with friends from Brittany and Paris. Deniel would play traditional Breton music whilst the musician that they had hired—a renowned harpist would provide other music. 'St. Patrick's Breastplate' was one of the hymns Anne had liked as a child and wanted to have it as part of her wedding. She drew great comfort from that hymn when her mother had died, and it was a favourite of Father O'Brien's.

Loieza had completed the wedding cake the day before. It wasn't the usual one of currents, cherries, and icing that was usually served at Irish weddings but a *croquembouche*. It consisted of a pyramid of creampuffs covered with hard-crack sugar with lightly caramelized sugar spun around it like a golden spider's web —a sight to behold.

It was nine o'clock, and Anne was eating breakfast with her father and Efflam. A sprig of hawthorn had been left on her bed earlier that morning.

'Efflam, you never told me what this was for.'

'It's a medieval Breton tradition. Normally, you give it to your fiancée when you get engaged. It means that she is your chosen beloved for life. This is the *carré* that I brought from Brittany. This piece of white silk is held over our heads at the blessing, and it will be used to wrap our firstborn in when he or she is baptised.'

'What a wonderful idea,' Anne exclaimed.

Joe and Efflam then went to the Dunshaughlin Arms Hotel to get ready. Loieza came to help Anne get dressed at the farm. Anne's small waist was accentuated by the gown's gold apron, which fell over the rich burgundy velvet bodice and skirt. Anne's hair, normally plaited, was now a cascade of loose, deep red-gold wavy sunshine that fell to her waist. The light danced on the fine strands through the transparent tuile cap as it was pinned onto her hair. She wore the jewellery set which Efflam had given her on her graduation day. She glanced at the bracelet and fondled the pendant to remind her of the giver—not that she really needed reminding.

Loieza stood back and smiled. You look bonny, as they say in Scotland.

Anne smiled back at her. 'I'm glad you came. How can I ever thank you?' Then a look of profound sadness passed over her face as she fingered her mother's wedding shawl.

'What's wrong?' Loieza asked.

'If only my mam was here.'

'Oh heavens, I forgot! Your gift!'

'Gift?'

'These are for you and Efflam for your wedding, from your mother.'

'*My* mother? I don't understand?'

'I got you something from her.'

Anne opened the two small boxes. Each contained a heavy gold Claddagh ring.

'I thought you could use them for your wedding rings. That way you will be reminded that your mother's love is with you always, especially during both the special and difficult moments in your life.'

'They're beautiful. Thank you.' Tears welled up in her eyes as she glanced down at them.

'No, not now ... you can't get upset. Efflam would never forgive me.'

Anne hugged her and thanked her again.

'This is from me, Visant, and Efflam's grandparents.'

Anne opened the large brown paper packet to reveal a white cotton hand-crocheted double-bed spread and a small envelope with a cheque to help them with a deposit for their own place.

'This must have taken months to make. It's exquisite. We can't accept this. It's too much.'

'My dear, Efflam is my only son. Nothing is too much, and you ... you are my only daughter.'

Anne smiled at her. There was no arguing. Loieza was right. Père Benead had already arrived at Our Lady of the Holy Rosary Church and was in private consultation with the good Lord before officiating at the wedding ceremony with Father O'Brien. It was a habit born of many years as a priest in Brittany. His English was nonexistent except for 'sank you' or 'bless you.' Both of these phrases set him in good stead and helped him in almost every situation. He spoke Breton and French, and although he was proud of his Breton heritage, he understood that not everyone spoke Breton or French. Tolerance and kindness would overcome all obstacles, whether they are cultural, linguistical, or spiritual.

Father O'Brien genuflected, tapped Père Benead on the shoulder, and apologised for interrupting him, explaining that it was almost time. Though poor Père Benead couldn't understand a word, he had an inkling to what Father O'Brien was alluding.

'Bless you,' he replied, and got up and followed Father O'Brien into the sacristy to get changed.

Unlike Irish traditions of not seeing the bride before the wedding believing it to be bad luck, in Brittany the groom goes off to pick her up, accompanied by his friends and family. Dressed in traditional Breton garb, Efflam left with Joe, Deniel, and his relations and cousins. Joe had a smart black suit. It was quite a sight. Most of the villagers had been invited and descended on the small country church like a swarm of locusts.

Efflam walked with Joe and his family towards Hazelhurst Farm to escort Anne and his mother to the church. He was a little nervous. When they arrived at the farm, Efflam waited outside as Deniel knocked on the door. Loieza answered, with Anne following her. Efflam's jaw fell forty feet when he beheld the vision that emerged. She was without doubt the most beautiful girl he had ever clapped eyes on.

Efflam escorted his mother, and Joe accompanied Anne, followed by the dogs, Bob and Jassie. Anne had insisted that they be part of the ceremony. By the time they arrived at the beginning of the winding avenue leading to the country church, many of Efflam's cousins and friends had made their way there, lining it on either side and demanding money to let Anne cut the ribbons and Efflam remove the briars that obstructed their way to the church. The money collected would be given to the poor. It was so unusual for the villagers, and they joked and laughed, joining in the fun of teasing Anne and Efflam as they finally made their way to the church door. Efflam and Loieza waited outside as all the guests entered the church. Joe and Anne would be the last to enter. Efflam escorted Loieza to the front pew and waited with Deniel at the altar.

Anne took her dad's hand. 'Dad, I know I'm marrying the right person, but I'm a little nervous. What if I don't remember all the words?'

Joe draped the wedding shawl more fully around Anne's shoulders. 'Don't worry. There's no need to be nervous. Efflam's a nice lad. He'll look after you like your mam looked after me. Anyway, even if you do forget the words, they're all friends and family, and they'll be far too busy wishing you well and telling each other how beautiful you are to notice. Never say die, eh! Let's go in now. Ready?'

'Let's go.' Bob and Jassie followed behind Anne and Joe, their tails wagging behind them.

The *Breton Wedding March* was played, and everyone stood up as Anne entered the little church with her father. It was as though it were happening to someone else. She was aware of the smiling faces and recognised most or all of them but was so unaccustomed to being the centre of attention of so many people that she forgot to be nervous about the words and was worried only that she wouldn't slip and break her neck on the way up the aisle. It seemed longer than she had ever remembered it, but that was just nerves.

The wedding ceremony went off without a hitch. The priests each took their turns in Breton, French, and English. Father O'Brien started and ended the Mass with the sign of the cross in Irish. Just before the ceremony was over, the *carré* was held over the bride and bridegroom's heads for the special Breton blessing, followed by a blessing in Irish. The couple filed out of the church, stopping outside for a small cake and leaving a donation for the poor in its place. The guests followed suit as they made their way towards the marquees for their wedding lunch. First, however, the musicians had set up to play the Dans-tro Fisel. The ropes cordoning off the section had been dressed with flowers. The wooden floor would make it easier for everyone to dance. As Anne and Efflam entered the area, all eyes were upon them, especially Efflam's cousins and friends who couldn't wait to see if Anne had mastered this important part of Breton culture and tradition. They strutted like two peacocks onto the floor, and then their feet fell into a rhythm of hop-skip-jump faster and faster as though sparks were flying round their heels, finally whipping into a frenzied pitch. Their guests urged them on by clapping and cheering, until finally the dance was done. Efflam swung Anne around and kissed her. A huge roar of applause and approval rose from the crowd. They had been caught in a private moment of intense happiness and as a result grew a little embarrassed and red-faced. The applause was stronger still as they left the area to rest their weary feet.

Everyone began to walk into the area allocated for dancing, and the Breton guests started to dance the simple *Rond*. Irish people and the rest of the guests unfamiliar with the dance weren't sure what to make of it. Efflam's Breton cousins and friends split pairs, asking the Irish guests to dance showing each of them the otherwise simple steps until everyone joined in and had a wonderful time. Then, all of a sudden, the bell was rung to announce that lunch was ready to be served.

Wedding Menu

Miss Anne Myers & Monsieur Efflam D'Arvenes

Saturday, 27th July 1986 at 11.00 o'clock

Muscadet sur Lie   *Chinon*

Irish Smoked Salmon
Breton Crab, Celery and Fennel «Mille-Feuilles»
****

Mushroom Soup with Cream
French Onion Soup
****

Medallions of Irish Beef with Horseradish Sauce
Breton Lobster with Apples
Irish Lamb Cutlets with Mint Sauce
****

Gooseberry or Raspberry Tartlets with Vanilla Ice Cream
Cherry Clafoutis with Cream or Vanilla Ice Cream
(A variant of the Breton Prune & Raisin Pudding)
****

Tea & Coffee
****

While people enjoyed the sunshine and a little ice-cold Breton cider to whet their appetites and cool themselves down after dancing, they made their way to one of the enormous marquees, which was set out to accommodate the two hundred guests.

Speeches were made but were kept to a minimum, as everyone was pretty famished. Loieza had made sure that everything was balanced between Breton and Irish culture. She presided over the menu to make sure that everything was as it should be. Mrs. McGonigle had been asked to do the gooseberry and raspberry tartlets. Loieza and the two chefs had done the rest of the menu. The Breton lobster and crab had arrived the day before, packed in ice with the champagne.

By the time the day ended, Efflam and Anne were tuckered out. They thanked everyone and made their way over to the Dunshaughlin Arms Hotel, where they would spend the night. The following morning they would go to Paris and Brittany for their honeymoon and then decide on what to do next. It was going to be a new adventure.

Visant, Loieza, and both sets of grandparents decided to stay a little longer. Everyone had been caught up in the preparations for the wedding. They had never really spent much time seeing the wonderful countryside or endless sandy beaches. They had heard so much of Ireland, and they wanted to make the most of it. They rented a car and spent the next two weeks taking in the sights. They weren't disappointed.

Efflam awoke the morning after the wedding hardly crediting that he was now a married man. The commotion of the last couple of days was a blur. It wasn't due to drink, though plenty of it had been drunk; it was due in part to the realisation of a dream. Some people don't get that 'all-illusive dream,' whatever it may be. Efflam was one of the lucky ones. He smiled to himself, yawned, and stretched and called out to Anne.

'Mon petit chou ... (my little cabbage) where are you?' He snickered to himself at the rhyme.

Anne came out of the bathroom whilst brushing her teeth, her mouth full of frothy toothpaste.

'Here.' She smiled, and he roared with laughter at the sight of her. She realised that it wasn't her that he was laughing at but the sight of her with her mouth full of toothpaste trying to talk and not making one ounce of sense. She went back into the bathroom and decided that he wasn't going to get away with it. She took out a can of shaving foam and came out spraying it on him. They joked and laughed as she wiped it off his face. He looked like Santa Claus.

Then he got very serious. 'I love you, *mon petit chou*,' he said, and he kissed her tenderly. It was the promise of a new life together and a dream they would share.

They got washed and dressed and caught the bus to Dublin; from there they would take a taxi to the airport. No airport coaches existed. It was either the bus or a taxi. They checked their passports, money, and everything they would need to get there. They were unsure as to whether they had enough francs, but if not they could change money at a bank.

The passports were checked on arrival at Charles de Gaulle Airport.

'Madame d'Avennes?'

'Yes,' she replied a little worriedly to the immigration officer checking passports.

He looked at her questioningly because she had answered him in English but had a Breton surname.

'My husband and I are on our honeymoon.'

It was as though a light bulb had gone on in his head. *'Ah, bien sûr! Bon chance madame et monsieur!'(Of course! Good luck madame and monsieur)*

They had made reservations at the *L'oie d'or* (*The Golden Goose*) Hotel off the *Champs-Élysées*. It was outrageously expensive, but this was their honeymoon after all. At the same time, they would only be staying there for a week or so, and they intended to see the sights.

It was true that Anne had spent a month in Paris during the third year of her degree course, but this was different. They decided to brave it and see Paris by bicycle. It was the perfect way to travel, as there wasn't much traffic even in the city centre because so many Parisians had left the city for warmer climes. It was all so romantic and brought to mind the times that Proust had described in *Remembrance of Things Past*, which Anne had read with great gusto a couple of years previously. They took a bottle of wine with them, stopped off at a patisserie for two little cakes, and dropped into a bakery for a roll filled with ham and cheese and had lunch on a stretch of grass underneath the boughs of a great sycamore tree. They laughed and joked, running around like a couple of wild kids, kissed, strolled hand in hand, and held each other as though it were for the last time. This was the beginning for them, and it was for keeps. It was glorious as the sun shone incessantly. Anne had forgotten about Ireland, her dad, and everything else for the present. A moment of complete happiness caught her totally unawares. Sometimes, Efflam would catch her daydreaming, and he would ask her what she was thinking about. She'd just reply, 'Oh, nothing. Just thinking.' She was thinking how lucky she was, how gloriously happy and blessed she felt and that if she didn't fill up every moment maybe God would take it back, realising that she had been given more than her share. Perhaps she would wake up to find out that, it had all been a wonderful dream.

Efflam broached the subject of looking for work in Paris after their honeymoon. Anne was a little wary. She was unsure how she felt about moving to Paris. Initially, she had felt that it had been a good idea, but now she wasn't so sure. Efflam allayed her fears and said there was no need to make a decision immediately; there would be plenty of time. He had neglected to mention anything to her about the farm that he had seen in Brittany and his thoughts on buying it. This was an oversight, however, not done out of deviousness. He had simply been caught up in the graduation and the wedding and it quite simply had gone completely out of his head.

Efflam's accent had improved; he rarely said 'zem' or 'zat' anymore. Anne missed that. She had never viewed it as a defect in his pronunciation but rather a quirk of his that made him special. Efflam was nervous as they packed their bags to go to Brittany. He took the metro to his parents' apartment. They lived in Vincennes, on the southeast border of Paris close to the famous Bois de Boulogne. He went to collect his dad's car so that they could drive to Brittany and see everything that he held so dear to him. It was important that she see Brittany the way he saw it, but if she didn't, he wouldn't let her know that it bothered him. There were plenty of little guesthouses there and that all-important viewing of the farm that Efflam had his heart set on, but it depended on Anne and her reaction.

By the time Efflam came back to pick up Anne, she was ready and waiting for him. They paid the bill, thanked the concierge, and left. Anne noticed a change in Efflam on the drive to Brittany but decided not to remark on it. He was nervous and curt. She, on the other hand, raved about everything she saw and he seemed to relax a little. Finally, she asked him to stop so they could have a break, and she decided to have it out with him.

'Efflam, what's wrong? You're so tense—did something happen?'

'I'm sorry, I don't mean to be. I forgot to tell you something before we got married, but the graduation and the wedding swept it out of my head.'

Anne smiled, envisaging someone with a sweeping brush.

'What is it?'

'When I was in Brittany the last time, I went to look at a few farms, and I saw one which I think would be perfect for us.'

'For us to move to?'

'Yes. We could start a new life there, not in Paris or Dunshaughlin but in Brittany. Will you think about it?'

'Yes, my love. Is that why you were so tense, or is there more?'

'No, *mon petit chou*.' He kissed her gently. 'That's all.'

'Well, thank God. I was beginning to think that I had married a Jekyll and Hyde character. I was wondering when you would start turning into something subhuman, sprouting hair all over the place!'

They both laughed, and in a couple of hours' time Anne would see the other love in Efflam's life, the love he had been passionate about as a boy, an ardour that never waned but increased as time went by: Brittany.

Everything Efflam had told Anne about Brittany was unfolding before her eyes. She thought it a shame that not everyone could enjoy such an experience. She began to comprehend why Efflam was so ardently enthusiastic about it, with the rolling countryside and majestic mountains, the beaches, and sweeping sea surrounding them, the colour of which changed as the sun danced on the water or patches of cloud overshadowed it. The breathtaking views were quite literally awe-inspiring. Anne couldn't understand how this little jewel seemed to have been completely overlooked. Perhaps Bretons knew a fine thing when they saw it and were careful about over advertising. The culture, language, and people were distinctly different from the rest of France. These were a proud people, celtic, predominantly catholic, and fiercely protective of their heritage. They were warm, hospitable, and friendly, welcoming outsiders, albeit initially with a little trepidation, but nonetheless sincerely wanting to share their joy in Breton tradition and lifestyle.

Previously, many young people had left to find jobs in bigger cities such as Paris or Marseilles, lured by the money and possibility of success. Now, however, the tide was turning and young people were beginning to understand that there were many types of success and wealth. People like Efflam were finally coming home.

Efflam understood this all too well, and it was for this very reason that he wanted to return home to Brittany. He would always love Paris, Parisians, and their *joie de vivre*, but he was searching for something more lasting, and he had found it as a boy in Brittany and as a man with Anne. They stayed in a guesthouse for a few days, discovering and rediscovering Brittany. They walked for hours on the beaches and strolled through the countryside. It was a slower pace of life, much like Ireland. Bretons enjoyed living; they weren't caught up in the rush of life. They sampled it like a good wine to be savoured and respected. The other wonderful thing that Efflam enjoyed was Breton cooking. As far as he was concerned, there was nothing finer. Finally, the day arrived when they were to view the place that Efflam had his heart set on. He was nervous, but he knew that Anne would look at the project objectively. They drove to the farm where the elderly widow still lived. She spoke both French and Breton, but Efflam thought it would put her at her ease if he spoke in Breton.

'Madame Brevliet, I hope you remember me. My name is Efflam D'Avvenes.

I saw your farm with my cousin Deniel.'

'Of course, I remember you. Is this your charming wife?'

'Yes, but she doesn't speak Breton. She's from Ireland.'

'Is she happy about moving here?'

'I hope she will be. If we stay, I will teach her Breton.'

The old woman shook Anne's hand warmly and said, 'I hope you will be very happy together.'

Anne smiled, not having one iota what the woman had said to her but reading in her face that she was congratulating her in some way.

Anne and Efflam walked through the farm, which consisted of a large barn, a small pond with ducks and geese, a cockerel, a few hens, two donkeys, and a Jersey cow called Lou Lou. Since Efflam had first seen the farm, the widow had acquired a kitten a few weeks old that had found a home in her enormous apron pockets and that peeked out every now and then. The farm certainly needed restoration, but Anne was careful not to voice her concerns whilst in the company of the owner. They thanked her and told her that they would let her know in a few days if the terms were acceptable. They spoke for hours, discussing the amount of finance necessary to turn the farm into a viable option. After a few days, they came to the decision that they would uproot and live in Brittany. This was going to be their home. She would have to make a living, but how? She couldn't practise law, but then Efflam came up with a solution. Couldn't she enquire about teaching at the University of Rennes, the differences between Napoleonic law and common law? After all, it might be very popular. Common law was practised practically everywhere in Europe except France and Belgium. Anne thought about it for a moment and decided that the only way to know was to contact the law faculty office in the university and make an appointment with the head of department.

The head of the law department thought it a very interesting idea, but whether she would have enough teaching hours to make it worthwhile was the problem. He decided to discuss it with the rest of the faculty members to see if they could put it on as a term option. They finally agreed. She had to submit lectures in advance so they could decide whether they agreed with her conclusions or not, what was more, the lectures would be in English. In this way, they would be in full control of what was being lectured.

Efflam was worried that the long journey from Morbihan to Rennes and back would be too much for her on top of the lectures and notes she would obviously have to prepare. She assured him that it wouldn't. After all, it was only going to be an option once a week for the first term to see whether it was worth doing. Even if it did take off, at most it would be only twice a week. Efflam felt better about it then. He didn't want to tire her out altogether. She would look into taking classes in French and Breton. She wanted to be able to converse with the locals in their own language without sticking out like a sore thumb. She didn't want to feel like some dumb cluck that couldn't have been bothered. She had to try.

Efflam submitted an offer on the farm, and this was accepted. Anne decided to start on the lectures and submitted four of the eight required. Her honeymoon had turned into work and the life ahead.

When the honeymoon was over, they returned to Dunshaughlin to iron out any unforeseen difficulties with her dad. There weren't any. Joe was glad for them both. He would miss them, but they had to strike out on their own and make a life for themselves. Deniel and two other friends came over to help crate anything they wanted to take with them and load it into the trucks they had driven over from Brittany. Anne wanted to take her dog Bob with her, but she was unsure of how Jassie and Joe would react. She decided against it. This was Bob's home with his mother, Jassie, and Joe. Besides, her dad loved Jassie and Bob so much that she hadn't the heart to separate them. There were scenes of tears, hugs, and 'I'll miss you' all round. It was difficult to witness and even more emotional to experience.

Months went by. Anne settled into the stunning region of Moribhan in Brittany and enjoyed lecturing at the University of Rennes, even if it was only part-time. Efflam too had embarked on his new life and had started to farm the land. Deniel and his cousins were as sound as their word and helped restore the farm to its former glory. It took almost five months to complete, but they all worked like mad men putting in every spare minute they could. It was perfect now. The new chicken coup had been erected, with fencing dividing up one of the fields into two paddocks as they intended on buying a couple of horses. They had cleaned out the pond, and the ducks and geese seemed quite at home. The geese were great at protecting the property, and the gander was certainly in charge as he took his job very seriously. The poor postman had been run off the property on more than one occasion. The barn had been totally cleaned and repaired. They had fixed the leaking roof of the house, and it had been rewired, re-plumbed, and painted.

Anne loved being in Brittany, but she wanted to see her dad at Christmas but didn't want to offend Efflam. She wanted to see Jassie, Bob, and all her friends. She felt a little isolated, even though her job in the University of Rennes took up some of her time. Efflam agreed that it would be a good idea and was very understanding. They would only be able to go for a week, as Deniel would take over the running of the farm while they were away. Anne was thrilled at the prospect of seeing her dad again and telling him everything about the farm. Perhaps he would come to visit, maybe, just maybe.

Joe, too, had fallen into the rhythm of life at his farm. He enjoyed his evening walks with the dogs, the banter at O'Neill's pub, and the kindness of his close friends, Tom and Teresa Mc-Closkey, without whom life would have been lonelier and more difficult. He loved his farm, though the love was tinged with sadness. He missed Mary more than ever now, with Anne gone. Everywhere he looked, he was reminded of her. Sometimes he would come bursting into the kitchen, dying to tell her of something someone had said or a funny thing that one of the animals had done, and he would realise that the light hadn't been switched on and Mary wasn't there anymore. It was being unable to share a funny moment or ask her advice on a matter that was bothering him. It was at times like these that were the most trying for him. They hit him hard, very hard.

Christmas arrived before Joe realised. Efflam and Anne were coming, and everything would be as before, well almost.

When Anne arrived with Efflam, Joe was surprised to say the least. She was pregnant, and Joe was over the moon.

'What is it?' Efflam had asked when Anne told him the news.

'How the devil should I know?' Anne retorted.

'Aren't there some sort of tests?'

'Look, I'm not going to have someone proddin' me about like a cow at a cattle market. I don't know. When he or she is born we'll find out then—plenty of time. You've always liked surprises. Well, you've got one now.'

Efflam turned a bit peevish like a little boy being told on Christmas Eve that he had to wait until Christmas Day to open his presents.

'But when exactly will it arrive?' he continued.

'I'm afraid I don't know *exactly*, but it will be around June.'

'Around?' Efflam replied, as though Anne should know automatically the exact day and hour of the birth; after all, she was the one having it.

'I'm afraid that the exact time hasn't been revealed to me as God is keeping it as a special surprise. He doesn't like to be rushed and does things in His own time,' she said to him with a decided note of sarcasm in her voice.

'Oh,' was all Efflam could manage. 'Sorry.'

'No problem. Men have yet to acquire a virtue called patience. Women, thanks be to God, acquired it when God put men on the planet. They had to or men wouldn't have survived.'

Efflam was a little mystified, couldn't quite work out to what Anne had been referring, but was wise enough to drop the subject and decided to calm her down by agreeing with her and saying 'You're right, *mon petit chou*. So right!'

Anne had dug a hole, and Efflam had fallen right into it, head first. Anne smiled. She knew that he hadn't a clue what he had said. He had just insulted his own gender to the hilt!

Joe, on the other hand, was an old hand at dealing with the fairer sex. He had had plenty of experience. When he asked, 'Any idea when the baby is due, luv?' and Anne replied, 'Around June,' he knew how to answer. 'That's great, pet. You never know for sure with these things. Don't work too hard and take it easy.'

Anne darted a look at Efflam as if to say, 'Learn from a master.'

Efflam dropped his head. He had an awful lot to learn about women. Being married didn't automatically give a man all the answers. It wasn't like doing a driving test, studying all the stuff beforehand, doing the test, passing it, and all of a sudden being able to drive. No, God wouldn't make it that easy. Perhaps He had decided that since most women had to run around and look after men, whether as a mother, sister, or wife, that the complexity of nature had to come into play. It was a hurdle that most men hadn't mastered after ten years of marriage, yet some were more adept at learning about their subject because they didn't let their pride get in the way and realised that they don't have all the answers. These, were the men who were the most successful, and Joe was up there with the best of them whilst Efflam seemed to belong to the learner driver category.

Anne had been a little tetchy with Efflam since she had become pregnant. She was sick in the morning and felt queasy most of the time. Her ankles had started to swell, and on top of that, it was going to be a big baby. She wasn't exactly looking forward to the birth, but she was looking forward to the arrival.

Christmas went off without a hitch, and Jassie, Bob, and Joe were delighted to see her. Father O'Brien dropped in with his sister-in-law, Maggie, as did Tom and Teresa McCloskey. It was almost like old times.

When Anne went back to Brittany, she felt more isolated than ever. It had been one of those romantic notions of going off to Brittany to live, and it was only now that she was beginning to realise it. It wasn't that she didn't love Efflam, but she was becoming snappy with him. She felt 'big as a house' and decidedly uncomfortable. Efflam wanted the baby baptised in Brittany, but Anne wanted Joe to be godfather and have the baby baptised in Dunshaughlin. It was a growing bone of contention between them.

Finally, Efflam relented. He was working on the farm during the day, and she was working in the university. Anne gave up work six weeks prior to the birth as she wasn't sure exactly when the baby would arrive. She had been asked to stay on after the law option finished to do some research, which she did.

Their little baby boy, Mazhe Joseph Visant, entered the world on 12th June in Brittany. They returned to Dunshaughlin two weeks after he was born to have him baptised in the Church of Our Lady of the Holy Rosary. It was a beautiful day, and the white silk *carrè* was part of his baptismal robe. Relations and friends alike attended the baptism. The child would receive a special blessing in Brittany to which all Efflam's relations and friends would be invited. But for now, this was Mazhe's special day in Dunshaughlin. There was a little reception at the Dunshaughlin Arms Hotel, and there was much 'to-do' made of the 'not so little' mite.

Anne spent as much time as she could with her dad. She missed him a lot and wanted him to see the farm in Brittany. Perhaps he would be able to give Efflam a few ideas from his vast experience. Joe wasn't so sure. He knew that someone would have to run the farm whilst he was away and was hesitant about asking Tom and Teresa to do it. He knew that they would have done it with a heart and a half. He didn't want to impose on them any more than he had already. They had been so kind to Mary and him.

Anne mentioned it again to him, this time in front of Tom and Teresa.

'Anne leave it for now, eh? I'll think about it. To be honest, I just don't see how it's possible.' Joe patted her on her hand.

'What do you mean, Joe?' Tom asked him.

'I can't leave the farm and the animals to look after themselves.'

'Don't be daft, man. Teresa and I will look after everything. We'll move the animals to our farm and there'll be no problem. Bob and Jassie will sleep in the kitchen with the four cats, and everyone will be grand.'

'Oh it's a lot to ask. I don't know.'

'You need a break, a little holiday. You haven't had any real break since your Mary passed on, Lord rest her. It'd be good for you. Why don't you go back with Anne and Efflam?' Teresa suggested.

'Well ...' Joe replied.

'Go on, dad, it's sorted. Please come.' Anne pleaded.
Joe turned to his friends. 'Are you really sure?'
Teresa piped up. 'Of course we're sure. Get a nice holiday.'
'I'd only be gone a few days.'
'Nonsense,' Tom interjected. 'Take two weeks and don't come back beforehand. The farm will still be here when you return.'

Joe looked at Tom searchingly to make doubly sure that he meant what he said and wasn't just being polite. Tom meant every word and reassured Joe.

'Fair enough,' Joe replied 'If you're really sure.'
'We are,' they both replied.

Anne was almost beside herself with excitement. She couldn't believe it.

Joe travelled back with Efflam and Anne a couple of days later. He was impressed with the farm and how hard Efflam had worked. Anne was thrilled to have her dad with them, and she didn't feel lonely or isolated. The family did the usual round of relatives after the special blessing they had for little Mazhe, and Joe settled into life in Brittany, enjoying every moment. He loved spending time with Anne, but he was looking forward to getting home and seeing the dogs and the rest of the menagerie. He could go home now in the sure and certain hope that Anne had married a fine lad, the right one for her. Joe noticed that Efflam supported her in as many ways as he could. He was a hard worker and a great help to her. He never took her for granted and constantly complimented her. He would often bring her a bunch of wild flowers after a day's work. Joe was content to go home. He was sure that Efflam would look after his daughter and give her the best he could. He thought, *A new generation has been born. Anne and Efflam are like Mary and ma'self all those years ago.* He needn't be so anxious. Sure, he would fret about her; it was natural, he argued with himself, but he needn't worry quite so much. She had truly met her match. Efflam would look after his Annie now.

Chapter Nine

Joe was glad to get back to the farm. He enjoyed his break in Brittany, but he didn't feel Mary was with him there. Regardless of whether she was gone or not, he had a sense of her belonging to the farm. Somehow, a part of her was present. The memories were still thick and fast, and Joe clung onto those to get him through the days.

Jassie was getting older. Her muzzle had just started to turn a little grey, belying her age. Bob and Jassie still accompanied Joe to O'Neill's after finishing for the day on the farm. He would go for the walk, the banter, a pint or two of 'the black stuff' but most of all, for the company.

The days were filled with work, and the evenings were spent at the local pub staring into the fire and puffing on his pipe. It was as though he were just existing, rather than living, but he put a brave face on it and was always in good humour. The local barmaid was a nice girl, bright and bubbly, who knew how to draw a pint of 'the black stuff' more ably than most men did. He often chatted to her with the dogs curled up under the chair and would tell her about his family and the farm. Often she would stand, listen, and talk about her own family, or they would share a joke together.

On Saturday night, after saying goodbye, he left the pub, puffing his pipe on his way home. As usual, the dogs were walking beside him. He hadn't walked more than two hundred yards when suddenly out of nowhere a pickup truck steamed around the corner. Its lights on full beam nearly blinded Joe. He put his hands up to protect his eyes, transfixed in horror as he realised what was about to happen. The driver was 'drunk as a skunk' as he veered from one side of the road to the other. Then bang, wallop, and a yowl followed. The driver ploughed into Joe, and he was thrown onto the bonnet of the car, smashing his face on the windscreen and slumping to the other side of the car and down onto the pavement.

Jassie had been walking on Joe's right, and so, suffered the complete impact of the car. Joe's body protected Bob as he had been walking on his left. Jassie lay under the wheels of the car as it had spun around completely, overturned, and was now lying on its side with the wheels still spinning madly. The driver was trapped and groaning with pain. The loud bang could be heard in O'Neill's, and customers came running out of the pub to see if they could be of any help. Joe was a well-known *local*. An ambulance was called. Joe's pulse was checked, and he was still breathing. Some kind soul put a coat underneath his head, and another held his hand and talked to him. The driver couldn't be helped as he had slipped into a state of unconsciousness and no one could get to him, as it was his side of the truck that was pinned to the ground. They would have to wait for the fire brigade to get cutting tools to get him out. The sirens of a Garda car, fire brigade, and ambulance screamed down the road on the way to the accident.

The barmaid noticed Jassie underneath the car. 'Ah, God, help her, the poor dog,' she cried, hardly daring to look, and burst into tears. Jassie was dead. Bob was still alive, albeit totally traumatized by the whole situation. One of the locals brought Jassie's limp body to the pub. Joe had been packed into the ambulance as it hurtled off into the dead of night with flashing lights and screeching sirens. Bob was brought into the pub, and the barmaid rang the local vet.

'Hello, Mr. Hegarty? It's Angela at O'Neill's pub. I'm sorry to call so late, but there's been a terrible accident. It's Joe Myers. Jassie, his dog, was killed outright, but Bob is completely out of it. Could you come straight away?'

'Sure. Where is he?'

'He's at O'Neill's, poor thing. I don't know if he was hit, but he's scared witless and shaking like a leaf.'

'I'll be there as quick as I can.'

The vet arrived a quarter of an hour later and saw to the dog. The barmaid, Angela, knew that Tom McCloskey was a good friend of Joe's and rang him to tell him what had happened.

Tom arrived up, collected Bob and Jassie, and drove home. He put Jassie's body in the barn that night. The following day she would be buried beneath the apple blossom tree on Joe's farm. Bob stayed in the kitchen, shaking half the night. Tom was so worried that the dog would go into shock that he wouldn't leave him. He petted and talked to him through the night. Finally, the dog fell asleep and Tom with him. The following morning, he took Jassie's body out to the farm and buried her underneath the large apple blossom tree, which Mary had loved so much. Teresa was in absolute floods of tears and couldn't see the sense of some idiot who had had too much to drink could do so much damage. In an instant, their lives had been changed forever.

Tom went to the hospital to see Joe. He was very badly injured. The doctor didn't hold out much hope. He wasn't a young man, and he was bleeding internally. He regained consciousness and was told that Bob was okay.

'What about Jassie? I'm worried about her, poor oul' girl.'

Tom lowered his head and bit his lip. 'I'm sorry, Joe. Jassie didn't make it. She didn't suffer, though.'

Joe's head flopped back down on the pillow. The twinkle from his eyes seemed to disappear then and there.

Tom went back home and rang Anne in Brittany to tell her what had happened. He told her that he would look after Bob and the farm. She thanked him, arranged the first possible flight home, and arrived in Dublin, taking a taxi to Beaumont Hospital. She spent the next few nights checking on her dad and was with him virtually round the clock, except when Teresa came to relieve her. Efflam couldn't leave the farm, though he would have like to. There was nothing he could have done. Joe was in the Intensive Care Unit, receiving the best possible attention. The chaplain gave him the Last Rites in case he got any worse and heard the mumblings of a confession.

Early Wednesday morning, Joe awoke with a little jolt, which woke up Anne, who had been sleeping in the chair beside him.

'How are you feeling now, dad?'

'I've a very bad headache. Jassie's gone, you know.'

'I know, dad, but she's in a better place.'

Then Joe tried to sit up a little and patted her hand. 'You'll be all right, luv. Efflam's a fine lad.'

'Thank God,' Anne replied.

Then Joe smiled broadly and suddenly his eyes became wide and bright like a little boy on his birthday. 'Ah ... Mary,' and he closed his eyes and heaved a long sigh. Joe was gone, gone to that better place.

The doctor walked in and saw that Joe had just passed away. He drew the curtains around the cubicle and checked his vital signs to make sure.

'I'm sorry.'

'Thank you, doctor, for all you did and all you tried to do.'

'I'll leave you alone for a moment.'

Anne nodded, and in the privacy of the small cubicle, she put her head on the bed and sobbed like a little child. She had no one in the world now, no one except Efflam. The doctor had rung Tom and Teresa, who were now en route to Beaumont Hospital.

They rushed into the ward and the staff nurse directed them to the cubicle.

'He's gone. My ... my dad's gone,' Anne exclaimed between sobs.

Teresa held her for a long time, rocking her to and fro. 'I know, luv. It's going to be difficult, but we'll help you and so will Father O'Brien, Maggie, and all who love and care about you. Come on, now, and we'll get a nice cup of tea. Let's go for a little walk, eh? Tom will keep an eye on your dad and say a few prayers, won't you Tom?'

'Sure will. Don't worry, Annie. It'll be all right.' He took out his rosary beads and fingered his prayers on each one.

Teresa and Anne went out to get a breath of fresh air and a cup of tea with plenty of sugar. Taking a handkerchief from Teresa, she blew into it, wiped her eyes, and gave it back to her. It was one of those strangely funny moments when Teresa looked at it as if to say;What do I do with it now? It was all the more tragic because in other circumstances she would have laughed. She only smiled at her, rubbed her back, telling her that things would look up. They called Efflam to tell him what had happened, and he said that he would be on the next flight home and would leave their son with his aunt. He would ask one of his cousins to run the farm whilst he was away and told her not to worry, that he would be there as soon as he could.

The prospect of arranging her dad's funeral was a daunting task. Mary had more or less arranged her own. Tom and Teresa got in touch with the same funeral directors, Branigan's in Dame Street, that Mary had used and requested that the body be removed to the Church of Our Lady of the Holy Rosary, Dunshaughlin, and then on for burial in St. Mary's Cemetery, Co. Meath, to be buried next to his wife.

The next day, the obituary was printed: *Myers: Joseph, devoted husband of the late Mary and beloved father of Anne. Father-in-law of Efflam, grandfather of Mazhe. Sadly missed. Family flowers only. All floral donations to The Poor Clares. Removal at five o'clock on Thursday to the Church of Our Lady of the Holy Rosary, Dunshaughlin. Funeral on Friday at eleven o'clock, followed by burial at St. Mary's Cemetery, Co. Meath. May he rest in peace.*

The notice appeared in the *Dunshaughlin Gazette*, the *Irish Times*, and *Irish Independent*. Anne chose three hymns, 'St Patrick's Breastplate,' 'Abide with Me,' and 'Nearer My God to Thee.' The boys' choir at the local national school would sing at the Mass.

Efflam arrived at about one o'clock, a couple of hours after Anne had told him, and caught the bus from Busarus straight to Dunshaughlin. Anne had gone down to Dunshaughlin with Mr. and Mrs. McCloskey. Following the issuance of a death certificate, Joe's body had been removed from the hospital. It would arrive the following morning in the church. Efflam's thoughts wandered back to years before when he had made the journey to Dunshaughlin for the first time. A lot had happened since then. This journey was not as happy as the first one. He remembered Anne's constant babbling chatter and kissing her to keep her quiet. He smiled to himself. No, this was a journey of a different kind. It was to say goodbye to good friends and family and to help his wife, who had now lost both her parents.

How could he ever cope? He thought to himself. Was he ready? The bus pulled up outside Hazelhurst Farm, and Efflam got off. He pushed open the gate, which still squeaked. *I suppose it was one of the jobs Joe never got around to doing*, he thought, and he smiled to himself.

Anne was in the kitchen as Efflam opened the door and called out, '*Mon petit*—. Before he could say '*chou*,' she had run over to him and was hugging and sobbing at the same time.

'*Mon petit chou, mon pauvre petit chou (my little cabbage, my poor little cabbage)*. It will be all right.'

'How am I going to get through tonight?'

'Don't worry, we will do it together.'

The funeral was like a rerun of her mother's funeral. The little church was packed to capacity, but this time it didn't rain. It was just cold and damp. Bob joined in the ceremony too. He was part of the family. Bob had his own grieving to do as he had lost his own mother. He had become very introverted and afraid at the smallest noise. He would cower underneath the chair or in a corner and shake incessantly. He lay down in the middle of the aisle as the prayers for the removal were recited. Then it was over. Efflam, Anne, and Bob, followed by Tom and Teresa McCloskey, left the little church, and walked home. No words were said. The household tasks were done as though Anne were a robot.

The following day was surprisingly bright and sunny. Anne had gone to Father O'Brien to tell him that although she was angry at the stupidity of the drunk driver, she wanted him to know that she had forgiven him and not to blame himself anymore. At the intercessory prayers for the faithful, Anne went up to the podium. 'For the driver who drove the pickup truck, may he find peace of mind in the knowledge that he has been forgiven as our heavenly Father forgives us. Lord hear us.' There was absolute silence in the church. Anne repeated '*Lord* hear us,' almost angrily, and then a loud response followed as she stared out into the packed church as her eyes welled up with tears, but she refused to let them roll down her face.

The usual 'sorry for your loss' and handshakes were the conclusion of a traumatic ceremony. The stream of cars followed the hearse to St. Mary's Cemetery, in Co. Meath. All the mourners returned to the Dunshaughlin Arms Hotel and had soup, sandwiches, tea, coffee, and little cakes afterwards. By the time Anne got back to the farm, the fatigue, worry, and heartache descended upon her like a great cloud, and the only energy she had left was to go to bed. She was exhausted. What would she do now? She couldn't think about it anymore. She would think about that tomorrow.

Anne couldn't think about the farm. It was too much to take in. Perhaps she might rent it, asking Mr. McCloskey to hold onto Bob and the rest of the animals until everything had been sorted out. She was unable to cope with it all. Yes, that's what she would do. Joe's Will left everything to Anne with the exception of Mr. Magoo, the cows, and Joe's pick-up truck, which he had left to Tom and Teresa. Anne asked Tom to arrange rental on the property until she could come back to sell it. She had to go back to Brittany to escape, so that the accident and the death of her dad and Jassie would become a distant memory.

Brittany did little to alleviate her grief after her dad's death. He was everywhere. It didn't help, either; that she had got pregnant so quickly again after Mazhe was born. She began to think that she didn't want the baby, and even at times grew to resent it. Anne's mood swings became extreme until it got to the point that Efflam was afraid that she would snap. When her daughter, Mary Loieza, was born, she couldn't understand how she could have resented such a little miracle. Mary was underweight but healthy. Anne sank into a deep depression after the birth and had the 'baby blues' for some time afterwards.

Efflam persuaded Anne that the only way to overcome her depression and her dad's death was to go back to Dunshaughlin. It would be her only salvation. This time Efflam, Mazhe, Mary, and Anne would go together. Whatever ghosts they had to face, they would do it as a family. Anne rang Mr. McCloskey to thank him for looking after the four cats, Bob, and the rest of the menagerie.

'There's no need to thank me. They're part of the family.'
She told him that she intended to take them back with her. He said that he'd miss them but understood. They intended on coming back at the end of the month. She was going to ask Father O'Brien to baptise their little girl. It would be a final farewell for the couple. They would sell everything and uproot to Brittany for good.

Anne rang Father O'Brien, and he said that he would be only too delighted to baptise her little girl. 'Mary Loieza,' he said, 'a fine name. Yer mother would be proud as punch.'

They would stay at the farm until it could be sold. That was the plan at least. The following few weeks melted into each other as Tom worked hard on his own farm. The tenants of Hazelhurst Farm had been already told of the possibility that the owner intended to sell shortly, so, when they were informed, it was no surprise.

Bob went everywhere with Tom, and they had started to forge a real friendship. Bob had started to overcome his nervousness and wasn't as jumpy as before. He often went to O'Neill's with him, but they didn't walk. He would trundle along in Joe's old pick-up truck, the dog sitting beside him on the front seat sticking his head out the window to enjoy the wind and the scents in the air, and then they would park outside the pub. He thought walking that same stretch of road where Joe and Jassie had met their fate would have been too traumatic for the dog.

Bob helped Tom on the farm and started to get back into his old routine. He missed Joe, but he knew Tom and felt comfortable with him. He hoped that he would spend the rest of his days with Tom. They were very kind to him, and he was always the centre of attention. It was a life not unlike that with Mary and Joe. Tom wanted Bob to get over his fears and helped him do that by keeping him so busy that at night he would be so tuckered out that he would fall asleep.

One morning bright and early, Tom packed a lunch and a flask with him, got into the truck, and whistled for Bob. 'I should be back before dark,' he shouted to Teresa.

'Take care of yourself, and don't hurry.'

'Don't you worry. I have Bob to look after me. Don't I, Bob? There's a good fellah, up you get.'

They set off for Trim, where Tom wanted to buy some supplies, and he thought he might get a little fishing in at the same time.

'What about a couple of salmon for tonight's supper? Eh, fellah?'

Bob barked at him as if to say, 'You bet.' He sat on the front seat with the window rolled down a little as usual, and stuck his nose out the window enjoying the fresh air. Tom bought his supplies and stopped off at some friends to purchase a new clutch of laying hens. He loaded everything else into the pick-up truck and decided to spend the rest of the afternoon fishing. Bob raced up and down the banks of the river Boyne, chasing one bird or another, and having the time of his life. He acted as though he thought he was helping Tom fish as he ran into the water, but as soon as he hit the water, he ran out again and stood on the banks, barking at the fish like a lunatic as if to say, 'Hurry up, for crying out loud and stop wasting time. Jump on the line. I want some of you for my dinner.' Then he would run up and down the banks, chase his tail, and generally act like some sort of a nut! It was the first time Tom saw the dog actually enjoy himself after Joe died.

Tom caught two large salmon despite Bob's fishing talent and put his fishing tackle and basket with the fish in the back of the truck; that way he would be assured of salmon for dinner in case Bob got it into his head to start without him. The truck bumped along over the uneven roads, avoiding the potholes galore. It had become a game with them.

'Here's another one. What do ya' think, boy. Will we run into it or avoid it?'

They were enjoying the trip on the way home when suddenly a car pulled out in front of him. Tom swerved to avoid him but hit the oncoming car. No one in the oncoming vehicle was injured, but Tom had a gash on the head when he hit the steering wheel. He felt dizzy and was concerned about Bob. The dog started to bark and howl until the ambulance arrived which was added to by the screeching of laying hens in the back of the truck. What a commotion! The ambulance arrived in record time, but Tom couldn't seem to get his balance as was helped into the back of it. People stopped to help, the Gardai were called and took note of the accident and the position of the vehicle. Bob hopped out of the open passenger window into the back of the truck and hid himself underneath the tarpaulin. He remembered what had happened to Joe and Jassie and started to shake all over. In all the commotion, no one noticed the dog. He had been forgotten.

After an hour, a towing truck arrived to move the truck off the road and bring it to a local garage. The man towing the vehicle checked the back and saw a clutch of hens and what he thought was a fox under the tarpaulin.

'Here you ... clear off leave those hens alone.' The dog didn't move. 'Didn't you hear me? Clear off!'

The next minute the tarpaulin was pulled back and the dog shot out of the back of the truck like a bullet from a gun. Bob was alone in a strange place for the first time in his entire life. He hadn't a clue where he was. He thought of the afternoon, the fishing, and running up and down barking at the fish. He made for the freezing rushing river. It was the last place he remembered being with Tom. He had to get home. The river was deep, cold, and very wide. English Shepherds aren't very good with water, and Bob was no exception. He started and stopped, not sure, whether he could make it, but finally decided to brave it. It looked more dangerous at night, than in the afternoon because Tom had been with him. This was something that Bob would have to do on his own. After what seemed like an eternity, Bob made it to the other side, almost drowning in the process.

The Gardai called into Teresa and informed her of the accident.

'Is he all right?'

'Yes, but he has a fine gash on his head.'

'What happened?'

'The other driver was too impatient and pulled out in front of him. He thought he could make it but didn't.'

'What about Bob?'

'I'm sorry but there was no one else in the truck with him. Who's Bob?'

'Our English Shepherd.'

'I'm sorry, but no dog was found in the truck and it's already been towed. We were told that there was a clutch of hens but that's all.'

Teresa got to the ward of the hospital and saw her husband lying on the bed with a large patch over his face.

'Thank God you're all right'

'Bob. Did they find Bob?' Tom asked nervously.

'No Tom. We can have a look tomorrow, but I don't think so. Bob's gone.'

'God, how am I going to explain that to Anne?'

'She won't blame you. It could have happened to anyone. Maybe Bob will find his way home.'

'I hope so.'

After a few days, Tom was released from the hospital, told not to drive and take it easy. A search party of friends was set up to look for the dog, but he never appeared. The day came when they had to ring Anne with the terrible news.

'Anne, this is Tom. I'm really sorry.'

'What's wrong?'

'It's Bob. There was an accident, and he was with me. He was left behind when I was brought to hospital. We sent out a search party for him, but no one has heard a thing. I'm afraid that the worst has happened. He's not used to fending for himself. He's so traumatized, even if he did make it I doubt he would survive on his own.'

'Oh, God, no. Not Bob! I will be coming home soon. Please keep searching for him.'

'If we do find him, you will be the first to know.'

'Don't blame yourself. You did the best you could. Thank you.'

It was as though the last vestige of her family had been obliterated. The memories of Joe and everything that had happened came flooding back to her. Efflam didn't know just how much more she could take, but it had to be faced head on whether she wanted to or not. They had to return to Dunshaughlin and the sooner the better.

Efflam had to talk to someone to take over the running of the farm. He spoke to his aunt and explained the situation. Deniel would move onto the farm and would run it full time. The sanity of his wife was in jeopardy and he wasn't taking any chances. She needed to go home and face the past; only then would she be able to let go. Efflam and Anne moved into Hazelhurst Farm with their two children. Anne hadn't had her daughter baptised yet as she was hoping Bob would show up. She thought that maybe he would find his way back to Jassie's grave. She looked for him everywhere but to no avail.

Months passed by and still he didn't show, finally, she concluded that he wasn't going to. *He was lost, true but why didn't he come home? Maybe had been knocked over, or wasn't able to deal with reality of what had happened anymore. Who knows why he didn't, but that was his decision,* she thought. The farm's squeaky gate was repaired, together with the thousand other little things that hadn't been seen to. The farmhouse had been painted and any necessary work had been done to it to obtain the maximum price. When the farm was sold, it would mean that the last tie with Dunshaughlin had been severed. The day came for the sale, and it realised more than had ever been anticipated. Efflam and Anne were happy with the price of the house. The farm had been good to them as a family. The livestock, hens, chickens, and geese were given to Tom and Teresa, and the only animals left to move besides the furniture were the four cats.

Anne and Efflam had their daughter's baptismal the day after the sale. There were lots of pictures and happy smiles. Still, at the back of Anne's mind she wondered about Bob and if he was okay. If he wasn't, perhaps he would be found and brought home, if not, maybe he would be cared for and loved and given a new home. Sometimes animals can't face up to so much pain, she thought. She wondered if he might have needed a break too, to start a new life with a new family.

'Please, God, look after Bob.' She lit a candle for her friend.

There would be a little farewell/baptismal party in The Dunshaughlin Arms, and after that, they would leave for Brittany. She had said goodbye to everyone and had faced her demons and resolved to conquer them. She had said goodbye to the ghosts of her past, to the memories of her mam and dad and their wonderful life. Now she had to face up to the life she had with Efflam. No longer could she be torn between two countries. She had to start again and begin to live.

Chapter Ten

Bob made it across the rushing river that night, nearly drowning in the process, but was so traumatised that he had completely lost his sense of direction. Instead of going towards Dunshaughlin, he was walking away from it ... and home.

Over the course of the next few months, Bob started to live in outhouses, travelling by night. He had to be careful. It was well known that stray dogs got hungry and ran in packs, killing sheep. The farmers who owned them kept strict vigil and wouldn't be afraid to shoot any dog to protect their property. Many a dog met his fate that way. Bob was intent that he wasn't going to be one of them. Tom had underestimated him. He would prove to be a survivor. As the months went by, Bob became more confident in dealing with other dogs. He was still terrified of trucks, cars, and any loud noises to such an extent that he would run and hide until either the noise had subsided or the vehicle had left. He started to feel abandoned. He was unaware of how worried Anne and Efflam had been about him and that they were hoping that he would return so that they could take him back to Brittany. He kept thinking about Jassie and Joe, but important things like fighting to stay alive took priority.

Winter was hot on its heels. The constant driving rain made it almost impossible to see on the roads. When Bob had been hit by a car, the angry driver just screamed out, 'blasted dog,' but he kept on going, unperturbed by what he had done. The reckless driver was one of the many thoughtless people he would encounter. Bob had overcome that and further abuse from numerous others. Sometimes, he found it difficult to walk and hopped every now and then, but at least nothing had been broken. The pain he felt was due to swollen muscles or strained tendons.

Whatever happened, he carried on relentlessly, trying to get home. At night, he roamed from house to house, stopping outside a door and scratching at it. The minute it was opened, he would dart into the darkest corner. The person would shout out, 'who's there?' and would close the door and Bob would repeat it until the owner realised what was going on and said, 'Want something to eat there, fellah?' The dog would bark as though answering, and the owner would leave a plate of something outside the door. It was this hand-to-mouth existence that helped him get through each day.

On one of his usual rounds, the rain had been driving particularly hard. He made his way to a barn to escape it, crawling through two broken planks in the door. The woman who owned the cottage was an elderly widow who lived on her own. She kept a few hens, a horse, and a cow in the barn. Bob had stayed a few nights, intent on moving on. He scratched around looking for food without any hope of any. The widow seemed careful about leaving anything lying around to attract rats, but the animals seemed fed and well looked after just the same. He had become very emaciated. He was exhausted and starving when she discovered him shivering in a corner of the barn as she went to check on her animals.

'What have we here? Hello, young fellah. C'mon, you look half starved.' The dog wouldn't move.

'Will you not come in out of the cold and have something to eat by the fire?' Bob stayed where he was. The more she approached him, the more he tried to bury himself into the corner. He whelped, giving her warning her to keep her distance. He wouldn't approach her no matter how much she tried to coax him.

'All right then, pet, don't get yourself into a sweat. I'll bring something out here and get a basket with some straw so that you'll be more comfortable.'

The woman went into the cottage, returned with a basket, and filled it with straw and a tattered blanket. She disappeared again only to return with a large plate of warmed stew and a bowl of milk. She decided that she would try to make friends with him, but Bob didn't want any contact. He had encountered the darker side of humanity by being abused, kicked, shouted at, and struck with stones. He didn't want the same thing happening again. Could he ever learn to trust again? He drew back from her every time she went near him. She was kind and gentle, leaving a plate of warmed stew every evening with a drop of milk to build him up a bit. This continued for two weeks, so after a while, he started to trust her. Bob started to improve once more. He was afraid of his own shadow, or so he thought.

One night, after the widow left him his usual stew and milk, he was settling down to snooze when he heard the smash of a glass pane. He peered through the broken planks in the barn door only to make out a large figure entering the house. There was no light on, and the man crept in with a torch, scarcely making a sound. Bob was curious and wanted to find out what he wanted. He had never seen any man around the cottage before and thought it peculiar that no light had been switched on. The man left the back door ajar as he crept about the house, shining the torch as he went. Bob stood in the doorway, unsure of whether he should enter or not. Then the man made for the stairway and sneaked up the stairs, carrying a large bat. Wincing every time he heard a step creak in case of discovery, Bob crept behind him, waiting at the bottom of the stairs to see what he was going to do.

The man placed his hand on the handle of one of the bedroom doors, and as it opened, the old woman said, 'Who's that? Who are you? What do you want?'

'Where's your money, missus?' he said menacingly.

'I haven't got any.'

'Come on, now, I don't have all night or do you want a taste of this then?' He waved the bat around and then raised his hand ready to strike out, and the widow screamed.

By this stage, Bob was halfway up the stairs and then bounded up the rest of the way, forgetting all his fear. The kind woman (*'mrs. plate of stew and bowl of milk'*) was being attacked, and he wasn't having any of that. The burglar wasn't expecting anything and lost his balance as Bob lunged at him, landing the burglar on the floor. The man, terrified, looked straight down the throat of a very angry dog who growled, his lip curling, demonstrating a very healthy pair of white teeth. His tongue protruded through his teeth as though relishing the next meal.

'Get him off me. Get him off.' Any movement and Bob would issue a blood-curdling throaty growl and would start barking at him, so the burglar decided to stay still. The widow, still shaking, mustered up the courage to call the Gardai.

'Keep him at bay there, fellah.'

Bob stood on the burglar's chest, eyes flashing intently, displaying his sharp teeth as he growled every time the man decided it was time to get up.

It was a blessing that the Garda station was only five minutes up the road as Bob was still on the burglar's chest when the Gardai arrived. They entered the bedroom. The burglar thought it took an eternity for them to arrive and for the first time in his life was relieved to see the Gardai despite the predicament in which he had found himself. He was so terrified of the dog that he was frozen to the spot.

'Get him off me. Get him off me,' the burglar shouted to the Gardai.

When the Gardai made a move to do so, Bob snarled at them, and then quickly flashed his attention to the burglar reminding him of exactly who was *really* in charge of the situation as he gnashed his teeth. The perspiration was pouring down the burglar's face as he envisaged the dog taking an almighty bite out of his throat and blood spurting in every direction.

A few minutes later, the widow came up the stairs.

'Is he vicious?' one of the Gardai asked the widow.

'What do you think?' the burglar shouted.

The widow smiled. 'It's all right, fellah. It's over now.'

Bob got off the burglar's chest and walked over to sit beside the widow, (*'mrs. plate of stew and bowl of milk'*). She petted him as he wagged his tail, his ears back, delighted to have saved the day. He looked as different as chalk from cheese. One minute he was a guard dog on duty, the next he looked as if a child could have pulled his tail and he wouldn't have minded one bit.

'He's a fine guard dog.' The sergeant looked at the bat on the ground beside the burglar.

'Had any other ideas besides robbing the place, had you?' He continued sarcastically, 'You were lucky we arrived when we did or perhaps you would have been *his* dinner, he looks kinda' hungry. What do you think?'

'That damn dog bit me.'

'Dear, dear now, who says so? You? You should be grateful he didn't cause you any *grievous* damage.'

'Grievous?' the burglar replied, stupefied. '*Long* lasting, *very* long lasting, know what I mean?' The sergeant looked at him straight in the eye.

'You're lucky that the dog stopped you dead in your tracks. I imagine you'll do time for this. But if you'd killed her with that bat, your life'd be over. You should be *thankful*. That dog has done you a great favour.' The sergeant smiled at the woman as the sergeant's partner led the burglar away in handcuffs.

'I didn't think she had a dog like that or I'd have never gone near the place,' he said to the sergeant's partner as he was being led down the stairs.

'Should have thought more then, shouldn't you?' was the partner's reply.

'That dog of yours has certainly earned his keep tonight. I doubt you'll be bothered with the likes of his sort again. We will be in touch regarding witness testimony. I don't think the dog will be required to testify.' He smiled.

'We will keep a patrol car in the area over the next couple of days just to make sure that no one else gets any funny ideas. If you feel uneasy, give us a ring.'

'Thank you very much for all your help.'

Bob stayed close to the woman for the next few days to make sure no other strange men decided to call. He was satisfied that she was safe as the Gardai dropped in to make sure she was all right. Bob had to start back on the road again. He had to try to get home. The following morning he left early. He had repaid the *'plate of stew and bowl of milk'* woman as best he could and decided to move on. He thought the woman would be good to him, but he couldn't stay; he had to find his own way home.

Later that morning, the widow went into the barn and called him. 'Fellah, here fellah.' She was so disappointed that he had left and had hoped that he would have stayed. She felt a great sense of loss and started to become scared at the slightest noise.

'I suppose he was trying to get home and stayed for a little while to get his strength up,' she explained to the sergeant who had been on duty the night of the burglary. 'Now I'm terrified to go outside my door. I just go out to feed the animals and go back in the house. I feel like a prisoner in my own home. At least when I had that little fellah I felt so much more secure.'

'It'll take time but you will get over it.'

'I doubt it.'

The sergeant dropped in on the elderly widow quite often but could see that she continued to be very shaken and so decided to do something to take her mind off it. One of the local farmers had English Shepherd pups for sale. He went to him and explained the situation. The farmer was only too pleased to help and gave him one. The following evening he called up to the widow and knocked on the door.

'Oh, it's you, Sergeant Sullivan. Come in, won't you?'

'I just called in to ask you if you would have room for this little fellah who could do with a good home by the fire.' Out from under his arm the sergeant produced a shivering puppy of about two months old wrapped in a little towel.

The widow's eyes filled with emotion. 'Oh, Sergeant, that is kind. She put her hands to her face to stop the tears from tumbling down her cheeks but wasn't quick enough.

Clearing his throat, he said, 'I take it you'll be able to look after him then.'

'God bless you, Sergeant.'

'I'll still call in every now and then to make sure you don't have any unwanted visitors. You can't get rid of me that easily.'

'Thank you so much, Sergeant. God bless you.'

The widow closed the door with the pup in her arms. Her fear melted away. Now she had someone to look after and who would care and guard her. She would no longer feel scared. The pup would grow up and be her guardian angel just as Bob had been on that fateful night.

Weeks went by, and the hand-to-mouth existence that Bob had known so well returned like an old enemy to taunt him. He was ready for it this time, though, and had become more astute. He realised that not everyone he met was cruel. There were cruel people, sure, but there were just as many kind ones around to balance it out. You just had to wait to discover what type they turned out to be.

Bob's injury played up every now and then, especially when he got into a dogfight. The gaunt emaciation resurfaced. He was unrecognizable from the fine healthy animal that lived with Joe and Mary, which seemed like a lifetime ago. The wind and driving rainy weather continued without any signs of letting up. He had become utterly exhausted, moving from one place to the next. He was forever rummaging for food as he limped into the side entrance of country pub and restaurant called *The Raven's Rest*. A barmaid sat on the side step of the kitchen, smoking a cigarette. She saw him and called over to him.

'Hello, young fellah, and what's your name? Lost your way, have you? I bet you could do with something to eat. You're *so* scrawny. Hold on a sec.'

Bob of course hadn't a hint of what the girl was going on about, but he decided that he would take a chance. He was fearful but remembered about his time with '*mrs. plate of stew and bowl of milk*' and decided to take the risk. She disappeared into the kitchen as Bob put his nose in the air as the smell of roast beef wafted out the door.

'Frank, are there a few odds and ends we could give my new-found friend here?'

'I dunno. You know Mrs. Baker. She's very careful and as for that husband of hers, God, he'd skin a hide off a flea and expect to be well paid for it.'

'For Pete's sake, Frank, I'll pay you for the few scraps.'

'That's not what I mean.'

'You know what, Frank? I'm sick to death of having roast chicken every day for the past three months, so he can have *my* lunch. After all, the Baker's are so stingy, they give you the cheapest possible thing to eat... chicken! The dog might as well enjoy it 'cause I can't stand the smell of it.'

'You can't do that, Karen. You've lost too much weight already.'

'No point in both of us being skin and bone.' Karen retorted.

'Make sure it's a good big piece of breast. I'm *really* hungry.'

Karen sat on the step waiting for the chef to cut a large piece of roast chicken for her. Chicken and potatoes with a little gravy were put in a dish for Bob. He was afraid and untrustworthy but thought that he had to start to trust someone if he was to survive. The next few days followed suit, and Bob appeared regularly. At lunchtime, a big burly chef, Frank, appeared in a white uniform and went into the backyard. Bob went ballistic. Karen followed him out.

'What's wrong with him?'

'He's scared stiff, but he's also protecting his territory.'

'I just wanted to give him some leftover chops.'

'Changed your mind then, have you?'

'I thought we could be friends.'

'Look, put your hand over mine and the scent of my hand will mask yours. Then he might trust you.' It worked. Frank held out a chop, and Bob teased it out of his hand and ate it hungrily. After a couple of days, they became firm friends.

'Maybe we should get him to a vet. What do you think, Frank? He's shivering all the time. He doesn't look very well, kind a' sluggish. Maybe he's caught something.'

'What will we do with him, *then*?'

'Let's take one step at a time? When will you be able to take us?'

'*Me?*'

'You're off tomorrow. What about then? Frank, you're a true friend. Thanks.'

'No problem,' he replied.

He was wondering when exactly he had agreed to go to the vet with Karen and Bob. He went into the kitchen, scratching his head as he mulled this over and still couldn't quite figure it out.

'Now then, young fellah, we are going to the vet tomorrow and try and sort you out. When we've done that, we'll buy a doghouse so that you have somewhere to sleep and then you'll get a new name. I don't think you had better tell Frank, though. He doesn't know what he's let himself in for.' She petted Bob and went inside.

The following morning, Karen went to Mrs. Baker and told her about the dog.

'Mrs. Baker, I wonder if I could have a word with you.'

'Yes, Karen.'

'Well, there's this stray dog and he's sort of adopted me and Frank and we were hoping to keep him. I could get a doghouse, and he could sleep in the backyard, and he'd be a good guard dog.'

'Who'd feed him? I don't want to be landed with some stray.'

'I will. I'll look after him.'

Mrs. Baker thought that Karen had a point. A guard dog would be a good idea. It would keep the backyard protected, especially during Saturday nights when the disco was on and drunken yobos came around looking for easy access to drink, and to boot, it wouldn't cost her a penny. What did she have to lose? She always looked for the advantage in every situation, but she had a kind spark that emerged every now and then.

'Mmm, all right, Karen, as long as I'm not going to be put to any expense, you can keep the dog.'

'Thanks, Mrs. Baker.'

Karen went through the kitchen looking for Frank.

'Frank, Frank.'

'Here I am.'

'I've just spoken to Mrs. Baker. She's agreed that we can keep dog.'

'We? Now just hold yer horses. I never agreed to take the dog. *You* agreed.'

'Come on, Frank. You like him don't you?'

'Course I do, but ...'

'Well, then, that's settled.'

'Are you sure you're only nineteen? You seem to have the knack for getting what you want, and the other fellah doesn't know he's been roped in until he's trussed up like a chicken grinning like an idiot, and almost thankful at the prospect.'

Karen smiled and then winked at him.

'Don't exaggerate, Frank! By the way, you're right. I'm not nineteen.'

'I knew it. You couldn't fool me!' He shook his head, delighted that he had discovered her secret.

'I've just turned seventeen. Don't tell the Bakers or I'll get the sack. Anyway, there's a good vet the far side of Dunshaughlin. He's not too expensive, either.'

'What? You're kidding. Seventeen. God, I'd hate to see you when you turn twenty! Anyway, how do you know about the vet?'

'I asked one of the locals in the pub, and he told me Cormac O'Shaughnessy in The Veterinary Clinic was the best place to go. It's a mile or so outside Dunshaughlin. He gave me directions. Most of the farmers go to him. I've never known a farmer to squander money, have you?'

'No.'

'Well, then, let's stop hangin' about and go.'

Frank put Bob in the back seat with Karen. He was shaking and shivering all over. As they drove along, the sign 'Welcome to Dunshaughlin' passed them by.

'Frank, slow down. It can't be far from here. Look! There's a church.' The sign read 'Church of Our Lady of the Holy Rosary.'

'That's it, Frank! It has to be near here. Oh, look! It's a christening!'

Bob raised his head, unaware of the christening taking place outside. The car drove past, leaving Anne, Efflam, and Mazhe behind as they were having photographs taken of their daughter on her special day. Bob had come so close to going home, so very close, but now, it was simply a matter of survival.

Chapter Eleven

As they drove past the Church of Our Lady of the Holy Rosary, Bob left part of his own life behind. This of course was done without his knowledge, which was probably just as well. Many things in life happen without our immediate knowledge of the situation in hand. Perhaps it was for the best; after all, Bob would have only reminded Anne of her past, especially of her dad, as he had been so close to him. Now she had to make a complete break, a new beginning.

The Veterinary Clinic wasn't far from the church. Karen brought Bob in to see the vet. As it happened, there weren't any clients in the waiting room, which was a bit unusual. Frank waited outside in the car.

'Have you been here before?' the receptionist asked Karen.

'No, this is my first time.'

'What type of dog is he?'

'He's an English Shepherd.'

'What's wrong with him?'

'I'm not sure. I want to get him checked over.'

'You can go in now.'

Karen went in to the veterinary surgery proper, and Bob was put on the table. Cormac O'Shaughnessy, the vet, examined him, checked his eye, which was gummed up and which had a small cut, his ears, and then his coat. The vet exploded.

'How could you possibly let a dog get into such a state? He is totally underweight. He has conjunctivitis; his eye is infected. He has mites in his ears, and to cap it all he is infested with mange. God only knows what other parasites he's infested with. People like you shouldn't be allowed to have animals if you're not going to look after them properly. I have a good mind to report you to the Association for the Prevention of Cruelty to Animals!'

After a few minutes, the veterinary surgeon regained his composure. He had lost his temper with good reason. Karen, however, was not part of the problem but the solution. She could clearly see that Cormac O'Shaughnessy had the welfare of the animals he treated first and foremost. He wasn't particularly interested in the feelings of his clients if they were in the wrong; however, this was not one of those times.

Karen said nothing; letting Mr. O'Shaughnessy rant on, and when a pregnant pause ensued, she started to explain.

'Well, you see—'

'Yes?' he replied rudely. He waited impatiently for this elongated explanation. He thought to himself. *'What's she going to come up with now? This had better be good.'* She looked at him apologetically.

'Well, you see. He's not mine. He's a stray. I brought him to see you on my day off to try to get him sorted out. I thought he needed looking after.'

'What?' the vet was flabbergasted. He wasn't expecting that at all.

'Yes, like I said, he's a stray.'

The vet sighed. 'Oh, I'm sorry. I shouldn't have blown my top like that. I see dozens of abused animals, and it just makes me so cross sometimes. Maybe this fellah will have a chance now.'

'That's okay. How were you to know?'

The vet gave Bob a couple of injections, wormed him, cleaned his ears and his eye infection, and gave her drops to alleviate the conjunctivitis.

'This is Allergen. It gets rid of mange and general parasites. Wash him in it, but don't rinse it off. Do it twice a week in the open air, and use gloves and a mask to protect yourself. You should begin to see a difference within a fortnight. Bring him back in three weeks, and I will have another look at him.'

'What do I owe you?'

Mr. O'Shaughnessy looked at her. 'Well, since you're trying to help a stray get a second chance. I'll just charge you the cost price of the medicine and forget about the rest.'

'That's really kind. I'm … Thank you. Thank you very much.'

'Bring him back in three weeks. Don't forget.'

'I won't. Thank you again.'

Bob, Karen, and Frank were making their way back to *The Raven's Rest* when Karen suggested making a small detour.

'Where do you want to go?' Frank asked.

'I want to buy a doghouse and some carpet to put in it.'

'Are you insane? He's a stray. He could leave at any time.'

'I don't think so. Anyway, you don't want him. So, he's *my* stray. Can we go?'

'Sure. There's a pet shop about three miles from here.'

They drove without another word and arrived at the pet shop. Karen bought the largest doghouse possible. Frank put it on the roof of the car and secured it with a rope so it wouldn't fall off. They drove a little further on where there was a supermarket and D.I.Y. shop. A furniture shop and carpet retailer stood side by side, and Karen told Frank to wait in the car.

She went into the shop and started looking through the carpets, called one of the assistants and asked for remnants. She explained that she wanted the piece of carpet for the doghouse on top of the car. He gave her a large piece and charged her £4.00. He rolled it up, and she paid him. She was very grateful that the assistant had charged her so little. It would seem that, that day, the vet and the carpet retailer had been touched by the plight of the English Shepherd who had the odds stacked against him and the girl who wanted to help him out. People can be quite surprising and do things, both good and bad, that seemed to be completely out of character. This was one of those days.

They stopped off at the supermarket as Karen stocked up on dog food, dog biscuits, collar, lead, and a few toys. Everything was brought back to *The Raven's Rest*. Bob was washed and disinfected. The doghouse was set up with the carpet and toys.

Mrs. Baker saw all the carpet and commented, 'That would have been perfect for the bathroom upstairs.'

'Ah, well, I think the dog needs it more,' replied Karen with a sarcastic smile.

Exhaustive efforts were made to find out if anyone owned the dog, but no owner could be found, so Karen decided that she would keep him.

'What are you going to call him? The kitchen staff all had their own ideas about a name.

'What about Spot?' said one of them.

'Who ever *heard* of a dog called Spot? Butch is a much better name,' said another.

The youngest of the staff piped up. 'He's not a Pit Bull Terrier! Rover is ideal. He's a sheep dog, after all.'

'Thanks for your suggestions, but I've already decided what I'm going to call him. His name is going to be Ragsy!'

'What type of name is that?'

'When he's completely cured, has a shiny coat and is the picture of health, it will remind me, and him, of how far we've come together and how lucky we were to find each other.'

Bob barked. It was of no concern to him whether he was Bob or Ragsy. The name mattered little, as long as it was accompanied by plenty of tender loving care. Weeks went by and Bob, or Ragsy, if you prefer, settled into his new life. Karen was really kind to him. He was brought back to the vet, and Mr. O'Shaughnessy was very pleased with the results. He recommended that she return after a month.

There was a disco every Saturday night at *The Raven's Rest*, and Karen would work behind the disco bar after the pub closed. She often worked until four o'clock and would have to be up early the following morning to do stocktaking and to make sure everything was as it should be. When the disco had closed and the stragglers were leaving Ragsy would slip in the side door, lie down, and wait for Karen to finish just as his mother, Jassie, had done with Anne years before.

He was hardly ever left on his own. One of the kitchen staff would come out into the yard, have a smoke, and pet him as they sat down on the step. He was Karen's dog, sure, but he was *The Raven's Rest* mascot as well.

The family that owned the *'The Raven's Rest'* had four grown up children. James was the oldest, twenty-five or twenty-six, strong as an ox and a real lady-killer. He was tall, very good looking, with a down-to-earth personality. They had two daughters, Marjorie, was blonde, pretty, slim, and pleasant to be with, a year or so older than Karen. Then there was Delphine, who was still in school, and the total opposite of her outgoing sister. She was a little overweight, with dark brown bobbed hair and John Lennon glasses, a typical teenager going through 'the terrible teens,' so sure of everything one minute and totally flummoxed the next.

Last but not least, there was Christopher. The less said about him the better, a weedy individual who thought himself better than anyone else. He wasn't tall and had what one could only describe as an insipid personality. He enjoyed bullying people and making them feel inferior. His exploits didn't finish there as his attitude spilled over to his treatment of animals. He was the sort of person who, by his appearance was forgetful; his manner, however, was anything but. Karen couldn't stand him, but as he was her boss, she had to watch her step. Often, she might be washing her hands by the kitchen sink and look out into the yard only to see Christopher 'hiss' at Ragsy like a snake and shout at him. The dog, naturally, took an instant dislike to him and every time Christopher walked into the yard, Ragsy would bark incessantly as though he were a burglar, and he wouldn't stop until he left. It was a 'blessing in disguise' because it was precisely because of this that Christopher didn't go into the yard too often.

Mrs. Baker was relatively pleasant, the one who really ran *The Raven's Rest*. She was a tall, slim, overly tanned woman with blonde hair that was always impeccably coiffured. She was very smartly turned out, with manicured nails and make-up that was flawlessly applied. She worked hard and ran the establishment with precision. She was a bossy woman, and her word was law. Mrs. Baker liked Karen, who she regarded as a hard worker. If Karen were needed, regardless of whether it was her day off or not, she would help out without any extra pay. She thought of it as a quid pro quo. Mrs. Baker had allowed her keep the dog without any fuss, so she felt obliged to her in some small way.

Mr. Baker was a tall man who always wore a farmer's cap. He smoked incessantly, had a red bulbous nose, and was very weather-beaten. He had an equally red wiry moustache and had the terrible habit of constantly twirling the ends of it. He looked like he had spent all his life on the land. Many people couldn't quite comprehend how a man like that came to marry a woman like Mrs. Baker. Karen could though. They were like chalk and cheese, true, but were well matched and seemed to be very comfortable in each other's company.

Each one, (with the exception of Delphine) had his or her own BMW. James' was black, Christopher's red, and Marjorie's blue. They were all spoilt, but some of them had more redeeming qualities.

It was a time when money was very tight for most people. To say that the Bakers were 'loaded' was an understatement. They lived in a very large house on a hill, with palladium columns. It would have reminded anyone passing by of the plantation property known as Twelve Oaks in *Gone with the Wind*. It was a stunning property with plenty of land around it, and it was a credit to whoever had built it. It was not situated in America's Deep South during the American Civil War but near Athboy, Co. Meath, in the 1980s, which made it seem out of place and time. Some of the farmers who were not as wealthy passed it by and laughed at the presumption of the owners of building such a house in a location like Athboy. Karen didn't think anything of the kind. She thought it a beautiful house, built with love and a great deal of care. *Good luck to them!* she thought. *It wouldn't be my cup of tea, but I'd bet that any of the farmers who don't have it wish they did!*

The Raven's Rest was a popular nightspot. Stragglers would be seen leaving after four o'clock, having enjoyed themselves thoroughly. After the end of one particular night, Ragsy was seen being bungled into someone's car with a crowd of yobos the worse for wear with drink. The car was stopped from leaving. Christopher dragged one of the yobos out of the car. Scrawny as Christopher was, he wasn't afraid to take on someone twice his size. He was never one to be crossed, not under any circumstances.

'Here you, what the hell do you think you're doing?'
'Whadera mean?' the yobo replied, completely legless.
'That dog belongs to *The Raven's Rest*. What do you think you're doing with him?'
'I thought I'd bring him home.'
'Bring yourself home. You're barred! Out you get, Ragsy.'
'Don't come back here ever again. As for your friends, they had better watch themselves. I'll be keeping a close eye on you lot.'

Ragsy got out of the car, and Karen was called.

'Christopher wants to see you *now*,' one of the staff told Karen.

'Yes, Christopher. Did you want to see me?'

'I've just saved your dog from being carted away by a load of drunken idiots. Keep him tied up in future.'

'God! Thanks a lot. I will,' she replied gratefully. Karen had to find another solution. She couldn't run the risk of the dog being taken by a load of drunken yobos on a Saturday night and possibly hurled out the window speeding down a motorway.

The answer came sooner than she had thought. On Friday, Frank promised to look after Ragsy as though he were his own. Karen had to go to Dublin for her parent's twenty-fifth wedding anniversary get-together. She had been given the Saturday off, which was unusual. She hadn't been home for three months. Her dad came to collect her, and as soon as she got home her mother kept telling her how thin she was and that she looked exhausted. She was advised to give up the job and go back to do her Leaving Cert. exam.

'I'm working now. The only reason I'm here is for your twenty-fifth and no other. Anyway, I can't leave. I have a dog now.'

'We have a dog here. You can't have a dog,' her mother replied.

'Who says? I'm not leaving him, so you can just forget about me leaving that place.'

'I want you to return to school to do your Leaving Cert. exam.'

'No way.'

'Karen, it's a dead end job. Do you want to be a barmaid all your life? Think, girl, think.'

'Even, if I did think, I'm not leaving my dog, and that's final!'

'Do you want me to go back now? Dad, could you drive me back, please?'

'Stop all this. Let's have lunch. We will have a think about it afterwards.'

'Karen, your mother just wants what's best for you and nothing else. Will you think about returning to school to do you're Leaving Cert. exam?'

'Sorry, dad, not if it means that I have to leave my dog.'

'Maybe you can find him another home.'

'I've spent all my wages trying to get him well. He was really sick. He had mange, and no one wanted him except me. I tell you what. I'll ask, but that's all. If I can't find a home for him that *I* would be happy with. I'm not coming home and that's final. Okay?'

'Fair enough,' he replied.

Karen returned to *The Raven's Rest* the following morning after her parents' twenty-fifth wedding anniversary. She was very depressed. The arguments at home didn't help, either. She knew that her mother wouldn't let up until she got her way. However, Karen had absolutely no intention of letting Ragsy go without one hell of a fight. First, she had to see if it was possible to get him another home, one that *she* would be happy with. She told Frank about everything.

'What are you going to do?'

'Try to get him a better home, I suppose. Let's face it. I don't want to be in this place when I'm forty.'

Karen asked the kitchen staff if any of them would be able to take on Ragsy, secretly hoping that they wouldn't be able to. It turned out to be 'no go.' No one could take him. They already had dogs and their families couldn't afford it. Their families lived far away, in Limerick, Cork, or Kerry and they had left home in search of work in Co. Meath. Karen rang home and told her father the news.

'I've tried to get him a suitable home and there is no chance. People live too far away, don't have the money, or have dogs and don't want to know.'

'I see. I understand. I'll have a word with your mother and see what she has to say.'

'Look, dad, there's no more to say. That's it.'

'Ring me back at the weekend, and we might have a solution.'

'All right, dad. I'll ring you at the weekend.'

By this stage, Ragsy was indeed the picture of health with the exception of a bald patch on his back. He was happy. He had come a long way, but there was still a long way to go. Karen sat on the step outside the kitchen, petting the dog.

'If only people could see you the way I do. They don't know you at all. You deserve a good home with a nice family. If only I could take you home myself. Oh, Ragsy, what am I going to do? Things will work out. I'm sure they will,' she assured Ragsy. 'Don't worry.'

Although Ragsy hadn't been Karen's constant companion from the time she started in *The Raven's Rest*, she felt as though he had. She wouldn't let him down or betray him; she just couldn't. She rang home at the weekend to find out what the 'solution' was going to be.

'Hi, dad, it's Karen.'

'Karen, your mother and I have been talking. We both want you to come home and go back to school.'

'I can't. I told you why.'

'I know. It's to your credit that you have done so much to help that dog, and I won't stand in your way. That's why, I ... I mean your mother and I ... well, we have decided that you can bring him home with you.'

'*What?*'

'But, on the proviso that he gets on with Poochie. He may even help her. She's very depressed lately because she's on her own so much when we're out working. It's only on that proviso!'

'Okay, dad. It's a deal.' Karen put the receiver down and went out to Ragsy in the yard.

'Ragsy, you can't fight with Poochie. I can only bring you home if you don't fight with her, okay?'

Poochie was an eight-year-old Cairn Terrier bitch. She had a sweet personality and was very trusting. She had been mauled by another dog when she was young, so naturally Karen's family was apprehensive that the same thing would happen again. It would be much more likely as a Cairn Terrier is so much smaller than an English Shepherd. If Ragsy did decide to have a go at her, he could do untold damage, but that was a risk Karen's parents were prepared to take. Karen went to Mrs. Baker to give in her notice.

'I'm leaving, Mrs. Baker. My dad's coming to collect me in two weeks' time.'

'Oh, I'm sorry to hear that. What are you going to do about the dog?'

'I'm taking him home with me,' Karen replied.

News went round the local farmers about Ragsy and the beautiful dog he was. Many a farmer came into the pub and remarked on his markings and his placid nature as he slept underneath one of the chairs, waiting for Karen to finish her shift.

'What are you going to do with the dog?' a local farmer asked.

'I'm taking him home' Karen replied.

'But that dog belongs on a farm. He's a working dog. I'll take him off your hands.'

'No, thanks. I'll take him home just the same.'

When Karen had finished her shift, she sat outside on the kitchen step smoking her cigarette. As she dragged on the cigarette and exhaled the smoke, a smile of satisfaction crept over her face. As ever, Ragsy sat beside her as she spoke to him in soft hushed tones. It was a quiet starlit night, with clouds lazily drifting past as she gazed intently upon them.

'You know what, Ragsy?' Karen said with her hand resting on his head. 'People amaze me. They can be so shallow. There's beauty right under their noses, and yet they can't see it. When you were sick and had all those diseases, no one even wanted to feed you. Yet now, you're well and stunning to look at, it's only now that they see what they've missed. I suppose people only see what's in front of them. They need special glasses to see what's behind a raggy coat or a dirty face. Why can't people look properly?'

Ragsy looked up at her, unbeknown to Karen; Ragsy knew exactly what she was on about.

'Don't think it's only animals that suffer, though. People can look right through you because you're too fat or too thin, or you're not pretty or perfect enough, and yet they're the ones missing out on so much and don't realise it. It's a shame people only *look* on the outside and don't *see* what's on the inside. They miss what's really important. If only there were glasses to help people see properly. I feel sorry for people like that, don't you? Just as well we're not myopic or whatever you call it, eh? Better put you to bed. It's a long day tomorrow. Goodnight, Ragsy.'

Chapter Twelve

The following day, Karen packed her belongings. She had called a taxi to go to The Veterinary Clinic in Dunshaughlin with Ragsy. She had promised that she would return after a month so that the vet could check his progress.

She arrived at The Veterinary Clinic and asked the taxi to wait for her to bring her back to *The Raven's Rest*.

'I'd like to see Mr. O'Shaughnessy, please.'

'He's with someone at the moment. Can you wait?'

'Oh, yes. I need him to check my dog first, anyway.' The person came out with a cat and Karen was told to go in.

'Mr. O'Shaughnessy, I know it's only been two weeks, but I would like you to check Ragsy.'

'Why? Is there something wrong?'

'No, not exactly. I wanted you to check him over as I'm taking him home to Dublin with me.'

'To Dublin?'

'Yes, he's coming home with me. We have a large back and front garden, and there's a boys' school very close by where they have about five or six acres where he can exercise. We also live very close to Sandymount beach, which runs from Ringsend to Booterstown. It's at least four miles long, so there will be plenty of room for him to run around.'

'Your parents don't mind?'

'Well, let's say that I have twisted their arms, so to speak, but they're happy I'm coming home.'

'It'll be a new beginning for him, a new family, and a second chance. I'm glad for him and for you.'

'It'll be a new beginning for both of us. Thank you for everything you did. You didn't charge me half what you should have. I am grateful. I wasn't paid much, so it was more appreciated than you can ever imagine.'

'Not, at all. Keep up the Allergen treatment. Don't worry that he has lost patches of hair on his back. He'll recover. He'll be fine. Make sure that you take him to your own vet and tell him what treatment he has had. I suggest that you take him in about three weeks. He's had all his jabs so don't worry. Here is a list. Good Luck to both of you.'

'Thank you, Mr. O'Shaughnessy. Thank you very much.'

Karen left The Veterinary Clinic. She took the taxi back to *The Raven's Rest*. Her dad was to collect her at half past two, and it was almost twelve. She thought that she had better get a move on.

The kitchen was a hive of activity as the lunch hour service was about to start, when she went in, everyone stopped. Frank stepped forward.

'Karen, we're all sorry that you're leaving. We'll miss you and Ragsy a lot, so, we all chipped in and bought something to wish you both well. We couldn't wrap it, but we thought you would understand.' The next moment, he produced a large cane basket with a duck down pillow sitting at the bottom of it. It had a red-checkered blanket on top.

'We thought that since you had spent so much on him already that we could at least chip in for this.'

'I don't know what to say. I ... thank you all so much. We'll miss you too.'

The staff told her to take care of herself and wished her luck.

Then Mrs. Baker could be heard in the background.

'Where are the waitresses? They should be outside taking orders! Where is everybody?'

The kitchen reverted to its previous humming activity as Karen closed the kitchen door and went up the side stairs to the bedroom she shared with another barmaid, Tessie. Ragsy followed her up.

Everything was packed, and she was ready to go. A box of dog food, dog biscuits, and treats were placed on the end of the bed. She sat on the side of the bed and looked around the room. It was totally devoid of her personality. It was as though she had never been there at all. She had stripped the linen from her bed. A chair, a wardrobe, Tessie's dressing table, and her bed were the only other items in the room.

She was glad she had come to *The Raven's Rest*. She had discovered Ragsy, a lifelong friend, and for that reason, if no other, she hadn't wasted her time. Now a new journey was about to start for both of them. Karen took the box of dog biscuits, treats, and the rest of the paraphernalia downstairs. Her suitcase stood beside the door. She was playing in the yard with Ragsy when Frank stuck his head around the door.

'Your dad won't be here for a while. Do you want some lunch?'

'What is it?'

'Well, it's ...'

'Let me guess.....chicken.' They both said 'chicken' together and laughed.

'I think I'll pass. Even Ragsy is sick of chicken! We have had it every day for the last four months. There's only so much you can do with roast chicken. Thanks for the thought, though.'

Karen took Ragsy's lead and decided to go for a walk. She was gone for an hour. When Karen arrived back at the pub, she made sure that everything was ready and sat on the step, smoking a cigarette. She must have looked at her watch ten times, waiting for her father to arrive. Finally, his car pulled around the back of the yard and drove up to the kitchen door.

'Beep, beep.' Karen waved at her dad and ran over to the car. Ragsy decided that he wasn't going to be left behind and bounded over beside her. She opened the passenger door, and before she could turn around, Ragsy had wormed his way in the door, jumped on the front seat, and started licking her dad all over his face. Ragsy had lost his fear of men.

'What's all this? Who's this?'

Ragsy didn't give him a chance, licking him all over his face.

'Who are you, then?'

Ragsy barked a couple of times, his tail wagging twenty to the dozen.

'Let me guess. I know now. You're Ragsy. Is that right?'
The dog barked excitedly twice or three times as if to answer, wagging his tail like crazy. It would seem that Ragsy was aware of how important this meeting with Karen's father was, and he had passed with flying colours.

'He's a real beauty, Karen, and so affectionate.'

'Well, I think he's learned a lot, and so have I, about people, I mean. There are good ones and bad ones. They aren't always what they seem.'

'Give people a chance to redeem themselves. They may amaze you. Life can be very surprising. You've been running away from it for the last four months cooped up in this place. You know very well that this isn't for you. I know you aren't all that pleased about going back to school, but at least you'll have a chance to make something of your life.'

'It wasn't just that. It was—'

'Things happen for a reason. I know that you wanted to get engaged to Richard. I've nothing against him. He's a nice lad from a good family and thinks the way you do, but what type of future would you have? He works in a pub in New York. Is that what you want, to be a publican's wife? Perhaps it's for the best. You're so young. You have your whole life ahead of you. How do you know what's going to happen? Chin up, eh? It can only get better. A year from now you'll be saying Richard? Richard who?'

'I suppose,' Karen answered, rather depressed.

'What goes around comes around. Life is a circle, good and bad, day and night, birth, and death. The seasons of the year have to wait their turn. Even winter has to give way to spring. Something that seems dead in the winter revives in the spring. Where there's life, there's hope. Don't forget that,' her dad warned her.

'I didn't know you were a philosopher!'

'Is that what I was doing? Well now, I didn't know that either. Imagine. I may become the next Nietzsche.' He laughed.

'Dad?'

'Yes, Karen.'

'I hate to put a pin in your balloon, but don't you think one Nightse I mean Nietzsche or whatever his name is, in the world is enough?'

'Perhaps you're right, Karen. The world isn't ready for my genius yet!' He laughed heartily. 'Let's go home, eh?'

'Yes. Let's.'

They secured the doghouse to the roof rack, using plenty of rope. The suitcase and cane basket were put in the boot of the car. Karen was glad to be leaving. She would miss Frank. He had been good to both of them. Frank had asked that she bring Ragsy back to see him. She had agreed but knew in her heart that that would never happen. She had no intention of ever returning to *The Raven's Rest*.

Mrs. Baker had told Karen before she had given in her notice that she would have to pay for coal out of her £45.00 weekly salary. It cost about £7.00 per week. The grate used up a lot of coal as the house was very cold. That was enough for Karen. She had already decided that she was going to give in her notice, but she had felt bad about letting them down. When she heard that she would have to pay for coal out of her meagre salary, she didn't feel guilty at all. She had been informed that the reason why her salary was small was because half of her salary went towards food, gas, heating, and electricity. She had heard of people getting blood out of a stone, but that was pure exploitation! Mrs. Baker kept going on about how much tax she paid for everyone. In all her time there, Karen had never seen a tax slip but assumed that they had paid tax, as Mrs. Baker never stopped going on about it. It was only when Karen got home that she discovered that they had never paid tax for her at all. She had been paid under the minimum wage so she wasn't eligible to pay tax and so neither was the employer. They had done nothing strictly illegal—immoral maybe—but she felt cheated and lied to and was glad it was finally all over.

Karen sat in the back of the car with Ragsy for safety reasons. The window had been lowered a little so he could stick his head out the window and feel the breeze ripple over his fur coat. He hadn't a clue where he was going, but he was content in the knowledge that he was going with good people who would look after him. He would never again know a day of hunger or loneliness. It was a new adventure.

They drove through Phoenix Park and the City Centre crossing the River Liffey towards an affluent suburb of the south side of Dublin known as *The Embassy Belt.* The cold winter sun glistened through the trees. The bright blue sky could fool a person into thinking it was summer, but this was belied by the biting wind. The trees shed their leaves of russet, gold, green, and brown as they mingled together to make a patchwork quilt of glorious colour, leaving behind spindly twigs on naked branches like an old woman's fingers. They drove down by the side of the *Church of the Sacred Heart,* where Karen had so often dropped in to light a candle and say, 'I'm in a bit of a hurry, but I thought I'd just pop in to say hello.' She looked back nostalgically at the church, reminding her that she was nearly home. It was as though everything was in a time warp. Nothing had changed at all. The car continued down Ailesbury Road, and after a few left and right turns, the car swung into the sweeping driveway of the house where Karen and her family lived.

'This is it Ragsy. We're home.'

Ragsy was a little unsure. He waited for Karen to get out. The suitcase and box were removed from the car as Ragsy bounded up the driveway. The door opened as Ragsy ran in, waiting for Karen to follow him in case he wasn't supposed to.

'In you go.'

'Mum, look isn't he lovely. Oh, mum he's beautiful.' Karen's sister Laura squealed with delight. She jumped nervously to one side. 'Oh, mum, have a look.'

David, Karen's brother, yawned as he made his way downstairs. 'He's here, then?'

He did not seem particularly bothered until the dog ran around him in circles, and then all of a sudden his interest piqued.

'Now, Karen, if he doesn't get on with Poochie, that's it! God, he's awfully big,' her mother said as she sidestepped him.

'I know. He may seem big, but he is as gentle as a mouse. He wouldn't hurt a fly.'

'Flies or mice, as long as that is crystal clear.'

'It is.'

'Good.'

As they opened the kitchen door, Karen's heart started to pound. She thought that everyone in the house could hear it, as she was afraid that it would leap right out of her chest. Well, this is it. If he fights with her, he'll have to go. If not, he can stay. She said a quiet 'Please, God,' and opened the door.

Ragsy wasn't expecting anything when he bounded into the kitchen. He stopped dead in his tracks when he saw the Cairn Terrier roll over on her tummy to welcome him. If he wanted to 'go for her' that was the moment. Karen stood close to Ragsy.

'Ragsy, this is Poochie.'

Poochie wagged her tail as if all her birthdays had come together. You could have cut the air with a knife as everyone waited to see what would happen. Then Ragsy tried to jump up on Karen's back to avoid Poochie. That broke the tense atmosphere as everyone erupted in laughter.

It was obvious from that time that they would be the best of friends. Ragsy was still very apprehensive as to whether this was a temporary arrangement or a permanent home. He followed Karen around like a lost sheep, afraid of letting her out of his sight in case she would disappear altogether.

'Karen, what are you going to call him?' her mother asked.

'His name's Ragsy.'

'Rag what?'

'Ragsy. RAGZEE.'

'You can't call a dog that. What type of name is that?'

'Well, that's his name, and he seems quite happy with it. I'm not going to start calling him something else and start to confuse the poor fellah.'

'I still think it a very odd name to call a dog.'

'You're right. It is odd, but we're an odd pair, odd as two left feet.'

Twilight was already setting in as the clock had been turned back recently. Winter had truly arrived. Whenever Karen's mother swept the kitchen floor, Ragsy would dart from one side of the room to the other. It would take a long time for him to realise that he had found a safe refuge, a place to be himself once more.

He would mope about all day waiting for Karen to return from school, and then he would revert to his old self and be like a puppy. After a few months, he fell into a routine, and a great relationship developed between Poochie and Ragsy. There were three steps leading from the garden patio to the back garden, which was set on half an acre. Poochie had begun to suffer from arthritis and found it difficult to get up the steps. Ragsy would go down to the step nearest the ground, put his nose in between her back legs to push her up the step. Then he would run up to the top step, bark at her, as if to tell her to get a move on, go down to the next step and repeat the process until she had finally managed to get up all three steps. It was hilarious to watch.

Ragsy was a new lease of life for Poochie, to say the least. No one realised at the time how truly depressed she was. Although she had arthritis, it didn't stop her from enjoying herself. The days fell into one another, and soon spring was on the doorstep. Ragsy, by this stage, had totally immersed himself in the family. Karen's mother was no longer worried about large dogs. She had been apprehensive about dogs in general until they had Poochie, and then her fear transferred onto larger dogs. Ragsy dispelled that fear relatively quickly. He was so gentle that if Karen's mother wanted to give him a piece of ham or chicken, he would take the corner with his teeth and tease it out of her hand. He was aware of her fear and didn't want to add to it. He was a very good-natured animal, gentle but protective.

Karen's Leaving Cert. exams started at the beginning of June. The house was on tenterhooks. Everybody was afraid to say anything to her as she locked herself in her room trying to get her study done. She was up early and went to bed late. She hardly said a word to anyone, lost in her own thoughts. She would walk Ragsy early in the morning, as he wasn't the most sociable dog in the world. If he came into contact with any other dog, it was world war three! Perhaps it was because he had

had to fight to survive, and he didn't want to lose what he had now. Days passed, and one exam followed another. Finally, the ordeal was over.

A great cloud lifted from the house the day the exams were finished. It was as though the whole family could breathe again. Karen decided to take a week or so off and then would look for summer work.

'Have you decided what you going to do?'

'I don't know.'

'What about university?'

'What about it?'

'Wouldn't you like to go to university like your sister? You could go to U.C.D. That's a lovely university and just up the road.'

'I'm not interested in more studying.'

'Wouldn't you like to be qualified?'

'In what? I just want to enjoy my life. It hasn't been exactly a showstopper so far. There must be more to life than books!'

'Well, as a matter of fact, young lady, there is. There are jobs where you stand on your feet all day. You could work in a pub working every hour God sends. Oh, sorry, you've already had a taste of that! You could work in a shop where your feet are hanging off you at the end of the day or you could be a secretary and be unlucky enough to have a bloody-minded boss screaming at you endlessly, telling you how hopeless and stupid you are. I know some bosses are fair, but who's to say that you'd be blessed enough to get one of those! Yes, I must say there are plenty of interesting jobs crying out for people who aren't qualified and want to step into a mindless rut.'

'It can't be as bad as that. You're exaggerating!'

'Do you think so? Step this way, ladies and gentlemen, and watch someone throw her life away simply because she won't listen to her mother. You think about that, young lady, and tell me in five years time if I wasn't right! God, I could shake you, if I thought it would make any difference, but I know there isn't much point 'cause I know it won't.'

Karen went to bed that night thinking about what her mother had said. Was it as bad as she made out? Would she be better going to university? She tossed and turned. Maybe she shouldn't have come back to Dublin; it might have been better to stay where she had been. Richard returned to her thoughts like an old song. She had difficulty getting him out of her mind. She had to do something to keep her mind active. Perhaps it was a good idea to go to university. She had no intention of working in a shop, a pub or being somebody's slave at a typewriter, no way José. Karen decided to think on it. She would make her mind up when she came back from her early morning walk with Ragsy.

The following morning, she went out early and sauntered along Sandymount beach, throwing sticks to Ragsy to keep him occupied. She went back and forth along the beach, thinking of what to do until finally she came to her decision.

'Mum?'

'I've decided.'

'Oh yes? What have you decided?'

'I'm going to apply for university. I mightn't have enough points to get in. I need to apply for the CAO form, and it may be too late.'

'Nonsense, here it is.' Her mother produced a CAO form for Karen to fill in.

'What! You knew all along. That pep talk was done to make me sit up and take notice. Go on, admit it!'

'Admit what? It was necessary for you to come to your senses. Believe it or not, girls of eighteen don't have *all* the answers even if they think they do.' Her mother smiled at her.

'You're a crafty one. I'll have to watch you in future,' Karen retorted.

'You'd never see me coming. An avalanche could fall on you and you wouldn't know it, until it hit you.'

'Oh you! I never thought you were so devious!'

'Devious, me?' her mother replied as though butter wouldn't melt in her mouth. 'I don't even know the meaning of the word! Devious? What a cheek!'

Chapter Thirteen

Karen applied for Trinity College, and her mother asked her why she hadn't applied for the University College Dublin as well.

'If I don't get Trinity, I don't want to go, and that's it!'

'Why are you so stubborn? How do you know if you don't apply to both? Wouldn't you have more of a chance?'

'You don't understand. I don't want to go to University College Dublin. If I am going to university, I want to go to Trinity. You still *want* me to go to university, I take it?'

'Don't take that tone with me, young lady. You'll do what you're told, and that's it.'

'It's a nice university, but it's not for me. It suited Laura, but it doesn't suit me. I'm not going to apply to U.C.D., and that's final.'

'You'd be lucky if they took you. Who says you'll get Trinity? Maybe all the places for snotty-nosed little brats like you are gone. What will you do then?'

'I don't know. Anyway, I'm not a snotty-nosed little brat. That's a horrible thing to say.'

'I say it the way I see it.'

'You obviously haven't read the book 'How to make friends and influence people.'

'It wasn't in print when I was in my prime!'

'*The Bible* wasn't in print when you were in your prime!'

'What a cheek! You need a clip around the ear.'

'I suppose you're brave enough to give it to me, are you?'

'I'll have less of that young lady. I am your mother, after all, and I deserve a certain amount of respect.'

'Don't make me laugh. What about MUTUAL respect.'

'Fair enough, okay, let's call a truce.'

'What are you going to study anyway?'

'Languages.'

'Are you going to teach?'

'I don't know. I haven't decided yet. Anyway, I have to be admitted first. Maybe I won't even have enough points to get in, and then this whole argument will have been absolutely pointless. I don't want to talk about it anymore.'

The following few weeks passed without much altercation except for the possibility that Karen might not get into university to study anything at all. The letter finally arrived to tell her that she did in fact get a place in Trinity, and the cutting atmosphere of house reverted to one of placidity. Trinity was very close to Dublin 4. You could have almost walked the distance!

It wasn't to be the only change in the house. No, an immediate one loomed and that would have a dramatic influence on Ragsy's life. The neighbours next door had bought a beautiful tan and white Cocker Spaniel called Dandy. He was a Dandy all right. You'd stand to look at him.

Poochie and Ragsy were in the garden, lolling about like they usually did when Dandy found his way in. That was it! Poochie was 'in season,' and that only added to the situation. Ragsy didn't notice Dandy at first, but then all of a sudden he appeared out of nowhere and all hell broke loose. It was like world war three had been declared. The two dogs went at each other hell for leather. There was no let up, and Poochie stood there wagging her tail as she was being fought over and the other two were trying to tear each other to pieces. Blood spurted everywhere as all that could be seen were tails and heads intertwined with yapping and growling in between.

When Karen's mother heard all the commotion, she couldn't believe it. She was gob-smacked and stood motionless in horror. Then she ran out the kitchen door whilst the two dogs were going at it hammer and tongs. She turned on the garden hose full blast and sprayed them with torrents of water. It hardly made a dent in the entire furore. Laura came out with a large bucket of ice-cold water and threw it over them. That did the trick! They had had enough. The boys from next door took Dandy, with his mangled ear, home to recuperate, and Laura grabbed Ragsy by the collar. Ragsy was still growling at Dandy, not realizing that he had also been a casualty with a piece bitten out of his tongue. Laura forgot her nervousness through sheer anger. What a nightmare! Ragsy was taken to the vet, his tongue still spurting blood.

'What happened?' Dr. Rafferty asked as he examined the dog.

'You won't believe it!'

Laura explained what had happened as Dr. Rafferty listened intently.

'I wouldn't be too cross with this fellah if I were you. He was protecting his home, and he saw Poochie as being threatened by an outsider. This fellah takes his job of protecting his territory very seriously. It would certainly make any potential burglar think twice about venturing into your home.'

'I wouldn't mind, but he's fine with people. It's just dogs.'

'If he feels threatened or feels that his owners or home are under attack, he'll warn the outsider first, normally by barking antagonistically. It's a natural instinct. If he feels there is no threat, he will be as gentle as a lamb. I can't stitch the tongue. It will heal itself. He will be all right. I'll give you some antibiotics in case he doesn't feel well, but I wouldn't worry too much. He'll be his old rascally self in no time at all.'

A few weeks later, David and Ragsy were playing in the field belonging to the boy's school nearby, as they did every afternoon after school. They had spent most of the afternoon running around acting like two idiots. They were both tuckered out, lying in the grass taking a breather. Then, Andrew, a friend of David's, came up to him and asked him to play tennis.

'No thanks, I'm knackered.'

'Come on, David, just for half an hour.'

'Well, okay,' He said reluctantly.

They made their way over to the tennis courts and started banging the ball back and forth. After fifteen or twenty minutes, things got out of hand.

'That was out!' Andrew shouted.

'No way! You must be blind.'

'That was out! You're cheating!'

'I won that match fair and square.'
'You wish!'
Andrew went over to David to hit him with the tennis racquet. Ragsy saw Andrew as he raised his racquet when David's back was turned, and just as the vet had predicted, Ragsy issued a blood-curdling, throaty growl. David turned around and was shocked to discover that Andrew was about to wallop him with the broadside of his tennis racquet. It wasn't done in jest but in earnest. Ragsy growled once more, showing his teeth as his lip curled back.

'Put the racquet down on the ground slowly and step away from me. Don't make any sudden movements,' David warned.

Ragsy didn't take his eye off his target as he continued to growl. Terrified, Andrew did exactly what he was told without question.

'Thank you, Ragsy. Good boy. I'm fine. Don't worry,' David reassured him. The dog was delighted to have protected his family once more and ran about like a mad looney, wagging his tail, sure in the knowledge that he had saved the day.

'Are you nuts? Never do that when Ragsy is around. He doesn't know if you are joking or not. He thought you were attacking me, so he protected me.'

'That dog is a menace. He should be put down.'

'That'll go down well. You were trying to hit me broadside with a racquet because you couldn't beat me fair and square at tennis. I can imagine who will come off worse with your dad. You or Ragsy! Want to make a bet?'

'No. No I don't. Let's leave it be. I'll make a deal with you. You don't bring Ragsy when we're playing tennis, and I won't lose my temper when I lose and try to hit you broadside with the tennis racquet. Okay?'

'Okay, but remember you were the one who wanted to play tennis, not me. Ragsy just came out for a run.'

'You win.'

They walked home together, friends again. It was a valuable lesson that Andrew never forgot. It isn't wise to be perceived as a threat when an owner's dog is around. It could have been nasty, he thought. Naturally, he didn't know that Ragsy was 'all bark and no bite'—well, almost, and wouldn't hurt a fly, but the threat was enough to keep Andrew in his place.

Weeks passed, and preparations were being made for Christmas. There was still a month to go, but Karen's mother was very organized and liked to have everything done in advance. There would be a large family get-together.

Presents were bought, wrapped, and put away. Puddings were boiled, and the Christmas cake was made and iced, taking pride of place on the kitchen shelf wrapped up in greaseproof paper to protect it. The day came for the Christmas tree to be bought and Karen, David, and Laura picked out the largest one they could find.

'I hope you know that you're the ones who are going to do all the decorating. I'm not getting into it,' their dad warned them.

The house was in a tizzy. You would have thought Christmas was the following day! The tree was finally brought into the dining room and put up. The smell of fresh pine needles filled the room as well as the floor as they shed incessantly onto the carpet. Karen and her siblings spent hours decorating the tree and put frosted cobwebs all over it. The tiny coloured bulbs were turned on, some of them glowing in the darkened room, whilst others twinkled. The Christmas lights added their own splash of magic as the whole family erupted in applause.

'It looks stunning. Well done, everyone!' Their mother praised them enthusiastically.

The biting winter had come in like a lion, and a stock of coal, oil, and wood had to be brought in. An ample supply of logs was stacked at the side of the house in a large box. The coal shed was full, and almost everything was ready.

'We're nearly out of heating oil. What will we do?' Karen's mother asked her husband.

'Maybe they will be able to deliver it. It's still a few weeks to Christmas.'

Karen's mother rang the heating oil company and explained that they had just realised that they would run out of heating oil shortly. The receptionist understood and said that she would organize a delivery that week. The side gate was left unlocked in case no one was home when the oil tanker arrived. The oil man was filling the tank in the back garden just as Karen's mother drove up the driveway. She gave him a cheque and wished him a Happy Christmas as he left. An hour or so passed, and she called Ragsy and Poochie in from the back garden for their tea. Poochie made her way down the steps to the patio near the kitchen door, but Ragsy was nowhere to be seen. Karen's mother went into the garden, closing the kitchen door behind her and checked the garden. No Ragsy. She walked around the side gate only to discover that it had been left open. What was she going to do? Karen came in about an hour afterwards, and she broke the news.

'Karen, Ragsy has escaped!'

'What do you mean *escaped*?'

'Well, the oil man came to fill the tank and I only discovered Ragsy was gone when I called them both in for their tea. I left the side gate open and forgot to close it after the tank had been filled. I'm really sorry.'

'He can't have got far. When was the oil man here?'

'I can't remember, an hour ago, maybe two.'

'Look at the receipt. It must have a time punched on it.'

'Here it is, ten past three. That was over two hours ago, and he still isn't back. You'll never find him. It's pitch black. What are we going to do?'

Karen's mother, Emily, started to panic, but Karen stayed in control.

'We can't do anything for the moment. We will just have to wait and see and hope that he finds his way back home.'

The house was as quiet as a mouse. The following morning early, Karen and her father looked all over Ballsbridge, Baggot Street, and beyond, but Ragsy was nowhere to be seen. She started to get worried about him. Maybe he would be run over or left lying at the side of the road somewhere. Worse still, he could be dead or the victim of some vicious prank. Her mind somersaulted, darting backwards and forwards over things that could have happened to him and others that could have prevented him from getting back home.

'There is no other alternative other than to ring the Cats and Dogs Rescue Mission. Maybe he was picked up.'

Karen's dad enquired, and no dog fitting Ragsy's description was found or dropped into the Rescue Mission. They were back to square one again.

'What are we going to do now, dad?' Karen asked, pleading him to come up with some bright solution, which didn't seem forthcoming. The family sat down to their tea all glum-faced as though someone had died. Then out of the blue, Karen's dad shouted out.

'I have it. I have it!'

'What, dad? What?'

'We'll put a reward in the newspaper.'

'Do you think it will work?'

'Work?' He looked at Karen as if she had lost her marbles. 'Of course it will work! Have you ever known money not to work? If he's out there and there's money to be had, mark my words he'll turn up.'

£100.00 REWARD
LOST
ENGLISH SHEPHERD ANSWERS TO THE NAME 'RAGSY', BLACK AND WHITE WITH TAN MARKINGS ON HIS EYES AND NOSE. LAST SEEN ON
14th DECEMBER IN THE VICINITY OF
AILESBURY ROAD, DUBLIN 4.
FAMILY DISTRAUGHT - £100.00 REWARD FOR RECOVERY. RING 01 679936

Karen's dad started to get second thoughts that his full proof plan would work. By the time Saturday had arrived, his exuberance had waned totally. He didn't let on to anyone in the family, exuding an air of confidence that he was sure it would succeed. He had become the consummate actor, even though the family was quite aware that nobody had phoned. The advertisement had been placed in the *Irish Times* and the *Irish Independent*. Now, all they could do was wait. Karen's dad was immersed in weeding the garden when the telephone rang.

'Emily, will you get that? I'm in the garden.' Karen's dad shouted to her mother. It rang a few times and rang off. He washed his hands at the garden tap and went inside. 'Emily, did you hear me? Emily?' Then he saw a note on the kitchen table.

Gerald,
I didn't want to disturb you in the garden, as you seemed to be enjoying yourself so much. I've put a large leg of lamb with rosemary in the oven. It should be ready by about eight o'clock. Don't touch the temperature gauge! It's supposed to be very low. I've gone to do some shopping in town and will drop into the supermarket and pick up some groceries on the way home. Don't get into trouble while I'm away!!!
Love Em.

No one was in the house. He had thought that Karen's mother was still at home. *Maybe that was someone about the dog*, he thought. *I'm sure they will ring back*, he reassured himself. No sooner had the thought flashed across his mind when the telephone rang again.

'Hello?'

'Hello. Did you place an ad in the *Irish Times* about a missing English Shepherd?'

'Yes, we did.'

'Well, we found him. He was trying to cross the Stillorgan Duel Carriageway and we stopped to pick him up in case he got run over.'

'Thank God. Is he all right?'

'He's grand. Will you be at home this evening?'

'Yes, yes I will.'

'We live in Kildare so we should be in Dublin at about half past seven. Is that too late?'

'No no. Not, at all.'

'Can you give me the address?'

'Certainly, it's ...'

Karen's father gave the young man the address and waited until half past seven. He wasn't fit for anything and kept pacing up and down. He looked at the note again, which Emily had left. '*Don't get into trouble while I'm away!!!*'

'I'm beginning to wonder if she's a fortune teller,' he thought to himself. 'Maybe it isn't the same dog but just looks like him.'

He was so rattled that he ended up getting a whiskey from the sitting room cabinet to settle his already frayed nerves. The house was deserted. It was just as well, Gerald thought, in case it was a hoax. A dark blue Volvo estate pulled up outside the house. The outside light was on as he peered out the window, he thought that he had perceived a shadow. Perhaps, someone was coming up the driveway. He opened the door before the young man got to it.

Ragsy broke free and hurtled his way towards him, running around Karen's dad like whirlwind.

'Take it easy there, fellah, easy there now.' Ragsy barked, chased his tail, and ran around her father once more and barked again excitedly.

'It's easy to see that he's home,' the young man remarked, smiling.

'I can't thank you enough. We've been going out of our minds with worry about him.' Karen's dad handed over the £100.00 without another thought.

'My mother and I knew he must have belonged to good people. He missed you so much. The first night he just whined, but when he thought he would have to stay with us for good, he wouldn't stop howling and yelping all night. It was obvious he was unhappy, as it got worse and worse. When we saw the advert in the newspaper we knew it had to be you.'

'Thank you very much.'

'Happy Christmas!'

'It will be now. It'll be a Christmas to remember! Happy Christmas to you, too!'

Karen's dad closed the door. He asked Ragsy all kinds of questions, not expecting an answer; just reassuring himself that Ragsy was finally home. He poured himself a scotch and sat down thinking to himself beside the crackling fire. Ragsy was equally comfortable, chewing on a bone and stretched out on the rug, when the key turned in the front door.

'Gerald, are you there? Could you help me with some of the parcels, please?'

Ragsy sat up when he heard the door open and looked at Karen's dad. Then as soon as he heard Emily, he bounded out the door and into the hall, barking furiously.

'Oh, Ragsy, you're home. Oh, thank God you're all right. Gerald, isn't it wonderful?' Emily turned to Gerald to be reassured; he nodded with a smile of complete satisfaction.

'Karen is going to be over the moon. This is going to be a great Christmas after all. You little nut! You had all of us worried half to death!' Emily petted Ragsy as he followed her into the kitchen. She set the table and started to put the groceries away. The smell of roast lamb wafted through the hall. Gerald took the groceries and parcels from the car and brought them inside. Dinner was almost ready when Karen walked in, leaving her things in the hall. She heard a whimpering noise from the study.

'Mum, why is Poochie locked in the study?'

She must have followed your dad in there this morning; she must have got locked inside by mistake. Poochie ran into the sitting room and started barking like something deranged.

'What's wrong with Poochie? She's acting really weird. Poochie, come on, we'll get you something to eat. Poochie! Poochie!. Where are you?'

'Karen, she's probably found someone amusing to play with,' her mother replied. Karen hadn't noticed that her mother said 'someone' and not 'something.' When she went into the sitting room, Ragsy was playing tag with her on the floor.

'Ra ... Ra ... Ragsy! You're home and you're okay!' Ragsy bounded over to Karen, nearly knocking her off balance.

'Dad, did you see?'

'We've been getting reacquainted,' her dad responded.

'But how?'

'I told you, the special wording in a lost and found advert is 'reward and money,' much like 'open sesame.''

'You're very cynical.'

'Not really. Cynicism is a matter of practice!'

The Christmas that followed was the most cheerful one any of the family had ever recollected.

The next few months slipped by without any problems, and exam time came around once more. The house reverted to tip-toeing around Karen, as televisions were lowered and everyone tried to keep as quiet as possible. She passed her exams with honours, but as she was studying French and German, she was told that she would have to spend her summer holidays abroad, practicing her languages. Emily had friends in Bordeaux where Karen could spend a month in the beautiful wine region practicing her French. However, she would have to go to language classes in Berlin, as her German needed some work. She would miss her family, home, and the dogs, but she would be home by the end of August and would be able to relax in September in Ireland.

Karen was packed off to Bordeaux and said her goodbyes so dramatically that you would think that she were off to the Himalayas—never to be heard from again. After her month in Bordeaux, she would travel from Bordeaux to Berlin by train and fly from Berlin home to Dublin. Karen was looking forward to coming back to Ireland before she had even left home.

Six weeks passed, and during all this time, David brought Ragsy every afternoon to the school field for a run. He would come home and give Poochie a short walk. He had noticed that she had seemed rather low in herself. David was worried about her.

'Mum, I think there is something wrong with Poochie.'
'Why do you say that, David?'
'She's acting really queer. Maybe we should take her to the vet.'
'I'm sure it's nothing. She's probably missing Karen.'

The following Wednesday evening, Emily remembered what David had said. She noticed her shivering in the basket, and the kitchen was warm. She thought it very strange and decided that it would be best to take her to the vet just to make sure that she was okay and not getting a cold. When Emily brought Poochie to the vet, he did an x ray and he noticed something rather unusual but didn't want to say anything to Emily, until he had the results from the tests, which he would have on Friday. Emily was told to bring her in to see him then.

'Emily.'

'Yes, Dr. Rafferty.'

'I suppose you've noticed that Poochie isn't as mobile as she was and must be having a few unwanted accidents.'

'Yes I did, but that's just age isn't it. She's just getting older isn't that all?

'Well, I afraid not. What age is she now?'

'She's about ten and a half.'

'She is suffering from renal failure. She's in a lot of pain. The kindest thing you could do is have her put down.'

Emily couldn't believe it. The dog had been part of the family for so long. What would they say? At dinner on Friday evening, Emily broke the news.

'Poochie is very ill. She has renal failure and is in a lot of pain. She could continue on for a while, but her suffering would only be prolonged. Dr. Rafferty says the kindest thing to do would be to put her out of her misery. I think he's right.'

Everyone protested except Gerald, who was just stunned by the news, as it had been his brother, Teddy, who had been a breeder of Cairn Terriers and who had given them the dog as a gift.

Emily continued, 'We can do it tomorrow. We can all go and say goodbye and be with her when she goes. She won't feel anything. She'll get an overdose of anaesthetic, will fall into a deep sleep, and won't wake up. When it's over, we can take her home and bury her in the garden. That way she will always be with us. We can't be selfish about this, and we have to be strong. We have to think what's best for her.'

There were no further objections, just a wall of cold silence. The following morning, the whole family went to The Veterinary Clinic in Donnybrook to say goodbye.

'It won't hurt her, will it doctor?' David asked, his red eyes welling up with tears and his chin trembling. He snuffled and wiped his eyes and nose with his sleeve. Emily looked at him.

Now was not the time to tell him to use a handkerchief. She kept silent and looked at Gerald.

'No, David, you can talk to her if you like and pet her to reassure her. That will help. I promise you it won't hurt her. She's just going to go to sleep.'

'Okay.'

Dr. Rafferty gave Poochie the anaesthetic as David stroked her and told her to be a brave girl. Then a few minutes later, she closed her eyes. The hot tears ran down his face as he looked at his mother and she looked back. No, this was not a time for words of reassurance. This was a time for feelings.

They drove home in the car with the lifeless body of the Cairn Terrier wrapped in a soft blanket. Gerald had dug a deep hole in the garden and put a little stone with her name and age on it. David was dressed in his school uniform and took out his tin whistle as he tried to play something on it with little success as she was being lowered into the ground. Everyone stood around, said a prayer, and covered her with soil. She was buried with the same respect as a dead hero returning from *The Great War*. The truth of the matter was that the whole spectacle was so touching that it would have melted hearts of stone.

The next few weeks dragged. Ragsy was moping around the house on a quest to find out where Poochie had hidden herself. He returned to his introvert self. At night, he would hide his head underneath the garden shed with the rest of his body in full view. It reminded everyone of an ostrich. He was dealing with grief in his own way, and no one made any comment. He had had great fun with Poochie; she had been his friend and now she was gone. Karen returned home full of the joys of travelling and her exploits abroad only to be met with the devastating news. She said nothing more but went upstairs to her bedroom in silence, and she lay down on her bed and sobbed until it seemed there were no more tears left. Nothing would ever be the same again, nothing.

Chapter Fourteen

Christmas had been and gone. Weeks passed, and finally Ragsy came to the realisation that Poochie wasn't coming back. Karen and her family helped him through patience and understanding. It took some time, but he eventually emerged from the introversion that was his way of coping with life-changing situations.

David, on the other hand, hadn't coped well at all. He would take Ragsy for walks in the school field after school had finished, but the previous boisterous prankster had transformed into someone very different. It had affected him more than anyone else; after all, Poochie had been his dog. Ragsy and David became firm friends, but he knew that the English Shepherd belonged to Karen, and he needed to feel loved by his own dog. He felt the loss of Poochie very keenly. This stifling atmosphere continued for some time.

It was February, and the ground was frozen solid. Every morning Emily and Gerald would go out to feed the birds twittering about on the patio.

'We are going to have to do something about David. This can't continue,' Gerald said.

'I know, I got a call from his form teacher yesterday saying that he was cheeky to a teacher and started throwing paper airplanes all around the classroom. He was totally out of control. She had to send him to Mr. Montgomery, the Junior Dean, for a lecture.'

'Does Mr. Montgomery want to see us?'

'No, I explained that he was going through a difficult time and that it had been reflected in his behaviour at home as well. She said that she had already spoken to Mr. Montgomery and that there had to be a logical explanation for his outburst. She wanted to find out was anything troubling him at home and that was why she had called me. She said that David always handed his homework in on time, but lately, every time she asked him for it, he would say that he had left it at home. He didn't seem too bothered if he was sent to Mr. Montgomery for another lecture. She was getting worried about him as it was so out of character.'

'We'll have to think about what to do,' Gerald said worriedly.

'Let's leave it for now and see how things pan out.'

'Okay.'

They went inside and carried on as though no discussion had taken place.

On Friday afternoon, the phone rang.

'Good afternoon. Could I speak to Mrs. Murray, please?'

'Yes, this is Emily Murray.'

'Mrs. Murray, this is David's form teacher. I need you to come down to the Junior Dean's office straightaway.'

'What's the matter? Is David all right?'

'Yes, but he's been caught in a very serious incident, one which the school cannot condone in any way, shape or form.'

'I'm on my way.'

Emily drove to the school straightaway. She was ushered towards the Junior Dean's office. David was sitting outside, red eyed, with his head drooping. He looked up at her. She glanced at her son as she passed by, mouthing the words, 'What did you do now?' David looked back at her blankly and dropped his head again. She followed the form teacher to the Junior Dean's office.

'Mrs. Murray, I'm sorry we have to meet under such serious circumstances, but we have to resolve this situation,' Mr. Montgomery said sternly as he extended his hand to shake hers and gestured to the chair.

Frantic, Emily replied, 'Why? What has he done?'

Ignoring the question, the Junior Dean continued. 'Normally, under such circumstances we would suspend the pupil and in some cases expel him for such behaviour. However, there are other factors in this case to be considered.'

'What has he done?' she repeated, irritated.

'He was caught smoking behind the swimming pool with some of the older boys who were egging him on. They will be punished severely.'

She sighed, relieved. 'Thank God,' she said under her breath.

'Mrs. Murray?' Mr. Montgomery questioned as though he hadn't quite heard her correctly.

Emily cleared her throat. 'Hmm, but he's only eleven!'

'David says that he is very sorry. He did it as a joke. I believe he means it. We can't be too hard on the boy after his bereavement. It's hit him very hard.'

'Oh, yes, of course.'

'Please extend my sympathies to the family.'

'Thank you,' Emily replied a little puzzled. 'That's very thoughtful.'

'I trust that you will deal with the matter over the weekend.'

'Thank you, Mr. Montgomery. I appreciate it. I am sure he will be a different boy on Monday.'

When Emily got home, she called her husband's office and asked him to come home early. She told him that they would have to have a long talk with David, who had been sent to his room in silence. When Gerald arrived, he wanted to know what all the fuss was about.

'I don't know where *your* son gets it from,' Emily started at him.

'What?' He followed Emily into the sitting room, taking off his overcoat. 'Typical. When he's in trouble, he's my son. When he's won medals or captain of the junior rugby team, he's yours. What on earth are you on about?' He loosened his tie.

'Here, you'll need this,' and she handed Gerald a small scotch. He stared at her.

'Is it as bad as that? What has he done, blown up the chemistry lab?'

'Wait till you hear. I think I'll have a scotch, too.'

'But you hardly ever drink! For Pete's sake! What's going on?'

'I was called by David's form teacher this afternoon and summoned to the Junior Dean's office.'

'Whaaat? What for?'

'I'm getting to that. Give me a minute.' She took a large gulp of scotch and continued. 'He was going to be suspended. For smoking.'

'Smoking? He's only eleven, for God's sake, and even we don't smoke!'

'I know. Can you believe it? I nearly died, but it was the lead-up to what he had done that I could hardly contain myself. When I discovered what he had actually done, it was a relief. If he had shot the President, it couldn't have been dealt with more seriously.'

'God, I'm glad I'm not still in school.'

'You haven't heard the best of it.'

'You mean there's more?'

'Oh, yes. As I was leaving, the Junior Dean said that David was very sorry and he believed he had meant it.'

'Good,' Gerald replied.

'I haven't finished yet. Then he said, 'We can't be too hard on the boy after his bereavement. It's hit him very hard.'

'Bereavement! What bereavement?' Gerald asked. 'Has someone died that I don't know about?'

'Just listen, will you? Anyway, as I was saying, naturally, I thought he meant Poochie, but when he said, "Please extend my sympathies to the rest of the family," I knew that there was something fishy going on. So, I asked David on the way home if he had any idea why Mr. Montgomery would say something like that. David apparently explained to him that his best friend had died. Even though it had happened in August, the reality was only hitting him now. He said that he had grown up with her, that she was an important part of the family, and that it had affected us all very badly indeed. Then in his innocence, David said, "he's not all bad. He has to be strict, you know." Wasn't that kind of the Junior Dean to say he was very understanding?'

Gerald couldn't control his laughter.

Emily continued. 'You better not say anything to David. He doesn't realise that the Junior Dean completely took it up the wrong way.'

'You're right. We will have to try to remedy the situation. Maybe we should see about getting him his own dog. That might set him straight.'

The following morning, Gerald went into his study and shut the door. He had resolved to phone the Cats and Dogs Rescue Mission.

'Hello. Is that the Cats and Dogs Rescue Mission?'

'Yes, how can we help you?'

'Well, it's my son. His dog died in August, and he's very cut up about it. We thought we might get another dog to help him get over it and at the same time give a dog a second chance rather than buy one.'

'Where do you live?'

'Ballsbridge.'

'Do you have a garden?'

'Yes, we do, a back and front garden. The back garden is completely enclosed and is on about half of an acre.'

'We do checkups before we release dogs to make sure that they will be well cared for. Will that be a problem?'

'Not, at all. I want to make it a surprise for my son.'

'We have someone in that vicinity this afternoon. Is that all right?'

'Great. I didn't think it would be so quick.'

'We don't like delaying the chance of one of our dogs or cats getting a home. It's very stressful for them here, so we like to move as quickly as possible, provided everything is in order.'

David was out playing rugby and so was none the wiser about the man from the Cats and Dogs Rescue Mission coming to view their property. He arrived shortly afterwards and was introduced to Ragsy, who looked healthy and happy but a little forlorn without any playmate.

'Is it all right?' Gerald enquired.

'It's more than adequate. I see you already have an English Shepherd. Are you used to dogs?'

'We've had dogs all our lives.'

'Where would *our* dog sleep?' the young man enquired.

'She'd sleep in a basket at the far end of the kitchen with our other dog, Ragsy. I'm afraid it would have to be a bitch. Ragsy doesn't take kindly to male dogs. We decided to get one from your Rescue Mission rather than buy one, as I already explained to your receptionist. We thought it would be good to give a dog a second chance.'

'I wish more people thought like that. Have you any type in mind?'

'Do you have any Cairn Terriers?'

'No, I'm sorry.'

Gerald looked disappointed.

'But I think we have a dog that would be ideal for you. We have a Collie mix. She's young and very affectionate. She'd be an ideal companion for your other dog. She's only a year old and has already had two owners.'

'What's wrong with her?'

'There's nothing wrong with *her*! It's the owners. She's just unlucky, poor thing.'

'Why do you say that?'

'Well, she'll have to be put down at the end of next week unless we get her a good home. We haven't the resources to hold onto dogs indefinitely. Naturally, we try to do the best we can and re-home as many as possible, but we are overwhelmed sometimes. We don't put any dog or cat into a new home without checking out the property and the potential owner. We don't want the dog going from the frying pan into the fire!'

'Of course, but why was she sent back twice?'

'Well, the first owner was leaving the country and wanted to get rid of the dog. The second owner took her as a companion for her second dog. She hadn't had our dog any length of time when her German Shepherd was killed and the woman was reminded of him every time she looked at Sheila—that's her name. She's lovely. I feel bad about it. If I had my way, I'd take them all, but you have to be practical and think of the welfare of the animal. She has just been spayed so she's a bit groggy today, but she has the most affectionate character. I think you'd love her.'

'Maybe she'll be third time lucky!'

'I hope so. When can you come to see her?'

'My son is playing rugby at the moment. What about now?'

'Now?'

'Well, there's no time like the present. Are you going back that direction?'

'Yes.'

'Well, I'll follow you in my car, then.'

Gerald followed the young man in his car. The Rescue Mission itself was a foreboding-looking place, Gerald thought, as he was shown inside.

The young man explained, 'We are getting new premises. They're being built at the moment. It all depends on funding. We are constantly trying to get people to spay their dogs and cats. It's not fair on them. The lives these poor things lead you wouldn't wish on your worst enemy, but we do the best we can to help them. That's how I sleep at night, knowing I've tried to make a difference.'

The staff employed at the home were very pleasant and compassionate about the animals in their care. It wasn't looked upon as just a shelter. It was a temporary home for some animals, a permanent home for others, until their time came, one way or the other. Gerald walked through the corridor until he was shown into a long room with cages on either side. He would have thought that the noise of so many animals would have been rather deafening. It wasn't. The cages were large, clean, with plenty of bedding, food, and water. The concept was to re-home dogs and cats and not to keep them in temporary accommodation. When Gerald was taken down to Sheila's cage, she didn't move a muscle. Other dogs barked, jumping up and down and vying for attention. She didn't. She just lay down with her head between her two front paws, looked up at him, and then down at the ground. She had already had two homes she'd lost interest in people; worse still, she had lost her faith in them.

'Hello there?' Gerald got down on his honkers.

She still didn't move, looking at him as though she were checking him out.

'God, she looks very down.'

'Well, I suppose she has cause to be. Life hasn't exactly been a bed of roses for her, even *with* her affectionate personality.'

'You've sold me! If I left her here another minute, I wouldn't sleep a wink tonight.'

'Will you come this way and fill out the paperwork. There is a fee—is that all right? It just helps cover our costs.'

'No problem. Where do I go?'

'Just follow me.'

'Are almost all the animals in here strays?'

'Strays? You've got to be jokin'. They're mainly unwanted Christmas or birthday presents. Christmas is the worst! Some people just don't think. Their pets grow up and become too big. They're no longer cute and cuddly. Unfortunately, some owners die. You can't do anything about that; it happens. You'd be surprised what some people do. Pregnant cats being left on dual carriageways, dogs dumped out of car windows. Do you know we picked up a pair of kittens terrified out of their wits the other day? They were found in a partially closed refuse sack. The owner of a restaurant found them in one of his bins. He brought them straight to us. I'd like to put whoever did that into a refuse sack, tied and helpless, and see if they like it! You learn to live with the effects of cruelty, but you never get used to it. It's not all bad news, though. People like you come along and give them a second chance, or in her case, a third, and they have a new family, the possibility of a life with dignity and hope. Everybody deserves to have that opportunity!'

Gerald smiled at the young man, who was so matter of fact about it. Perhaps, it was precisely because he was so matter of fact about the situation that it affected him all the more.

'Do you still have the kittens?'

'Yes, they're recovering. Hopefully, they'll get a good home, too. The vet saw them this morning, and they will be put up for adoption in the next day or so. We'd really like to see them go together, but a lot of people only want one.'

'Could they go today?'

'Why?'

'Well, I know it sounds daft, but since you want them to go together. I could take them home with Sheila and me. What do you think?'

'It's kind of unusual! You haven't even seen them yet! I'd need to speak to the vet.'

'Could you ask him now?'

'Wait here a minute and I'll check.' The young man arrived back a few minutes later, smiling from ear to ear as though he had won the lottery.

'The vet said that since I'd already checked your house this morning and you were taking Sheila, he didn't see any problem with the two kittens.'

'Will Sheila get on with them?' Gerald asked the young man.

'They're so young, they won't pose any threat. You'd be surprised at mother nature.'

Sheila was brought out into a large room, still as quiet and depressed as ever. The two kittens were put on the floor. One of the kittens was a ginger, and the other was a tabby with a splash of white on his chest. They were very young. As soon as the young man put them on the floor, they started to 'meooow' but in a strangely clipped way as though their vocal cords hadn't fully matured. Sheila's interest was piqued, and she went over, checked them out, and lay down again. After a few minutes, the kittens tried to find their feet; they snuggled up to her and she started to groom them, licking them all over, knocking them off balance with her tongue.

'I wouldn't have believed it if you had told me' Gerald said flabbergasted.

'I know. People could learn a lot from animals. Live and let live, eh?'

The three of them were piled into the car. Sheila sat in the back with the two kittens in a small cat carrier.

'It's been an experience!' Gerald said to the young man as he was leaving. 'Thank you. Thank you, very much.'

Gerald stuffed a substantial cheque into the young man's hand. He looked at it and then at Gerald. 'To help with your work!' Gerald said.

The young man nodded, smiled, thanked him, and waved goodbye. Gerald and his little troupe drove off. None of them knew what the future would bring, but it had to be better than the past.

David hadn't returned from rugby when Gerald got home. He called Ragsy and put him in the back garden. He went to get Sheila, hoping that they would get on together. He needn't have worried. Sheila just stood there as Ragsy bounded about. After throwing the ball at them a couple of times and playing with them, he watched them run off to the end of the garden, chasing each other. Ragsy had been lonely without Poochie. It was wonderful that he had accepted Sheila so readily. Gerald went back to the car and brought the two kittens into the kitchen, where it was warm and cosy. He put them in Poochie's old basket and they "meooowed" but after a drop of warmed milk they settled down. The key turned in the door.

'David, take off those dirty boots. Don't go through the house in them, and go upstairs have a shower and change.'

'Do I have to?'

'David!'

'Oh, okay, mum.'

David did as he was told and disappeared out of sight. Gerald opened the kitchen door slightly and peered into the hallway.

'Emily.' Gerald beckoned to Emily with his finger. 'Em,' he whispered loudly, 'psst'

'What's all the secrecy?'

'Shussh, not so loud, come in here a minute. I don't want anyone to hear.'

'What have you been up to? What's going on?'

'Look.' Gerald pointed out the kitchen window as the dogs bounded about like two mad loonies.

'Whose dog is that?'

'Ours,' Gerald declared proudly.

'You're kidding.'

'No, and that's not all.'

'What have you brought home now, an elephant?'

'*Very funny*,' he said. 'Anyway, an elephant wouldn't have fit in the car!'
'What?'
'Come over here. See?'
'Have you gone stark raving mad?'
'No, just a little. I've had a really eye-opening experience this afternoon, and I wanted to make a difference.'
'What do you mean, "make a difference"?'
Gerald sat down and explained to Emily what had happened that morning. He wanted her to know why they had suddenly become the owners of two kittens and another dog and exactly why it was so important.
'I suppose I've made a difference too, then, since I'll be looking after them!' Emily said a little bewildered.
'You always have, darling, you always have,' Gerald replied, giving her a peck on the cheek. Emily opened the kitchen door.
'David, come downstairs. Your father wants to talk to you about something.'
'Do I have to? Anyway, you told me to go and have a shower. I'm doing something *really* important.'
'David Murray, come downstairs this instant if you don't want your backside warmed. Karen? Laura? Everyone is to come downstairs to the sitting room. Your father wants to talk to you all. *Now*.'
Everyone converged to the sitting room for the great 'pow wow'. Gerald explained what had happened that morning. He told them about Sheila and the two kittens. He thought David should be given the responsibility for his own dog. David couldn't believe it. He just sat there with his mouth wide open, and after a few minutes, it dawned on him.
'Yippeee!' He ran into the kitchen to see the two dogs playing in the garden. The whole family followed him in. The two kittens were picked up.
'Mum, ah look. They're so cute,' Laura declared.
'What are they called, dad?' Karen asked.
'They don't have any names, so that's what we are going to decide this afternoon. They have to be names of a pair of fa-

mous people. Each of us has two chances. Whoever thinks of the best couple wins.'

'Do the people have to be living?'

'No.'

David was called in and told about it. They sat down at the table as the family started to rack their brains.

'Fred and Ginger,' Gerald started off, sure, that his suggestion would win.

'Henry VIII and Anne Boleyn,' Karen proposed.

'Don't be daft. You can't call a cat Henry VIII and the other Anne Boleyn.' Laura chided Karen.

'Sorry, I wasn't thinking. What about Romeo and Juliet?'

Karen laughed at Laura's suggestion.

'What are you going to do if they're both boys? God, he'd never forgive you calling him Juliet!'

'Stop that you two. You're not helping.' Emily scolded them and continued. 'Gerald, we have to think of names that sound more suitable for their personalities. They'll be forever getting into all sorts of situations. Cats are renowned for it!'

Everyone seemed stumped at the idea. David was petting his new dog, Sheila, and Karen was stroking Ragsy as David piped up.

'What about Laurel and Hardy?' He was paying more attention to his new friend than the question in hand.

'That's it!' Gerald declared triumphantly. 'Well done, David. Laurel and Hardy. Priceless!'

The kittens and dogs became the heart of the Murray household. Every time Gerald looked at one of the kittens and the mischief they might get up to, he was reminded that the future might not have been quite so comical for either of them if he hadn't shown up at the Cats and Dogs Rescue Mission that morning.

The following Monday, David was back to his old self. The form teacher called Emily again at the end of the week to remark on how well David was doing and that 'that talk' she must have had with her son changed his whole perspective on life. He had reverted back to the boisterous prankster who was polite and did what he was told. He sent in his homework on time, and there had been no more nonsense.

Weeks drifted into months, and that dreaded task of washing the dogs was upon Karen once again. Ragsy hated it, whereas Sheila didn't mind it at all. Ragsy would try to get out of the bath anytime Karen had her back turned and wanted to get the shampoo or conditioner. By the time she had finished, the bathroom looked like a swimming pool. They both loved to be brushed and dried with the hairdryer. Ragsy would sleep upside down in his basket on his back with his feet straight up in the air. The kittens would snuggle up to Sheila, viewing her as their mother in her extra large basket, and would abandon Poochie's basket until they were much older. The dogs had different ideas of fun. Ragsy loved to run about in the school field. Sheila loved the beach.

Friday night was family night and that was sacrosanct. No one made arrangements to go out. They all sat about after dinner and played a board game or cards as the dogs munched on bones in the corner and the cats preened themselves. Everyone was included. Gerald and Emily were content with their extended family.

It was a good life. *You get what you put into it*, Emily thought, and that belief was reinforced when one Saturday morning there was a telephone call.

'Hello?'

'Hello?' answered Emily.

'Could I speak to Karen, please?'

'I'm sorry, but she's out with her brother at a rugby match. Who shall I say was calling?'

'It's Richard. Richard Coakely'

'Richard? My God, you've a nerve after all this time. It wasn't enough that you walked out on my daughter just before your engagement. She was so torn up about it that she went to work in Meath to get over you. I had one hell of a time trying to get her to come back home, and now you have the audacity to call her again. She's in Trinity now and is back on an even keel, thank God.'

'I didn't know.'

'Is that an excuse? I didn't know!'

'I'm really sorry. I didn't think that she loved me, and that was why I broke up with her. I can't stop thinking about her, and I wanted to ask her just to make sure.'

'Love you? By God, you put that poor girl through the ringer. You know she isn't the lovey dovey type. She's always felt things deep inside but never expressed them. Love you? God, I could kill you this very minute.'

'I know you're angry, but please don't put the phone down. I need to see her. Please. I haven't stopped thinking about her since we split. I'm miserable. I need her back.'

'Good. That's nice. Let's see how you'll cope.' She was still ranting on at Richard when Gerald walked into the hall.

'Emily, what's all the shouting about?' Gerald enquired.

Emily put her hand over the phone and said in an almost-venomous spit.

'It's Richard.'

'Richard? Richard who?'

'Karen's Richard. Remember?'

'Give me the phone.'

Gerald took the phone from Emily and in a very calm voice, he asked, 'What do you want, Richard?'

'I need to see Karen. I really do. I need a second chance. I miss her. I won't hurt her, I promise.'

'Is this going to be a prolonged visit to Ireland, or do you intend on taking off for New York again in the near future?' Gerald retorted in a sarcastic manner.

'I've given all that up. I'm working with my dad now, training as an auctioneer.'

'*Really?* As an auctioneer. Hmm.'

'Can I see her?'

'I don't know if she wants to see you or give you a second chance. You are not going to treat her like the dirt under your feet. Understand? If you don't heed my warning, you will have to answer to me. Have I made myself crystal clear?'

'Yes, Mr. Murray, crystal.'

'Good. I'll tell Karen. If she is prepared to see you again, she'll be walking the dogs on Sandymount beach, near Martello

Tower, this afternoon at three o'clock. If she doesn't turn up, you have your answer. Is that fair?'

'Very fair, but you *will* tell her?'

'I am a man of my word. Don't ever question that, young man!'

'Yes, of course, I didn't mean ... I mean ... thank you, Mr. Murray. Will you tell Mrs. Murray that I am very sorry, that I didn't mean to upset her?'

'Yes. Yes, I will. Goodbye.' Gerald put the receiver down.

'Are you insane?' Emily asked her husband.

'Emily, Karen has never got over that boy. She won't know how she feels until she confronts him and deals with the issues between them. She can't keep running away. You know I'm right. You know I am.'

'I suppose so, but everything was going so well.'

'Was it? She hasn't gone out with anyone since Richard. Anytime you mention going to a disco, she says she can't be bothered and watches TV or listens to music. Tell me, Emily, is that living?'

'I suppose I just wanted her to be okay.'

'I do, too, but sometimes we have to let go, and if she falls we'll help her to get up again. That's what life is all about, darling.'

'I just hope he doesn't hurt her again.'

'So do I.' Gerald hugged Emily as they walked into the kitchen. 'So do I.'

Karen came home with David after the rugby match. Gerald and Emily were waiting for her.

'Karen, I need to talk to you,' her dad said seriously.

'What's wrong? Has someone died? You look so strange. What's up?'

'Karen, Richard rang.'

'Richard? Richard who?'

'Richard.'

'Oh, that Richard.'

'He wants to see you. I told him I'd tell you. He said he didn't know if you really cared for him and that was why he broke up with you. He's in a bad way.'

'Let him go to hell,' She snapped back angrily.

'Karen, if you really felt that way you wouldn't have reacted the way you just have. Do you remember what I told you when I picked you and Ragsy up from *The Raven's Rest* that last day? I said one day you'd say Richard who?' He smiled at her.

'I remember. You said a lot that day. You said that I had to stop running away and that I had to face up to my life and give people a chance to redeem themselves. You're right, dad. Good and bad, day and night, winter and spring all make up life. How did you ever get to be so wise?'

'Life is the greatest teacher of all,' he replied.

Karen changed her clothes, got the leads for the dogs, and packed them into the car. 'Karen, why are you taking the car? I thought you were taking the dogs for a walk?' her mother asked.

'In case I need to make a run for it!' she replied.

Emily wagged her head from side to side and shut the door behind her. Karen drove down to Sandymount Beach, parking some distance away from Martello Tower. She checked her watch; it was ten past three. She didn't know if she should make a break for it or not. Her father's advice of giving people a chance to redeem themselves kept ringing in her ears. The tide was out. She got out of the car and walked onto the beach, letting the dogs off their leads. Sheila chased the waves, and Ragsy chased after her. Karen made out a figure sitting down on the steps beside Martello Tower with his head in his hands. The dogs raced ahead of Karen, and he looked up and saw them. He stood up and saw her in the distance. He was uncommonly tall and slim, extremely good looking, with black hair and piercing blue eyes. He made his way towards Karen as the dogs stopped and raced up and down after them.

'I didn't think you were coming,' Richard said despondently.

'Neither did I!'

They stood there looking at each other, not knowing what to do next but were suddenly distracted by a mother who was looking for her three-year-old little girl who had gone off exploring for shells. A look of relief crossed the mother's face when she spotted her daughter drawing in the sand.

'What are you doing? You'll get all dirty!' The child dropped the stick that she had been playing with and was dragged off home by her mother. Karen walked over, picked up the stick, bent down, and started drawing in the sand.

'My dad said I should give people a chance to redeem themselves. I'm not very good at that. He's right, though, about day and night, spring and winter, good and bad, birth and death.'

Richard hadn't a clue what Karen was on about and looked at her, puzzled.

'What about them?'

'They're cycles in time. You have to appreciate them for what they are. Wasting a good friendship or any relationship because of a mistake is as pointless as drawing circles in the sand. The waves just wash them all away.'

'What about us? Do you forgive me for being so stupid?' Richard asked as Karen continued to draw in the sand. She looked up, smiled at him with tears glistening in her eyes, and nodded. She stood up as he bent down and kissed her tenderly.

'I'm so sorry. I didn't realise how much I loved you until you were gone, and then I didn't know how to get you back,' Richard said.

'I'm sorry, too. I should have told you how much you meant to me. God, if you left me again I think I'd die. I love you so much that I can hardly breathe.' Richard kissed her passionately, hugging her as though his very life depended on it.

'I'm never going to let you out of my sight. I'm going to be around for a very, *very* long time, so you'd better get used to the idea.'

'Come on. We're supposed to be walking the dogs, remember?' Karen said, smiling, thinking that it was something of a minor miracle that he was there at all. They walked up the beach with their arms around each other and the dogs racing after them, leaving nothing behind except the child's drawings of *circles in the sand.*